The Gates of Paradise

THE GATES OF PARADISE

Taleb Alrefai

translated by Kay Heikkinen

Interlink Books
An imprint of Interlink Publishing Group, Inc.
Northampton, Massachusetts

First published in 2025 by

Interlink Books
An imprint of Interlink Publishing Group, Inc.
46 Crosby Street, Northampton, MA 01060
www.interlinkbooks.com

Originally published in Arabic in 2021 as *Khatf al-Habib* by Masciliana Editions, Tunisia.

Library of Congress Cataloging-in-Publication data:
ISBN-13: 978-1-62371-607-3

Printed and bound in the United States of America

My dear sister Hayat
Memories of a lifetime and inextinguishable
longing to be together

1

"Do not criticize God's own sun!"

He yelled that to my face. We were walking on the seashore, in front of my room in the beach house. I was annoyed by the blazing sun that burned our heads, and I had remarked, "The sun is like fire!"

He stopped and looked at me; his features began to alter, and it seemed to me that his chest became broader. A black beard grew, surrounding his face, and his headcloth slipped, revealing a completely shaved scalp. I did not understand why he was so agitated. He shook his finger in my face: "Do not criticize God's own sun!" He added, threatening, "Your punishment is coming, your punishment is coming!"

He was suddenly dressed as an Afghan. He left me on the sand of the beach, beneath the blazing sun, and walked barefoot into the sea. Another person appeared at his side, equal to him in height and indistinguishable in his broad chest, his Afghan dress, and the shape of his bare head. They went on wading into the sea. I don't know where the third one who joined them came from. Suddenly the number of people increased; they became a row and then rows, and then they turned into an army of men with shaved heads. They plunged into the sea, their voices thundering, "Your punishment is coming, your punishment is coming!"

I cried out, "Ahmad, Ahmad!"

No one looked back; the sea and the pounding waves swallowed my cry. My heart was shaken by a strange fright, and at that moment the color of the waves began to change, quickly becoming a deep blood red. The waves rose noisily and spray flew, hitting my face and my clothes. My breath was filled with an unpleasant smell of blood.

"Allahu akbar, Allahu akbar!"

The sound of the muezzin's call to the dawn prayer woke me, frightened and breathing hard. The dream had stained me with spots of blood, and I was surrounded by its rank odor. It was about five in the morning; the dream, still fresh, flowed around me. I raised my head from the pillow and sat up, trying to free my body and my clothing from the clinging moisture of the dream. *I take refuge in God from Satan the accursed!*

I looked around; I was alone in my large bedroom, and calm reigned in the house. My wife, Shaikha, was in her room. I ran my hand over my face, feeling for the spray of blood. I stayed as I was for a time, then I lay back and stretched out on the bed, the dream crouching silently beside me and the smell of blood in my nostrils.

I could no longer sleep. The question stretched before me—what message was this dream bringing to me? All my life I've believed that dreams bring messages. As the question stirred in my head and my heart, the image of Ahmad, grimacing and frightening, appeared before me. Where was he now? What was he doing? Had something bad happened to him? How had my son's affairs gotten away from me? He hadn't called me for some time, so what did he want by coming to me in a sea of foul-smelling blood?

Scraps of news about him come to me: he's a jihadi fighter in an Islamist group fighting in Syria. From the time he was little, he was the dearest to my heart, intoxicating me when I embraced him or wrestled with him. I would tickle his waist and legs, and the sound of his sweet laughter would ring out.

"It's not right for you to play with Ahmad and not the others!" Shaikha would whisper to me. I would smile at her, nodding in agreement, but objecting, "I love him!"

The dream frightened me—God protect us! I got up in a bad mood, the smell of blood in every breath, and went out to the living room. As soon as I sat down, the anxious thought came—could I be the reason for what my son has become? The sentence stung, aimed directly at me and filling me with the taste of bitterness and distress.

Shaikha was sleeping in her room. I had been in my early sixties when her snoring began to deprive me of the pleasure of sleep. I've slept lightly ever since I was a young man; I doze at the edge of waking, and the slightest movement, the softest whisper wakes me. She began to snore, and sleep eluded me; whenever I dozed off, her snores shook me awake. I would look at her, totally unaware of her own miserable noises. "Shaikha, Shaikha!" I would cry, and half asleep, she would answer, "Yes?" I would tell her that I couldn't sleep because of her snoring and ask her not to sleep on her back. She responded willingly and would turn over on her side, but it wouldn't be long before she went back to snoring, and I went back to my irritation as sleep fled.

Many nights, I would steal away with my pillow, careful not to wake her, leaving our bed and tiptoeing to the living room to stretch out on the sofa. But when I could no longer put up with her snoring and I was tired of sleeping on the sofa, I told her frankly, "I'm going to go sleep alone, in another room." A tear glistened in the corner of her eye, and all the stages of my life when she was beside me flashed before my eyes. She was silent, though her eyes reproached me with her love, telling me I was distancing myself from her. With tears in her voice, she said, "I'd like you to stay with me in our bed, but your rest is more important. I'll sleep alone."

When I was stretched out in the living room, the darkness felt my presence and surrounded me with specters of our memories. We had been married for nearly forty years. She had grown old, though she spared no effort to preserve the youthfulness of her body. Nonetheless, the dust-laden winds of time had scratched the bloom of her face and the flash in her eyes, as they had evened the curves of her body.

I remembered the day I returned from the company and saw a strange alteration in her face, something unusual in her eyes and her smile. "What happened to your face?"

"I had an injection of Botox in my forehead." I wished she had consulted me before she went; I love her as she is, I love the gentleness of her expression. "The doctor promised me that my face wouldn't change!" But the balance of her face, its kindness, had been disturbed. She threw me a fearful question: "Am I ugly?"

"No, no! But your face has changed."

We've spent many years in each other's company. Each of us has become familiar with the other, used to his way of looking and being, of breathing, of moving, and of choosing where and how to sit. We've grown old, and our relationship has also aged, becoming flabby and tired. I admit that I alone have prescribed our way of life; I was concerned with my business, my contracts, my accounts, and my travel, and she with raising our children and managing the household. It was a tacit agreement; I turned to my own concerns and she accepted willingly, understanding the nature of my work. My heart was comforted by a wife who loved me sincerely; the look of contentment on her face soothed me, and I was pleased by her compliance. But I realize now that I have been mistaken. My confidence extinguished my yearning, attracted me to my distant preoccupations, and weakened my relationship with my wife.

I feel a moist spray soiling my face, and a hateful smell of blood clings to me. I rise to stand before the living room window. Cold darkness envelops the large garden around the house, and the fronds of the date palm sway lightly. February is the most beautiful month in Kuwait, with its refreshing chill and gentle sun . . . I should practice my morning meditation, which alone gives me a clarity of mind that stays with me for the rest of my day. But the dream is still breathing beside me, walking with me, rising and falling in my chest, and the voices of Ahmad and his companions are ringing in my ears. A question looms: what's coming next?

I don't remember when I formed the habit of paying attention to what happens to me. The words of my grandfather, the sea captain, remain with me. I was a boy when he instilled them in me, his sight weak but his voice calm. "We used to go to sea without a motor, with only sails, the wind, and the mercy of the Lord of the Worlds. A captain must learn to pay attention to the messages sent by the wind, the stars, the darkness, and the smell of the sea. He must be alert to any sign that comes to him, for everything has signs, and fortunate is the man who learns to read what's coming—he expects what's waiting for him, and he prepares for it." Over the years I've learned to catch the whiff of a passing message and to ponder what secrets it might hold.

I washed my face to remove the traces of the dream still clinging to it. By force of habit, I went down the steps to bring in the newspapers. Recently I've begun to hate reading the papers; there's nothing but disappointing local news, corruption that hatches more corruption, a government that goes and another that comes, struggles among the sons of the one Arab homeland, terrorist attacks sweeping the world. A worrying thought comes to mind: someday I'll open the paper and see a picture of my son Ahmad in Afghani dress with his new name, Abu l-Fath al Kuwaiti!

A year and a half earlier Uthaiman had come to me, with a look on his face that I couldn't read, to give me the news. "Thanks be to God, Ahmad has become an emir, commanding a jihadi group fighting in Syria! His name is now Abu l-Fath al-Kuwaiti."

It took me a moment to absorb what he said with such obvious happiness. "Where did you get this news?"

He showed me a picture on his phone. It was Ahmad, with loose hair and a long beard, in the middle of a group of young men who all wore Afghan clothing and brandished machine guns. Below it was written, "The sheikh and combatant in the jihad, Abu l-Fath al-Kuwaiti, commander." I felt nauseated, and handed the phone back to him. A moment of silence passed between us before I looked at him, revealing all my antipathy and anger, and asked, "Are you in contact with Ahmad?" Something in his face quivered before he rushed to say, "No, no, I just follow the news of him!" I continued to look at him, refusal in my heart, doubting his tone of voice and unwilling to believe him.

That same evening I received a call from a friend who is the editor of one of the local newspapers. "Yaqoub, my friend, I'm sorry to bother you, but I have to tell you...." He informed me that he had received the news from a correspondent close to Islamist groups, and that he had kept it from being published, out of concern for my reputation and my relations. He ended by saying, "We don't want the sons of Kuwait to stand before the world as killers and terrorists!"

Who played with Ahmad's mind, who stuffed his head with the love of blood? He's become "the jihadi combatant, Abu l-Fath al-Kuwaiti"! I'm obsessed with the idea that it's not his fault. Shaikha and I raised him—did we fall short in anything, did we make him an appetizing prey for those who hunt their pigeons in mosques? Both of us sinned by neglecting his behavior, his transformation into a terrorist.

After I ate breakfast and washed, I stood before the brightly lit wall mirror in my bedroom. I adjusted my headcloth and the agal cords that held it, and the smell of blood returned to my nostrils. "What a sad face!" I murmured to myself. I took the bottle of cologne and sprayed a little on my neck and my hands. The specter of Ahmad with his turban appeared to me and settled in the top corner of the mirror. I turned my face away from him.

I was used to going to Shaikha's room every morning when I left; she would chide me if I left the house without saying goodbye. I hoped she was still sleeping.

"Yaqoub!" Her sleepy voice called me. I stopped, waiting for what she would say. She turned over on her side, then pulled herself from under the covers and sat up on the edge of the bed. "What time is it?"

"It's eight A.M." I had not wanted her to wake up!

"Don't forget that tonight is Abrar's birthday." She left the bed and walked toward me, her steps slow and her face sleepy.

"Your cologne smells good!" She was looking at my face with absent eyes. I embraced her, smelling the scent of sleep in her hair, and she whispered, "I love you."

I don't know why I remain silent in such moments. My tongue is mute and I experience a sort of irritation, as if my inability to answer taints me with failure, so I'm unhappy with myself and with her too. I avoided answering, asking instead, "What shall I bring to Abrar?" Her arms fell away from me.

I detest leaving the house late. For years I've felt an aversion to the ritual morning embrace; I wished she had remained asleep or had contented herself with speaking to me from her bed. She was looking at me, so I said, "Choose a gift for Abrar and call me so I can arrange for the payment." I turned to leave, but her voice drew me back:

"Where's my kiss?"

I felt my annoyance rising, but I bent down and touched her cheek and neck with my lips and said goodbye. I left her standing as I pulled my silhouette from the mirror in her room, fleeing as Ahmad's image pursued me. I nearly stumbled going down the stairs, between my exasperation and the smell of blood. I don't dislike Shaikha, but I can't embrace her every morning, or match the tenderness of her emotions. Sometimes I wonder why this is happening between us.

I opened the outer door of the house and my chauffeur, Bayoumi, rushed to take my briefcase and open the car door. "Good morning, sir."

"Good morning," I replied, taking my place in the rear seat. I said to myself that I would have left in a better mood if she had stayed asleep! I was pained by what our relationship had come to.

"The main office?" asked Bayoumi.

"Yes." The trip from my house in the Dahiya neighborhood to my office in Al-Qibla takes no more than ten minutes.

Today I'll meet the employees of the company. Uthaiman looked at me in amazement yesterday, commenting, "This is the first time you've asked to see the employees! Has something happened?" He remained standing, his thick beard framing his face, waiting for any clarification from me. I repeated, "You'll be with me tomorrow, and I will meet all the employees." He told me that the total number is fifty.

"Prepare a list of the names of the members of each department, with their names, their nationalities, their degrees, and the nature of their work. I'll meet them in groups of five."

"As you wish."

Uthaiman is Shaikha's brother. He has been working in my company for three decades, as deputy general director for finance and administration. He's like an octopus with tentacles reaching the leading personalities of religious groups and Islamic financial institutions, and that brings more tenders and important financial opportunities to the company. I keep him working at my side even though I detest him.

My black Mercedes advances slowly. Since the end of the Iraqi occupation, it has been my habit to trade in my car every year. As soon as the new model arrives, my friend who holds the Mercedes concession arranges to have a new car sent to me, after appraising the car from last year and taking it back.

Traffic covers the Riyad road; there's no set time for traffic in Kuwait. We stop at a traffic light and Liberation Tower and the Television Building appear in the distance. I smell a fleeting whiff of that young woman's perfume.

Last Monday morning when I arrived at the company, the security officer hastened to move a young woman away from the door of the elevator, placing his massive body in front of her and inviting me to enter: "Please, sir!"

Our eyes met, hers and mine. I glimpsed one side of her face and a flash in her eyes, and the scent of her captivating perfume touched me. I wished I could remain, to see her whole face and body. It was as if her look spoke to me of something unknown. Her hijab seemed strange, only a light covering hiding her hair. She looked away quickly, averting her eyes.

"Please, sir!" Bayoumi was indicating the elevator door. She was still hidden behind the security officer. I stepped in and her perfume followed me. As the door closed, I was surprised to see part of her face and her glance reflected in the elevator mirror. I thought about getting out, to meet her and learn who she was, but I remained beside Bayoumi, with her perfume between us. It seemed to me that a hidden appeal shone in her eyes and on her face, and it struck a chord in my mind. That day a vision of her appeared to me from time to time, and I felt her sitting beside me in the car on the way home.

On Tuesday and yesterday on Wednesday, I came to the company hoping to run across her in the morning, so I could allow her to share the elevator ride with me and contemplate what was behind her eyes. But all I met was the eager security officer, waiting for me. Once again, my mind was constantly distracted by her. The image of a passing young woman was invading my thoughts and confounding me! It was as if the look in her eyes spoke to me of more than one thing—I saw her smiling, and then turning her face away, and then with her eyes closed. I don't know why I imagined her taking off her head covering, so that I could see her radiant face. Something like an obscure memory came to me, as if I had met her before, taken her face in my hands, and kissed her forehead. She was barely the age of my daughter Sahar! The thought crossed my mind that perhaps she was a message, and I should follow it.

I was irritated by the thought of how preoccupied I had been by her during the last two days. I tried to push away her image but it resisted stubbornly, remaining before me, as the scent of her perfume came and went around me.

Yesterday evening I had been sitting unspeaking when Shaikha commented, "It's Ahmad's absence that's made you so silent." The scraps of news that reach me about him torment me, like a drill piercing my flesh. I don't know where he is, I don't know how to get him out of there and bring him back to Kuwait. I'm helpless, facing the question of how to extract him from the turmoil of terrorist battles. Oh, my son, how will you get out of Syria? I ask myself, shaken by the thought that while Shaikha and I and our children and our grandchildren enjoy peace and quiet, he is in the midst of explosions, killing, and blood.

My son is at the head of a terrorist group fighting in Syria! And here a young woman I don't know suddenly crosses my path and occupies my mind. A troublesome question occurs to me—what if she's not an employee of the company? All the employees register their entry by a fingerprint at eight o'clock. I remembered that I was at the elevator at about eight-thirty. If she's an employee, then she was late; I'll ask for the list of those who were late on Monday. But what if there was more than one, how would I know her from the name? But I calm myself, whispering, "I'll see her today among the others, and I'll recognize her."

My car turns north, making its way to the roundabout at the Sheraton.

Is it possible? I asked myself. Yaqoub al-Shiraa, CEO of one of the largest general trading and contracting companies in Kuwait, is preoccupied by a chance meeting with a young woman? I'm in my mid-sixties. How can a glance from a girl capture my thoughts, shake my heart? Is it possible that my spirit trembles in the hope of seeing her? What chord has this young woman struck, to awaken the melody of yearning that was slumbering in my heart?

Day and night, the shadow of Ahmad gnaws my spirit's very flesh. Now I turn my eyes away when I walk by the closed door of his room; I don't know how to extricate myself from these thoughts. And for the last two days, the shadow of this young woman has added to my tension.

In recent years, I've come to feel that women's bodies monopolize my covert attention. When a tender body passes before me, leaving perfume in her wake, I restrain my glances, hide my turmoil, swallow my desire, and keep silent.

My car smoothly pulled up to the entrance of the building housing the company's offices, and Bayoumi hastened to open the door for me. I wished I would find her before me, but when I stepped down, it was the open maw of the elevator that awaited me.

2

"We're silly to celebrate the time that's elapsed in our lives!"

Yaqoub said that at the beginning of the week when I reminded him of Abrar's birthday. His comment pained me. I looked at him and justified the celebration: "Rather we're looking forward times yet to come!"

"Jaya!" I called her to take the breakfast tray. She's my devoted servant, the one who raised my children. She's been with me for more than thirty years, never complaining for a moment and never once stinting in her service. Sometimes I feel as if she's closer to me than my sisters.

I don't know what's happened to me recently; it's gotten so that I hate being alone. Strange thoughts leap into my mind, frightening and upsetting me. For the first time since we were married, I yearn to be with Yaqoub. I look at him stealthily and see the worry in his face, hear his silence, and I wonder what could be preoccupying him. He has everything a man could dream of, so why is he sad and scowling most of the time? Why have his actions lately begun to hurt me, and even make me cry?

This morning as he was going to work, the scent of his cologne lingered behind him, pervading my room. Suddenly I was crying hard. I had said to him, "Your cologne smells good," but he didn't respond. He kissed me as if he were eating something unappetizing. When I stepped up to him, I sensed from his breathing that he was irritated with my closeness. Sadness stirred in my heart, and I stood still.

"Jaya!" Where has she disappeared? Tonight is Abrar's birthday.

I reach for the party list on the table. I've written everything down, for fear of forgetting. All that's left is to buy Yaqoub's gift for Abrar. After I arrange everything, my chauffeur, Dadou, will take me to the Salihiya market to buy a Rolex watch. In a little while I'll call the girl in charge of the music, to stress that she must arrive early to set up the speakers. She told me she would come at four. Abrar has talked to her about the songs she and her friends like and asked her to bring young Manayir with her to play the CDs, since she knows what the girls like.

The banquet manager of the Sheraton came yesterday and inspected the garden. He agreed with me about the arrangement and placement of the buffet, and about arranging the chairs for the guests, and he assured me that his workers would arrive at five. The head of the company that organizes children's birthday parties called me a little while ago, telling me that her workers were on the way. She told me that as soon as they arrive, they'll begin setting up the decorations and games for the children. Yaqoub spoke to the company and they sent Riyad, the Pakistani electrician; he has been in the garden since morning, extending the electrical connections and setting up lighting for the palms. I asked him to stay the whole day and not to leave until after the party, in case there's any problem.

When I glanced at the garden a while ago I found workers from the umbrella company working to set up temporary umbrellas, in case it rains. But the weather is clear today; I don't think it will rain.

"Yes, Madam." Jaya stood before me.

"Take the tray, and make sure that Sahar is awake. She's going to the university."

Naeema, the girl from the beauty salon, came yesterday afternoon to remove the peach fuzz from my face, to clean my legs, and to dye my hair. We agreed she would come today at five to set my hair and apply my makeup, and then she'll take care of Sahar's hair and face.

Yaqoub left without a word, as usual. It's hard for a woman to live with a man who's constantly silent, who doesn't know how to gladden her heart with a word, who doesn't know how to smile!

I'll get up, dress, and get ready to go out.

I've been oblivious for years, absorbed in pregnancy, giving birth, the children, the house, shopping, and travel. Now I realize that Yaqoub intentionally placed a bright blindfold of money over my eyes, so that I wouldn't notice how he drew away. If I asked for a hundred dinars he gave me two hundred, buying his distance with money. I was stupid to accept it!

I remember when he shouted at me recently. I was at the beach house, he was at home, and I wanted him to be with us, so I called him more than once. "When are you coming, dear?" When he came, his face was closed, and as usual he sat with us in silence. When Abrar and her husband left the table, I looked at him and asked, "What's wrong?"

As if he had been waiting for the question, he exploded and yelled at me. "I've had it!" I was frightened, but he went on: "What do you want to know? I've had it with you, with the house, with the kids, with the company, with your brother's interference, even with myself! It's enough that I've lost Ahmad."

At the time, I told myself, so it's the loss of Ahmad. At the sound of the shout, Abrar came to the door, but he chased her away. "It's nothing, go back to your husband and your kids!"

He looked back at me and continued his attack. "'Where are you, where are you?' Fifty phone calls! Fine, what do you want? What do we have in common, what do we talk about? We share a table, a few glances, talk of the market and brands and foolish shopping!" He looked up, pain marking his face, and shot out, "Nobody remembers Ahmad!" He turned his face away, as if to hide his weakness and defeat from me. "The day he left the house, he took my spirit with him."

As usual when he's angry, he finished what he had to say without waiting for a response. He got up and headed for the seashore to face it in silence, leaving me to my tears, his reproaches a burning coal in my chest.

When we were married, I realized that he's a man who loves his work, and I respected that. I chose not to pursue him, so as not to annoy him; but I did not realize that every day that passed added a brick to the wall of separation that rose between us. Now I can't take it any longer. After all these years I've discovered my negligence, I've discovered that I've lost my husband! When I meet him now, I'm always on the verge of tears.

I wish I had a friend I could open my heart to and reveal my pain. Each of my three sisters is busy with her life and her world. We're only brought together by our dull, weekly visits to my mother, where each one comes decked out in her own pathologies. My younger sister, whose room walls I remember as festooned with pictures of singers and movie stars, has become religious and started wearing the hijab, quickly followed by the black niqab that covers her face. She dragged her husband and her children along in her wake. For a while, her face would cloud over every time she saw me; she would point to my head and say, "God guide you, Shaikha! What a shame for this head and this hair to burn in the fires of hell!" She would mutter, "It's not right, it's not right!"

Once my youngest cousin came in, whom I had carried in my arms when he was an infant. He greeted me and I kissed him, just as I would my son Du'aij, and I was taken aback to hear her shouting, "That's not permitted—it's forbidden!"

That's when I exploded and yelled at her, "It's only forbidden in your sick thinking. It's only forbidden in your sordid views. It's forbidden because you're not a decent human being!" She froze in shock. "My hair, my clothes, and how I behave are no concern of yours!" I sprang up to leave, but my poor mother intervened.

"Please Shaikha, dear—I have nothing left of you children but these visits, so don't . . . " and she burst into tears.

I looked at her, now so weak, and said, "It's hard, Mother!" Then I left, trembling as I went out. I hated my sister, and I would avoid meeting her and her hostility again.

During the last two years our weekly visits have turned into a heavy burden. When my sister Mona was promoted to become the under-secretary of one of the ministries, everything in her changed: the look in her eyes, her way of speaking, her clothing, her purses, her watches, her shoes, even her way of sitting. She never stops talking about her meetings and her work with important officials, while we're left to look at her in silence and to fidget. Yaqoub interceded for her, at my request, with his friend the minister; when the decree announcing her promotion was issued, she called to thank him, but she didn't trouble herself to say one word to me. I found that strange, but I told myself that position changes people.

I don't know what's wrong with me—something has touched my spirit and I've come to hate being alone. I long for Yaqoub. I sit on the edge of a river of tears, and the least word makes my tears flow.

"Jaya, Jaya…" She must tell Dadou to get the car ready for me.

Sometimes I feel as if I have everything I want while having nothing: a husband, children, wealth, houses, servants, and travel. My sisters, the women in my family, and my friends are all envious of me, while alone I suffer from Yaqoub's abstention from any caress or endearment, from his endless preoccupations. From time to time, I sigh and complain to him of my hardship and my pain: "I'm worn out, I've had enough, and you're isolated from me!"

Every time, he gives me the same faint response: "I'm not isolated." He's silent for a few seconds, then he lifts his eyes and looks at me: "You know I love you." How often have I asked myself how Yaqoub loves me!

I sense that he's sad and depressed, drowning in a dark pool of silence. I know that he's pained by Ahmad's absence. Once he reproached me, saying, "You don't care about him!"

I found the accusation odd: "How can you say that?" He remained silent, so I poured out what was in my heart: "Ahmad is a young man, he needed you to stand beside him, you're the man, the father!"

His face flushed and he nodded. "You're right, I'm the one who failed him."

Has Ahmad's absence, together with the frightening news of him, added to the coldness in our relationship? Ahmad was difficult from the time he was born; I would have died giving birth to him, if it hadn't been for the doctor who saved me by a Caesarian section. From childhood on, Ahmad was silent like his father, content with his isolation and with following everything with his eyes. When I gave him a toy or a gift he would take it without emotion, as if he was required to take it, to the point that I was never able to tell if he was happy with it or not. He wasn't like his brother Du'aij in his manners, nor did he resemble either of his sisters.

Yaqoub was more attached to him than to any of the others. Whenever we sat alone together, he would reveal his delight in him— "Dear Ahmad, he resembles me!" I would look at him and find a strange smile on his face, as he told me, "I like his personality, his calm, and his silence. I'll put him at the head of our companies, and they will grow under his leadership." I would reproach him, telling him not to favor him over his siblings, but he would justify himself: "He's the dearest to my heart, but I won't stint any of the others."

He didn't listen to me or alter his favoritism for Ahmad. That's what made me pull away from Ahmad, perhaps unintentionally, the more his father drew close to him. When he became religious he changed, and a frightening look appeared in his eyes. He began to pursue me, his sisters, and the servants with his shouting, his reprimands, and his abuse. I began to fear him and avoid meeting him.

What dress shall I wear…?

"Yes, Madam!" Jaya's voice came to me.

"Have Dadou get the car ready."

Jaya is calm and silent like Yaqoub, hearing an order and obeying it without commenting. Maybe it's my fate to live among people who know only silence.

The Salihiya market isn't crowded during the day and I'm only going to one store, so it doesn't matter what dress I wear.

In recent months, in an effort to draw closer to Yaqoub, I've asked him more than once, "What's bothering you?"

"Ahmad. His image never leaves my mind. I'm afraid of him and afraid for him, and the news is not reassuring—every day he's in a battle!"

"You have far-flung contacts, why don't you try to bring him back to Kuwait?"

"I have tried but I couldn't. He's working with a terrorist group." It was the first time I had seen him so weak and broken. "Ahmad does not want to return."

Was it Ahmad alone who was on Yaqoub's mind?

I wore this dress last week. White is more appropriate for the morning.

For more than a year I've been meaning to organize my wardrobes. I don't even know what's in them anymore. But whenever I think of starting, it seems like an onerous chore. Even my shoe cabinet is full. I'll wear the white shoes. But maybe the brown shoes would go better with the dress, I don't want to look... Where's the green dress? My God, the wardrobe is stuffed with clothes! I'll organize it on Friday; we won't go to the beach house this week, and if we do go, I'll organize it on Saturday. I'll call Jaya to help me, and I'll give her the old clothes to send to her daughter in India. I have a lot of dresses I've never worn. Whenever I traveled, I went shopping.

My heart tells me that there's something on Yaqoub's mind.

Yesterday I came across a picture of Ahmad on one of our trips to Geneva. I began to look at him, the way he stands and his calm gaze, and it stirred my longing for him and my fear for him. My tears flowed, and I shook with repressed sobs. A black idea came to mind, but I cast it away and sought God's protection from Satan.

Has Yaqoub heard any news of Ahmad? I don't know how he slipped out of our hands; I wasn't expecting.... Now his name has become "the jihadi combatant, Abu l-Fath al-Kuwaiti." Any time I meet my friends I'm afraid of the scandal, afraid of hearing "Your son is a terrorist!" Sahar came to me once, her face pale, shouting, "May God not bless you, Ahmad!"

"What happened?"

She burst into tears, and told me that she was sitting with her friends when one of them lifted up her phone and asked her, "Is this a picture of your brother Ahmad?" She told me she had been flustered and confused, not knowing how to answer, and she had no choice but to deny it and leave them, embarrassed. She stared at me and asked, "Is it true that he's a terrorist, that he kills people?"

Her question frightened me. "No, no, it's not true!" She looked at me for several seconds before she took her tears to her room.

I remember the day Ahmad lit into her and chased away her friends. He shouted at her, "I'll kill you if you have a party!" That day I called Yaqoub to ask for help.

Fine. I'll wear this dress, with black shoes.

"Madam, the car is ready." Jaya's voice comes to me from the door.

"Let him wait."

"Goodbye, Mama!" It's Sahar's voice.

I call out, "Sahar, Sahar!"

"Mama, dear, I'm late for the lecture. I'll call you from the car. *Bye.*"

I look fat in this dress. It's gotten so I hate my body. A while ago, Abrar recommended an American trainer to me. She said she's fantastic, she comes to the house at set times, and she also works with a nutrition group. I hate being fat. I must preserve my body. When I ask Yaqoub if I'm still pretty, he always answers with the same word: "Definitely."

Tonight Abrar will be thirty-seven; nearly four decades have passed since we were married. My life has been peaceful, except for Ahmad. Whenever I asked Yaqoub to join us in some family occasion, he would excuse himself, choosing to remain at a distance and repeating "I'm depending on you." Rare are the pictures that show him with us. Last week, Abrar said to him, "I want a gift for my birthday."

He looked up at her and said, "Just ask." He was waiting for her request, but she got up and went to sit beside him. Then she kissed him and said, "I want you to come."

An embarrassed smile flickered across his face. "Certainly, I'll be there."

It has often occurred to me that Yaqoub hides behind his money, leaving it in his place. But money can't replace the presence of a person. We live in the same place, but we aren't together! Tonight I'll ask him to take a trip with me. We need to be together.

This dress is fine, and Dadou is waiting in the car. I'll choose a watch for Abrar and come back quickly to finish the arrangements for the party. I'll call Yaqoub from the shop to tell him the price, and he'll take care of the rest.

3

"Have Uthaiman come in," I said to Marwan, on the telephone.

Why am I rushing? I must appear calm. I hear a light tap on the door. "Come in!" Marwan appears, saying good morning and handing me the file of mail. I return his greeting. "Is there anything important?"

"You have a meeting at noon, you, Mr. Ismail, and the engineer Mr. Kareem, with the representatives of the Baghdad company. The papers for the meeting are ready."

"Fine. Have Uthaiman come first."

I turned my face away, looking at the mirror of the sparkling sea. My office on the twenty-seventh floor gives me a continuous view of it. Oil took us away from the sea, so it sulks and turns its face away from us. Kuwaitis' homes used to bathe their faces in the sight of it at sunrise, and bid it farewell when evening scattered darkness over it. Its waves were part of their gatherings in the evening and their songs, and it listened to the secrets of lovers among them. As the years passed, the people of Kuwait became distant from the seashore; the asphalt of Arabian Gulf Street stretched out like a giant to separate them from it. The sea came to be a specter of a distant past, with its sea captains, its divers, and its long voyages, a memory of struggles with terrors and frightening darkness in order to earn a bitter bite of bread.

When I was a child, all I knew was running on the sandy beach, swimming, and fishing. Kuwait was a small city, the mud-brick houses clinging to each other and the dirt roads narrow. My father's house was in the Qibla neighborhood, and I used to go with my mother to my grandfather's house in Sharq, walking in familiar streets. We would pass through Farjan, where we knew the people in almost every house.

"Your trip is at the end of next week," Marwan reminded me. I was surprised to hear him, as I had thought he had left. "Your trip to Masira, with Mr. Sami."

I looked at him. "Remind me at the beginning of the week."

"Certainly." He turned to leave.

I had forgotten that I had agreed with my friend Sami to travel to Oman for a fishing trip off the island of Masira.

The project my company is bidding on in Baghdad is worth thirty million Kuwaiti dinars, more than a hundred million American dollars, and we have been working on it for nearly a year. Ismail, my maternal cousin and partner in the company, and the Lebanese chief engineer, Kareem, have visited Baghdad three times. The idea gleamed quietly in my mind: my company is rebuilding Baghdad, while my son might be among those making car bombs or packing explosive suicide belts to cause destruction in it. I quickly pushed away the anxiety.

Yesterday, Ismail informed me, "The contract will be authenticated by the Department of Authentication in the Iraqi Ministry of Foreign Affairs, and by the Kuwaiti embassy in Baghdad." I was looking at him, while the image of that young woman was running wild through my head. He added, "Our company has deep experience in working in Iraq." He smiled and said, "And you hold the Saddam Hussein medal!"

I didn't like his comment. "Saddam has gone to hell, *an evil destination*, and his medal with him!"

He sensed my irritation, so he rose to leave.

I don't know where Ahmad is now. He might be in Syria or Iraq, and he might have crossed into Turkish territory. Someone is at the door. "Come in!"

"Peace be upon you." It's Uthaiman, carrying a folder. "The lists are ready."

I asked for Marwan, and when he came in I said, "Begin with the financial department, and bring in five employees at a time." He seemed not to understand, so I gestured to Uthaiman: "He'll explain."

They left together and I remained alone, anxiety crouching under my long dishdasha. Why am I so unsettled? Chairman of the board, with relationships stretching from Kuwait to the Gulf, the Arab world, Europe, America, and Japan. After working with me, many people have told me, "You've got charisma!" Maybe it's my name, my companies, my unusual height, the look in my eyes, my natural silence. But something strange struck me the moment I glimpsed that young woman near the elevator, something that weakened my spirit. Shadows of her have clung to me and suspended me on the edge of an enormous boulder of apprehension.

The door opened and Uthaiman came in. "Long may you live. The first group has arrived."

I had directed him to have each person identify himself, state his nationality, and give the department where he worked. "I want every employee to give me one short sentence stating the worst aspect of the company." I left my desk to sit at the head of the large meeting table, keeping silence over my secret.

As the first group came in, I read embarrassment in the employees' faces. I remained silent while Marwan and Uthaiman ran the meeting. I saw faces I had never seen before, and I made notes about some of the comments. I discovered that I have an employee from Senegal and another from Ukraine. Retreating into my own tension I examined the faces, groups coming and going, until Ismail came in with his beard and his loud voice, proclaiming, "Peace be upon you."

"And on you." Anticipating his question, I said, "It's not right for us to work with employees we don't know."

I sensed that he found it strange that I would plan this without his knowledge. Uthaiman was there, and he murmured, "I'll leave you."

I said to Ismail that our company's work is worth millions, that our projects are spread over Kuwait, Qatar, Iraq, Egypt, Dubai, Saudi Arabia, Jordan, Lebanon, Morocco, and Oman, and that matters in the region are unstable. A simple email could reveal the details, specifications, and prices of a contract, and we need experienced employees we can trust.

"It's a good step," he commented. "Uthaiman told me about it yesterday." This was not the first time Uthaiman had told Ismail what went on in my office. "Should I be with you?"

"There's no need for that." The words were intentionally cold. He reminded me that our meeting was at twelve-thirty. "Of course." I nodded to him, and he rose to leave the office.

I returned to my anticipation, though my irritation with Uthaiman remained. What will you do if you see her? The question surprised me, and I sat silently, following the groups as they came and went. Suddenly I saw her come in, with another woman and three men; my eyes met hers, and I felt an electric charge pass through my neck, shaking me. She seemed taller than I had imagined, with a sculpted body and a defined waist. I sat up in my chair calmly, seeking to throw Uthaiman off the scent of my interest in her. I stole a glance at her, to slake my thirst.... A piece of light fabric was still wrapped around her head, perhaps more firmly fixed around her face today. She sat with her back straight, placing one hand over the other. I looked at the green veins visible in her small hand. Suddenly the scent of her perfume permeated my office, jasmine, lemon, and gardenia.

One of the men spoke, and then she said, "My mane is Farnaz Qurmuzi, Iranian in nationality. I work as a computer specialist in the Department of Programming and Development." She spoke calmly and clearly, not looking at me but addressing herself to Uthaiman.

"What's the worst thing about the company?" I spoke to her in order to make her look at me.

She took her time, and I felt as if she swallowed hard. She lifted her face to me and our eyes met; she looked into my eyes and I reveled in her gaze, drinking it in, my heart bathed in joy and the scent of gardenia enfolding my spirit. She spoke once more, calmly, in her soft voice: "There's nothing wrong with the company." I took in her words from her eyes, from her face, from her scent. How I wished she would say more, but she stopped, and a sudden silence descended on the office.

I realized that I was breathing more rapidly than usual. A young woman with soft, bronze skin, black eyes, carefully drawn eyebrows, a delicate nose, and a beauty spot above her left lip. Something in her called to me; I was drawn by her voice and I wished she would stay longer in my presence. "You have nothing to remark?" I asked her again.

She simply shook her head and said, "No."

When her colleagues stood up, she looked at me and asked, "May I say something?"

"Please."

"I was not late on Monday...."

Before she had finished speaking, Uthaiman admonished her, saying, "Fine, fine, it's not important."

"Let her finish!" I cut him off brusquely, and everyone froze. My eyes and my heart were fixed on her.

"I had been excused for an hour to go to the doctor."

I nodded my assent. There was a moment of silence before Uthaiman moved, then they all followed him out of the room and the door closed behind them.

I felt I was being swept away by her, and that something mysterious was calling me, pulling me toward her. I was amazed to realize that I would have liked to get up and follow her out, to look at her face and stay close to her. I noticed that some perfume was settling near me.

Yaqoub! I said to myself, you're falling for an Iranian girl you don't know, when your son is fighting against Iran in Syria and Iraq! Slow down, Yaqoub, and pay attention—you don't know what's behind her. You can follow after her; start off, perhaps you will reach your heart's desire...but the danger is that you'll be lost!

Ahmad's journey had started from the mosque. I began to notice that he came home late, and when I asked him about it, he answered, "I'm attending Quran lessons, memorization and commentary, after the sunset prayer." At the time he was fourteen, in the first year of high school; for some reason, his answer stirred something in me. I made no objection, but the next day, after the evening prayer, I walked to the mosque near our house. The main door was locked; I looked for another entrance without finding one, so I went to the muezzin's quarters. When he came out, I asked, "How can I get into the mosque?" He examined me for a few seconds, as if he were trying to guess my intentions. Since I was wearing a dishdasha with a headcloth and cords, he led me to a small door next to his residence. "You can go in from here."

I went in calmly, concealing the worry alert in my breast. The courtyard of the mosque was empty except for a lingering aroma of incense, which I recognized. I saw a small door ajar and heard the voice of a man speaking. There was a little circle of perhaps ten boys surrounding the man. He was bearded, he had a dark prayer callus in the middle of his forehead, and he wore a white headcloth that flowed down over his shoulders. He stopped speaking when he saw me coming toward him. I asked, "What are you doing with the children?" "Say, 'Peace be upon you,' Brother." He spoke in a pretentious tone that I hate. I looked at him. "I'm studying some verses of the Quran with them, may God bless them." His accent told me that he was Egyptian. Since I remained standing, he rose to face me, and I saw that he was overweight.

"We meet together between the sunset and the evening prayers."

"What else do you do?"

Ahmad stood up, took my hand, and pulled gently, saying, "That's enough, Baba."

I remained where I was, facing the man, and he added, "Every Muslim has a duty to call others to God."

I ground my teeth in irritation, and he stepped back. "You're calling the children of Muslims to God?" My question surprised him. I warned him, "This time I'll leave you, but next time I won't let you get away." A muscle in his face twitched, and I shouted, "Get out of the mosque! Get out!"

The boys scattered, moved by fear, and he followed them without protest.

Ahmad walked beside me in silence, wrapped in his anger, and the moment we entered the house he hurried to his room. "Ahmad!" I stopped him. "I don't want you to attend these lessons!"

"Why did you shout at the sheikh and throw him out of the mosque?" His protest surprised me. "You humiliated me in front of the others. It was very embarrassing!"

"To hell with the evil sheikh!" I answered, overcome by anger. Since he was still staring at me, I softened my tone. "Son, please, don't let yourself be carried away by the likes of these!"

He turned back toward his room before I had finished speaking. His lack of response infuriated me, but I let it go, to avoid making things worse. That night, he did not sit with us for dinner. Perhaps this event was the first step on the journey that led to losing him.

Oof! Where is that smell coming from—the smell of blood in my nose?

4

Does it make any sense for me to desire a girl the age of my daughter?

I'm watching television in the living room, alone with the image of Farnaz: her way of speaking, her facial expressions, the look in her eyes, the beauty spot on her lip, all of her. The National Geographic channel keeps me company in my solitude.

It's Abrar's birthday; the music reaches me from the garden. Shaikha has been busy for over a week. "I'm going to throw a big party," she said. In recent years she's sought out any occasion to distract herself, with no objection from me.

"This is all heresy—it's against our religion!" Ahmad had been in high school the first time he yelled at his mother to protest against his sister's birthday party. I looked at him in disbelief, while he finished his grievance: "This is all a blind imitation of the Jews and Christians. It's wasteful and immoral; God preserve us from it!" Then he threatened his sister: "Next year I'll burn the garden and everyone in it!"

"Ahmad!" I shouted. "You're going to burn your sister's friends? What's gotten into you, have you lost your mind?"

"You, Father, you're the one who's responsible before God! The prophet said, 'Each of you is a shepherd, and each of you is responsible for his flock.'"

I was amazed by what I was hearing. He seemed like a stranger, in his insolence and his nerve. I looked at him, my youngest son, fearing what he would do to himself, fearing him, and hating the scowl of disgust on his face. It occurred to me to wonder what had lit the fire of savagery in my son's mind and in his words.

Ahmad was ferocious with us then, so how is he now, with others? Whenever I'm alone recently, I've begun looking for pictures of him online. The last time, I found one that showed him sitting behind a machine gun in an open truck bed. I stared at the picture for a time. His appearance frightened me; he had wrapped his headcloth around his head in a strange fashion, allowing his long hair to hang down beneath it, and his beard framed the grimace on his face. How had my son changed? I looked at the picture in dismay—is this my son? I was shaken, wondering how a person can become savage, turning away from gentleness to killing. A sudden fear struck me: does my son take part in cutting off people's heads, like any other terrorist? I hate even seeing a chicken butchered! I felt as if I couldn't breathe, and I pushed away the thought that perhaps it was my fault.

Sounds of music come from the garden, together with the noise of children's games and a little of the women's laughter.

This afternoon I was sitting at my desk looking at the distant expanse of the sea, when I was pulled back by the sound of the telephone. The screen told me it was Shaikha.

"I'm in the Salihiya mall," she said. "And I've chosen your gift for Abrar. It's a Rolex watch, gold with diamonds."

"Thank you. I didn't have time to go with you."

"It costs twenty-eight thousand dinars, after the discounts."

"I'll send you a check with the driver."

She objected quickly, "There's no need for a check. The merchant will send you a link on your phone, and you can pay from where you are."

"That's best."

I ended the call and the scent of Farnaz's perfume leaped into my mind; her image wavered before me, and I heard the melody of her voice.

Am I becoming infatuated with an Iranian girl? The phrase caressed my face playfully, lovely, like a rose . . . The tender thought pleased me, and a smile came to my lips. I tried to imagine her walking before me, having taken off her head covering. Once again, I was seized by a hidden certainty: something links her to Ahmad; she's a precursor for something coming, and I must follow the signs.

Abrar came this afternoon with her two children to have lunch at our house and get ready for her party. Then Du'aij came with his wife and his son (whom he named Yaqoub, after me), and they all came up to greet me. Shaikha invited her mother, her sisters, their children, her friends, my sisters, their daughters, and their daughters' children. Abrar sent invitations to her friends and colleagues from work, for them and their children.

A little while ago I went out to the garden and sat with my sisters Hissa and Dalal, near Du'aij. Women and girls and young children came to greet me, but I was annoyed by the music from the speakers and the shouts of the children's games. The moment Shaikha brought me a glass of orange juice I took it and stood up, excusing myself to go back inside. She smiled. "I'll call you when it's time to blow out the candles."

I went back to the television, to the National Geographic channel. As soon as I sat down, the specter of Farnaz came to sit beside me. I would have liked to go somewhere, anywhere, to be alone, but I know how affectionate Abrar is and how attached to me she is. She would be sad if I weren't there when her birthday candles were blown out and if I weren't in the picture beside her.

Before the meeting with the Baghdad company today, I spoke to Uthaiman. "I want to see the file of the girl who protested that she had not been late." I was careful not to mention her name, to give him the idea that she didn't mean anything to me.

"I reprimanded her."

"She didn't say anything wrong," I objected, intending to defend her from any possible harm. "I'd like to have a look at her file."

Farnaz is twenty-four, born in Kuwait, single. She joined the company nine months ago, with a secondary certificate and a further, two-year diploma in computer and secretarial skills. She's Iranian. It flashed into my mind that she must therefore be Shi'ite! It occurred to me to wonder how Ismail ever permitted the hiring. My son Ahmad is fighting the Iranians with groups dedicated to jihad, and here I sit huddled over my thoughts. Just what do I want from this girl?

I examined her personnel file. I was ashamed to remove her picture, showing her with her head covering, so I photographed it with my phone. I don't know what has made me go back to look at it more than once since I came into the living room. Every time, I look at the expression in her eyes and wonder what the secret behind it could be.

There were three representatives from the Baghdad company, who came with a fourth man from the Iraqi embassy in Kuwait. The entire discussion in this meeting focused on the two essential points dividing us: our company's insistence that all the bonds for the project be issued by an Iraqi bank, and that the Baghdad company be responsible for providing all the heavy equipment. Time and time again, Ismail had told me, "If we quarrel with them at any stage of the project and we withdraw, let them go to their bank to collect the guarantees, rather than coming to a Kuwaiti bank and entangling us with them." Kareem, the chief engineer, had also said, "If we quarrel with them, we won't be able to get any heavy equipment out of the project, they'll confiscate it all."

My mind was preoccupied with Farnaz. The meeting went on for more than an hour and a half, and for most of that time I was listening, following the ongoing discussion, as I knew I would have the last word. In order to end the dispute, I said decisively, "Let's come to an agreement." I paused for a few seconds, then I told the director of the company, "We will sign the contract as soon as you agree to the two conditions."

"But. . . ." He wanted to reopen the discussion, but I stopped him. "Please. I'm sure that your schedule is filled with important meetings, and there's no need for additional discussion. I stood up and looked him in the eye. "We will await your response." Everyone around the table stood up.

The director rebuked me. "Are you throwing us out, Mr. Yaqoub?"

"Excuse me, this office is your office. I'm buying your agreement."

"And we're buying your company's reputation and experience."

We shook hands, and they left with Ismail and Kareem to formulate the agreement.

Later, the financial director brought me the prepared contract. I read it, then I asked him to have the director of the Baghdad company sign it first, before the signature of anyone from our company, establishing the full acceptance of their side. Then Ismail signed in my place; I was careful that my name would not appear in any of the contract documents, so no Iraqi party could object that I had been among the supporters of Saddam.

The image of Farnaz was still clinging to me; I can no longer free myself of it! As I looked at her picture on the telephone screen, I thought back. There had been a few passing relationships when I studied in America, in New York, but I had lived my life for study and for work. I never had time for anything but thinking still more about work and financial transactions. I was then and still am amazed that someone can be satisfied with a job, a position, a given profit, or a monthly salary. My view is that every day dawns only for new work and new transactions.

A week ago, Shaikha was talking to me about the arrangements for Abrar's birthday party. My mind wandered for a moment, and she asked, "Where are you? You aren't listening!" I looked up and she added, "You've gotten old, Yaqoub, but your head is still spinning with projects!"

Abrar defended me. "Baba's still young, and his projects are successful and earn millions!" She got up to give me a hug.

When I came back from America, I worked in the National Bank of Kuwait for two years. I moved from one department to another; I would forget myself sometimes and work more than fourteen hours in a day. When I tendered my resignation and my immediate supervisor asked me why, I told him that I was going to start my own company.

I remember that it was maybe a year ago when Sami sent me a picture on my phone, showing a young woman baring her chest. I looked at her, with her breasts pushed forward, an appeal in her eyes, an invitation in her open mouth. But I deleted the picture and did not send any reply.

I don't know exactly when it was, maybe after I passed fifty, that I began to look stealthily at the body of any passing woman, reading its contours at the urging of my hidden desire. I began to wonder why a man desires the body of a passing woman when he's blind to the body of his own wife. What's the difference, when sex is the same?

Farnaz is soft, as if she had been dipped in the nectar of her perfume! The sentence escaped me, and I realized that I was in the living room, in front of the television, and that the music from the party in the garden had become louder. What do I want from Farnaz? I wish I could see her now.

"Baba." It was Abrar's voice. "Come sit with us, the weather is lovely."

"My dear, the children's noise gets on my nerves." What would Abrar say if she knew that I was hiding here to think about a young woman I'm captivated by?

"Where's my birthday present?" She reached out to me, a smile on her face.

"I'll bring it to you in a little while." She bent down to kiss me, then left quickly.

I won't see Farnaz for the next two days; Friday and Saturday aren't workdays, so not until Sunday.

How has this young woman stirred the still lake in my heart? What she said at the end of the meeting makes me think that she saw me at the elevator, and that she had prepared an answer to defend herself. Did she cross my path on purpose? Or is she a mystery I must pursue, following the traces?

"Yaqoub." Shaikha is calling. "Bring Abrar's gift and come out. We're going to blow out the candles."

5

"I'm sorry." Safi was apologizing to me, ashamed of her baby's crying. She gave him her breast.

I smiled. "Dear Safi, this was your room before it was mine." Anyway, when I think about sleep it refuses to come.

My father was late coming home tonight. We all waited for him, my mother and I, Safi, her baby Husain, and our forebodings.

It's been a month since Safi came home divorced, and she still has tears in her eyes. A little while ago my mother came to our room and urged her to pull herself together. "You're not the first or the last to be divorced, and now you're safe from that torment." Safi remained silent, tears running down her cheeks. "Your father's house will always be here for you." Then, betraying her pain, "My dear daughter, why are you crying? You'll hurt yourself and the child you're nursing. Muhannadi and his mother can go to hell! Your life is more important."

It's here in the Nuqra neighborhood that I was born and spent my life. We moved to our new apartment four years ago, after our old building, not far from here, was torn down. My father came to Kuwait in 1981, fleeing from the Iran-Iraq war. He was a young man then. He shared a room with one of his relatives in a residence for single men; then at the end of 1989 he went back to Iran and married my mother. No sooner had he brought her to Kuwait than Saddam attacked, so he always laughs with my mother and tells her, "You brought that devil Saddam to Kuwait!"

The year of the attack my brother Reza was born, then two years later Safi came, then I was born in 1994. My dear father is now over fifty-five. When we went to Iran to visit Reza and my grandfather two years ago, my grandfather asked my father to come back and settle in Iran: "I've gotten old and tired, son!"

Grandfather's words frightened me. After a few days I began to feel like a stranger, disliking everything I saw. I concealed how shaken I was by the thought that I was a stranger there, and that I wanted to go back to Kuwait.

I don't know what made me take a dislike to Muhannadi, Safi's husband, the first time I saw him. Safi told me that he's nervous, he turns into a monster when he's drunk, and he doesn't hesitate to beat her. His mother is also tyrannical, treating Safi as a servant and constantly causing trouble for her.

"I asked Muhannadi if we could leave and go live on our own," she confided, crying. "I thought his mother was someplace else, but she swooped down on me like a hawk, yelling, 'You wicked woman—trying to separate a mother from her son!'"

Safi told me the whole story. Some quarrel arose between her and her husband; she tried to placate him, but he held himself aloof from her, and the quarrel turned into a barrier, which quickly became hatred. Then his sister intervened and advised him to divorce her, so as not to lose his mother. He came into her room one evening, loaded with anger and alcohol, to pick a fight with her. He beat her, pronounced the formula of divorce, and threw her and her infant out into the street in the middle of the night.

Safi is two years older than I am, and I never wanted her to come home as a divorcée. For two weeks now, whenever I wake up at night I find her awake with her tears, in the gloom and the silence. I've begun to notice dark circles under her eyes, but I'm afraid to ask her if she's crying over her terrible luck in her marriage and divorce, or if she loves Muhannadi and is crying over leaving him.

I've been in bed for over an hour without a wink of sleep.

My father came home about nine o'clock. He looked exhausted, so I ran to take the bag he was carrying, and he smiled. "We're having kabobs; it was a good day." When we sat down to eat, he told my mother, "Thanks be to God, I worked all day, one passenger after another."

After dinner I washed the dishes and went to bed, in the room I share with Safi and her infant. I looked at her, wishing I could tell her that Mr. Yaqoub, the president of the company, was looking at me covertly today. It was the first time that the employees went to meet him. He has a large office, filled with light, and there's a view of the sea from every part of it. I noticed his bookshelves, lined with books, and a picture of him sitting next to a beautiful woman who must be his wife, with two boys and two girls standing behind them. My colleague Mervet was surprised by how calm I was before the meeting. "God protect us," she said. "We all tremble in front of him!"

Mr. Uthaiman, the deputy director, informed us that changes are happening in the company, and that the president wanted to meet personally with all of us. Mervet whispered to me, "Mr. Yaqoub has differences with Ismail. He wants to make sure the employees are loyal to him."

He saw me last Monday near the elevator. I had asked permission to be late, so I could take Safi and her child to the pediatrician. At the elevator our eyes met briefly, and his eyes held mine until the security guard came between us. I tried to explain the matter to him today but Uthaiman objected, and after work he called me to his office. He was annoyed and gave me to understand that I had overstepped by speaking about a private matter in front of the president, and that I alone would bear the consequences of my actions. His words frightened me.

I hear Safi's regular breathing. My poor, dear sister! She has wilted during the last few days.

After I graduated from the institute, I spent more than two years looking for work. My Iranian citizenship was a stumbling block on the way to employment, in spite of my Kuwaiti birth certificate. I remember one interview, when the president of the company told me, "Your qualifications are good; they're suited to the position, but. . . ." He was silent for a moment, looking at me. "The problem is that you're Iranian."

"I have no ties to Iran." He went on looking at me, so I clarified, "I was born in Kuwait, I've never lived in Iran, and I know nothing about it."

"But you're still Iranian."

I was going to say that if I had been born and lived a quarter of my life in America, I would have American citizenship! But I stood up calmly and left the office, thanking him.

My mother cried tears of joy when I was hired by this company. Out of my salary of three hundred and fifty dinars, I give one hundred to my mother, to help with household expenses and to spend on herself. I pay ninety for the installment on my little car, and I spend the rest carefully during the month.

My father works all day driving a small pickup. He leaves at five in the morning and doesn't get back until nine at night. He pays the rent for our apartment and the household expenses, then he sends something to his family in Iran, and sometimes to Reza. My brother finished high school in Kuwait but he could not enroll in any university, so he went to Tehran. A relative of ours there helped him enroll in the military college.

It would be a catastrophe for us if they fired me from the company. I've been there less than a year, and I haven't made any mistakes. I just wanted to explain things to the president. Of course he won't care about me, a man who's a millionaire and who owns several companies.

Mervet told me, "The company is going to sign a new contract in Iraq. Maybe they'll choose some employees to work there." The very thought of going to Iraq, even for a single day, scares me. My father would certainly not agree—he doesn't hate any other regime as much as he hates the Iraqi one. He can't forget his younger brother, who died in the Iran-Iraq war.

Fadi, the son of our Lebanese neighbor, proposed to marry me on his last visit to his family. My father asked him, "Have you come back to settle in Kuwait?"

"Oh, no," Fadi answered. He explained that he worked in an appliance repair shop belonging to Hezbollah, that his salary was excellent, and that he came to Kuwait to visit his family.

"You're out of luck then," my father told him. He added, "My son is in Tehran, and I don't want my daughter to go to Lebanon."

Fadi is a handsome young man and his financial situation is great, but something prevented me from becoming attached to him. A few days after he came to propose marrying me, after we finished dinner, my father spoke to me: "Farnaz. . . ." Our eyes met and he asked me, in his hoarse voice, "Do you agree, about Fadi?" His question surprised me so I said nothing, not knowing how to answer. He went on, "I don't want to stand in your way."

I got up and kissed his hand. "I want to live near you." I don't know where the next thought came from, but I added, "I love Kuwait, and I don't want to be far from it."

I'm stretched out on the bed, and Husain is sleeping like an angel. At the beginning of the week my father brought a crib for him, which Safi put beside her bed. He comforted her, telling her, "This child will be a consolation for us all."

Our apartment has two bedrooms, one for my mother and father and the other for Safi and me. There were tears in my mother's eyes yesterday when she confided to me, "I hope you marry a Kuwaiti." I smiled, and she added, "Maybe that way you could get Kuwaiti citizenship and have a house of your own."

Mother, where am I going to find a Kuwaiti husband? Even girls, lots of them will sit with me, thinking at first that I'm Kuwaiti, because of my color, my way of speaking, and my Kuwaiti dialect. But as soon as they find out that I'm Iranian, they withdraw.

There was Faris, Mother, that young Kuwaiti who kept after me for months. When I told you about it, you said, "Speak to him. Maybe God has destined him for you." After a call or two, I went to meet him; I sat with him in the cafeteria in the Rihab Mall, while you sat at a table nearby. He told me that he would finish his university studies in a few months, and that he was prepared to marry me. I was cautious as I listened to him, and as he was saying goodbye, he added, "Our next meeting will be at my apartment." I was surprised, and he went on, "I have an apartment where I study. It's quiet and safe from other people's eyes." I did not answer, nor did I tell you about it. He revealed his intentions during the next phone call, when he said, "In the apartment we can relax, and I can feast my eyes on the beauty of your body."

Oh Mother, where can a girl find luck for her life? It's not on sale in the spice markets, and neither beauty nor learning have anything to do with her luck. Safi is like a rose, but that loathsome Muhannadi beat her and threw her and her child out in the street. I want to find a man who won't torment me, a young man who will love me, one I can go crazy loving.

I must sleep! It's almost the middle of the night. But tomorrow is Friday so I'll wake up when I please. Maybe I'll go out in the afternoon with Mother and Safi, to cheer her up a little.

6

The sea is rough today.

I always wake up at five, no matter what day it is or where I am. Today is Friday, and calm envelops the house, the garden, and the street nearby. Shaikha is deeply asleep; yesterday she stayed up at the party with her daughters, her grandchildren, and her friends until after midnight.

I woke up with something like a swirl of worry gripping me. I was like someone who has lost something and looks for it everywhere, hoping to find it. I made my ablutions and prayed, then sat in my corner. I assumed my position of relaxation, closed my eyes, and entered the corridors of light and dark that compose my daily meditation, as silence surrounded my spirit. I had finished my journey when Jaya approached calmly and stood before me. "Good morning, sir. Shall I bring breakfast?"

I nodded. After breakfast, I felt as if I needed something I couldn't put my finger on; I couldn't stay in the house. I went out, got in my car, and drove. I don't know why I came to my office in the company.

It was a little after ten-thirty when I passed the neighborhood mosque. Ever since high school, I've stayed away from communal Friday prayers. At the time, I was bothered by what the imam of our mosque preached in his sermon. I moved to another mosque, but I found myself with the same feelings for a sermon that was repeated, and that was as far as could be from the events of the time, from its language, its issues, and its concerns. I stopped going to the mosque before I left for America, though I did not stop performing the prayer.

I've come to the company today in athletic clothes. The parking lot is empty, only the cold wind moving through it. The security officer was surprised by my presence and rushed to welcome "the bey," but I paid no attention to him and made my way to my office.

As soon as I sat down behind my desk, my hand reached for the drawer and took out Farnaz's file. I was surprised, and I asked myself if I had come because of her. I caught a whiff of gardenia, and in the distance flashed the sea, the blue-green waves slightly ashen and clashing. I turned back to her picture, with her headscarf and her gaze.

This morning I stood naked before the mirror in my bathroom and contemplated my body, talking to myself: "Your hair has thinned, Yaqoub, and part of it is tinged with gray. The lines on your forehead have not changed, but the lines from your nose to your upper lip have deepened, and there are gray hairs in your mustache."

Sami injected his cheeks with Botox, using specialized needles, last year. Some of the fatigue in his face disappeared, along with his sagging cheeks, and he regained his fresh look. At the time he advised me, smiling his new smile, "Go to her clinic; she's a smart doctor and uses the very best, the latest types of Botox in the world. It's very expensive, but the results are guaranteed." I looked at him and he added, "The prophet said, 'God is beautiful and loves beauty.'"

I smiled and answered, "No one can live his own life and someone else's too."

He laughed. "That's nonsense—old men's talk. Give yourself beauty to live! A lot of men all over the world have had cosmetic surgery."

Sami has been my closest friend since my student days. He's interested in life and never tires of repeating, "Life is a pleasure, if you know life!" He and I and Fadil all studied together in New York, our years abroad spent in the same apartment. Memories of that time fill our hearts and spring up fresh whenever we meet. Sami and I were satisfied with bachelor's degrees; Fadil came back with us, but he soon traveled to Edinburgh to complete his study by earning a doctorate.

This morning it crossed my mind to wonder if I can be linked in a relationship with a young girl—what connection can there be between a man in his sixties and a girl in her twenties? And then, what can happen between us? I was lost in my thoughts. What do I want from her?

I'm looking at her file before me. She was born in 1994; eight years earlier I had received the Saddam Medal, because I was part of a group of Kuwaiti businessmen who had each contributed a million dollars to support the war effort and the steadfast resistance of the Iraqi people to the Persian attack. Everyone kept saying, "Iraq is the guardian of the eastern gate," and I was convinced at the time that if Iraq fell, then Kuwait would not be safe. It's a memory with sharp edges, and whenever it stirs, it makes bloody wounds in my spirit!

There were three of us who went by special invitation to Baghdad, "the fortress of resistance to the Persian expansion," as the regime's mouthpieces kept repeating at the time. We stayed at the Hotel al-Rashid, but the day before our meeting with President Saddam, a military detachment came and took us from the hotel by night. We didn't know what roads the cars traveled. We came to a place that seemed to be a village, and we stayed the night in a palace. Each of us was in his own suite, every breath he took counted by the security services. In the morning we got into cars with tinted windows, which drove off fast and stopped only in front of a large palace. We waited more than an hour in a spacious hall, looking at each other in complete silence. After that we were asked to go through a metal detector, then an officer performed a body search on each of us and had us take everything out of our pockets. The accompanying officer gave us our instructions: we must remain standing when we went into his honor the president's reception room, until he gave us permission to sit; we must remain completely silent except when responding to a question directed to us by his honor the president; we must not kiss his honor the president or touch any part of his body; we must leave a distance of not less than three steps between us and his honor the president at the moment of his placing the decoration around our necks; we must look at the camera and smile for the picture. I found the instructions strange, distasteful, and clearly insulting.

A sudden terror seized my heart when my eyes fell on Saddam, sitting in his military uniform and smoking a cigarette. I felt as if he were surrounded by a sort of a halo. At the time I imagined that it was the halo of power or of a great historical personality, but later I realized that it was the halo of despotism and obsession with greatness, the halo that destroyed Iraq.

As we approached he stood up to receive us, greeting us in his condescending tone. "Welcome, a warm welcome to the gallant businessmen of Kuwait!"

His adjutant Abd Hamoud stood straight as a statue behind him. I was second in line. He clasped my hand in a strong grip, and when his eyes met mine, he said, "Brother Yaqoub, you have the body of a soldier!" I don't know what I murmured in response, but he added, "We are all soldiers defending Iraq the Great and the Arab nation. When Kuwait defends Iraq, she is defending herself." Then he included us all in his wolfish stare and said, "Iraq is your country, just as Kuwait is a part of our country!"

The adjutant had me incline my head, then Saddam placed the decoration around my neck, though I forgot to look at the camera and smile. This morning, when I bent my head in front of the mirror, I felt a pain in my neck.

How can I meet Farnaz? How ironic is it that the Kuwaiti businessman who admired Saddam and gave money to defend Iraq should be infatuated with an Iranian girl in his old age! And the greater irony is that my son is fighting in Syria against Iran... suddenly Ahmad's pictures assailed me, and the scent of blood came with them.

After the first incident at the mosque, Ahmad dutifully remained in the house with us for several days, though he was silent and resisted joining in any talk. I noticed that he had become more aggressive in his answers and interactions with his mother and his sister Sahar. He stopped her once before she went out and said, "You're not wearing a hijab? It's not right for you to go out with your head uncovered."

His sister was surprised and called her mother, but he yelled at Shaikha. She was afraid and did not argue with him, but she called me, and I called him and said, "I am the one responsible for her!"

"She's my sister, and paradise is forbidden to procurers! Also, God will not forgive us for keeping silent in the face of sin."

"She's none of your business, do you hear me?"

When I went home that day, as soon as I saw him I asked, "Did the person who taught you to be zealous about your sister's clothing not also teach you the verse, *And out of kindness, lower to them the wing of humility, and say: My Lord! Bestow on them thy Mercy even as they cherished me in childhood*?" He remained silent, so I repeated, "Your mother and your sisters are none of your business; I alone am responsible for them." His expression and his breathing showed his annoyance, so I went on, "The noble prophet told us, 'The most beloved to me among you and the closest to me in paradise are those with the sweetest character.' He did not say, the most severe or those who quarrel the most with their families."

"This is an indecent display; it's not right to be silent about it!"

It was clear that he had closed his mind to any word I might say, and that he had made his decision about his way of life. He let his still-developing beard grow long and he shortened his dishdasha above his ankles. Soon he began to absent himself again.

Since I knew the way, I went into the mosque the second time with my anger raging. The Egyptian man sprang up as soon as he saw me, and a shorter bearded man stood beside him, wearing a loose head covering without cords to fasten it. I faced the Egyptian and yelled at him, "Give me your identification!"

"And peace be upon you, and the mercy and blessings of God," he intoned, in that pretentious voice that I detest. I grabbed his neck and shook him violently, yelling, "Give me the ID!"

"Who are you and why are you attacking us?" The short man asked this in a Kuwaiti accent, trying to release his companion from my grip. But I pushed him away and tightened my grip, demanding furiously,

"Give me the ID!"

"Here." He handed me his identification card. I read his name: Abdel Shafi Muhammad; employment, accountant for the Hilal al-Rahma Company.

I pulled his dishdasha and ordered him, "Come with me!"

The Kuwaiti objected, "You have no right!" I pushed him again to get him out of my way, so Ahmad took hold of him and began to speak to him.

"Where are we going?" the Egyptian asked me, trying to free himself. But I dragged him with me.

"To hell!"

I left the mosque and the boys dispersed, with Ahmad and the Kuwaiti following me. I opened the front door of my car and pushed the man in, then quickly rounded the car and started the motor. He was protesting, "I'm studying with the boys, matters of their religion, and the community knows about it!"

I was agitated, so I shouted at him, "May our lord take vengeance on you and your community!"

When I took him into the police station, the officer knew me.

"Welcome, Mr. Yaqoub!"

I was still holding the man; the officer asked me to let him go and called one of the policemen to take him to detention. The policeman took him, and I went with the officer. I explained the situation to him, telling him that this man was an accountant who was exploiting the mosque to brainwash boys with extremist ideas, something that could be destructive. The officer was silent for a time, then he said, "Unfortunately, I have no power or cause to hold him in the station." I looked at him in amazement, and he clarified, "As you know, we apply the law. There must be some accusation or misdemeanor for me to hold him."

"Can you hold him until tomorrow?"

"It's difficult."

"I'll speak to the district commander or the deputy minister."

"As you wish."

I remembered that I still had Abdel Shafi's identification card in my pocket. "Keep him here for an hour until I return." Then, without waiting to hear his reply, I stood up and thanked him.

Someone is knocking on the office door. "Come in!" The door opened and the face of the security guard appeared. He asked, "Do you want to order anything, tea or coffee?"

I was provoked by his sudden entrance, and I raised my voice in anger. "Go back to your work at the entry, and don't come to office again unless I call you. Is that understood?"

"I'm sorry." He withdrew, embarrassment written on his face.

I'm alone in my office looking at the sea, as if I'm telling it a story.

When I returned from the police station I expected to see Ahmad, but he wasn't there. I asked Shaikha about him, but she said he had not come home.

Ahmad left Kuwait six years ago, without telling anyone what he intended. I learned from Uthaiman that he went to Jordan; from there he accompanied a young Saudi to Turkey, and they crossed into Syrian territory at Idlib. Now I know nothing about him except his nom de guerre, the fact that he has become the commander of his unit, and that he lives moving between Syria, Iraq, and Turkey with his group of jihadi fighters.

I'm alone in the silence of my office, where I hear the sound of the wind on the other side of the glass. The waves show how hard it's blowing.

It's as if I'm smelling Farnaz's perfume. What's happened to me? From one day to the next I've turned into an adolescent! I don't want anything from her. That sentence escaped me and sat facing me on the surface of my desk, then it winked at me and said, "She's like a rose, with captivating eyes, soft skin, a melting smile, a beauty spot on her lip, and a perfume of jasmine, lemon and gardenia." My longing to see her stirred, and I wished I were close to her. I went back to looking at the picture in her file. How can I interpret the look in her eyes, how can I understand the secret behind my attraction to her? I wish I could smell her perfume.... I turn back to look at the sea, and the anxiety returns: You've become a child again, Yaqoub, trying to spell out what's written on your heart!

Why have I come to dislike Shaikha coming close to me over the years? Why has the spark of our desire been extinguished, so we wander in darkness, silence, and regretful looks? Sami has an apartment where he receives his female friends. Sometimes I call him and visit him, just for a change. Once when I visited him, his voice rang out with happiness as soon as I sat down. "Your arrival is a good omen!" I smiled, and he continued, "Siham is on her way, she'll be here any minute." I noticed how joy seemed to pour into his spirit and show on his face. "She's a new friend. I worked hard until she gave in and I convinced her to come."

I stood up to leave. As I went through the door of the building, I met a woman entering unobtrusively, and it occurred to me that she was Siham.

My Cartier desk clock is looking at me. I've been alone in the office for more than an hour, gazing at Farnaz's picture as if I can't escape from the trap of her secret. A girl I've never known before—what has she set in motion in my heart and my spirit? Why do I care about her?

For the first time, I'm feeling the weight of time. I don't know how this evening will pass, nor the whole of tomorrow.

This girl appeared before me and rekindled the coal of Ahmad in my heart, as if my yearning for her fed on my yearning for my son. But is it possible that she could be a path leading me to him? I don't know what's happened to me—I feel as if I'm breathing hard and I want to cry.

I don't think it's a coincidence that my company is signing a contract in Iraq just as I've become infatuated with an Iranian girl. It's hard for Iraq and Iran to coexist in my heart. If I spoke to Sami about Farnaz, he would tell me to bring her to the apartment.

No, I won't say anything to Sami, I won't say a word to anyone. Her telephone number is recorded in the file in front of me; should I call her? But what would I say? One approach might be to apologize to her for the bother of the meeting—but why apologize to her, specifically? What would she say to the others? What would Uthaiman's reaction be, and how would Ismail interpret it, religious as he is?

I must forget the matter. I feel irritated. The telephone rings and it seems to me that it might be Farnaz. "Hello."

"Where are you?" It's Shaikha.

"In the office."

"Are you coming to the beach house?"

I hesitate for a few seconds. "I've got work to do. I'll come when I've finished."

7

I hate digging into my closets.

I came back early from the beach house today. When the sun set, I said to Abrar and Sahar, "I'm going home." Abrar looked at me in surprise, so I added, "I'm going to do something I've been putting off for a year."

"A romantic interlude with Baba?" Sahar teased me.

"I wish. I'm going to clean my closet."

"Oof, what a pain!" commented Abrar.

The room with my wardrobes is very large. I called Jaya to help me, asking her to sit with me. I don't know which wardrobe to start with. Yaqoub once said to me, "You have more dresses than there are days in the year."

I'll start with the one for daytime dresses, then I'll move to the one with dresses for special occasions, and last, I'll organize the wardrobe with evening wear. That leaves the shoe cabinet.... Only a few of my dresses are connected to some occasion with Yaqoub. On our honeymoon trip, we shopped together during the first week, and after that he said, "Excuse me, I hate shopping, it's a waste of time." From that day on I've chosen my clothes alone, and later he began asking me to buy his clothes, especially suits and shoes.

I remember once, maybe it was four years ago, we were alone in our apartment in London, and I suggested going out for a coffee. The driver took us, and after we had our coffee, we were strolling in the aisles of Harrod's. It was one of the few times he stopped me, pointing to a dress and saying, "That will look beautiful on you!" My heart leaped. I couldn't believe my ears. When I came out of the dressing room and stood before him, he smiled slightly and said, "Lovely!"

Where is that dress? The daytime dresses are the majority. I always choose the same colors, ever since I was at the university. Every person has specific colors, ones that call out to him, and I don't like to change the colors of my clothes. This dress was given to me by Sahar and I wore it once, maybe twice. I don't like it. "Jaya, this is a new dress."

"Thank you."

There is a distinctive aroma in my wardrobe. Ahmad told me once, "I love your smell." He's changed a lot in recent years; he's become a different person. Abrar and Sahar and I came to fear walking in front of him—he threatened me more than once, furiously: "Every part of your body that shows, God will grill it in the fires of hell!" The threat wounded my heart, but he went on, with a terrifying look in his eyes: "God will take vengeance on you and your daughters!"

"Aren't you ashamed of yourself, to speak to me like that?" I shouted that at him, and he studied at me for a moment, then answered,

"I should be ashamed before you, when you aren't ashamed before God?"

"I'll speak to your father so he can make you understand."

"Oh, sure, that tyrant who has no fear of God, who practices usury and who persecutes preachers!"

That was when I felt that everything in him scared me: the way he looked at us, his words, the tone of his voice, even his silence and his smell! I don't know how this happened to him. My heart tells me that he won't come back to us; maybe that's what's breaking Yaqoub's heart and grieving him.

I like this dress; I wore it often when I was working at the ministry. Some clothes never get old, they become part of me, so it's hard for me to get rid of them. I'll give it to Jaya so it doesn't hang here for more years.

When I was working at the ministry, I don't remember that I ever traveled without coming back with a gift for Yaqoub, but he usually traveled and came home as if he had never left Kuwait. On one of his trips he brought me a Chanel handbag. I was as happy as a child, and surprised that he thought of it. He said, "It's a gift for your birthday." I kissed him, though I suddenly wondered if Abrar or Sahar had called to remind him of my birthday. I thought about asking them, but I decided not to, telling myself that I wouldn't spoil the pleasure I took in the handbag Yaqoub had given me.

This dress has gotten tight. I hand it to Jaya, who stands silently, looking at me kindly. She came from India to work in my house when she was not yet twenty and devoted herself to helping me and to raising my four children, staying up with them whenever she was needed. That's why Du'aij and Abrar treat her so kindly, surprising some of my sisters and my friends. She has a daughter and a son from her husband, who died of cancer. When she came back from India last year, she confided to me tearfully, "I won't go back another time. There's no house for me there. My daughter built her own house with my money and so did my son, but they. . . ." She swallowed her tears. "My kids and my grandchildren are living their lives, and they want me to stay here in order to send them money and gifts."

What she said saddened me. I told her, "Stay with us as long as you like, even without working!"

Sometimes I wonder for whom I'm buying all these clothes if my husband pays no attention to me. It's true that I wear them on special occasions, and that a woman's spirit is refreshed when she puts on a beautiful dress. But the most beautiful thing any woman dreams of is a compliment or a loving word from her beloved or her husband.

What has made each of us neglect the other and hold back from him? From time to time I'm saddened by a feeling of regret and loss—why has our relationship become so weak and feeble? A few cold expressions of courtesy are the only thread connecting us anymore.

Sometimes when I hear my friends complaining about their daily conflicts with their husbands, I feel jealous. A little marital conflict is healthy, hiding desire and interest in the other. I grieve that there are no disputes between me and my husband, and what pains me even more is that there is no conversation at all between us.

At the beginning of our marriage he was busy setting up his company, and my time was taken by pregnancy, giving birth, and raising my children. But after Sahar started school, I became prey to isolation and loneliness, and boredom reigned over my days. I had graduated with honors from the College of Business; I complained to Yaqoub that I had gotten tired of sitting at home.

He arranged for me to be appointed to the Ministry of Finance, and by means of his contacts, he watched over my progress there. Sitting in my office, the day I assumed the position of assistant deputy minister, I felt my own worth as a woman and a person. I also saw clearly how people vie for favor from those in high positions! But work relations, meetings, and reports besieged me. I would come home at three in the afternoon, have lunch with my children, and then begin helping them with their schoolwork. I finished only when I was overcome by fatigue.

During those years I pulled away from Yaqoub, and he in turn was distant. Our relationship became anemic and dried up; even our sexual contact was scarce, and it became more miserable when he left me to go sleep alone. How that has tormented me! Many nights, I'm stirred by the thirst of my body and spirit, desiring his love, so I soak in a tub scented with honey or rose water, I put on my nightgown, I perfume myself, and then I go to his room, carried along by my desire. He will be absorbed in reading a book or a report or watching television. I go in and sit next to him, reaching out to embrace him, but he remains distant. Sometimes we exchange a few meaningless comments, and I slip in a suggestive word or expression, hoping he'll notice my desire for him and for union with him. I'm ashamed to be open about my needs. Little by little my desire cools, and I leave his room, discouraged. I go back to my room to sleep alone with my grief, and I wake up to a pounding headache.

One of my friends whispered to me her own experience, smiling. "He was oblivious, he wasn't about to understand a hint, until I started going to his room, lifting the covers, and slipping into his bed!" The idea pleased me when I heard it, and I resolved to imitate my friend. More than once I went to his room, but I wasn't able to impose my desire on him.

Poor women! They have to bear children, raise them manage their households, and go out to work, all the while preserving their bodies, constantly beautifying themselves, and always remaining in a good mood in order to please their husbands and to arouse their love.

I wore this dress once and hated it. I hand it to Jaya. She smiles affectionately, and says, "All your dresses are new, madam!"

"That's true, but I don't want to just leave them hanging. I don't like to look at them!"

Sometimes it occurs to me to wonder how the servants see us, when they know the tiniest details of our lives. Do they know the cost of what we buy? Do they know that it's several times more than their salaries? Does it hurt them that we enjoy the pleasures of life, while their families can't find enough to eat? We never stop buying and they see it all, they carry it to our rooms and throw the empty sacks in the garbage. Yaqoub has his own convictions, including the saying that "each person is born to his own fate."

For many years he excused himself from going with me to our children's schools, saying he had a meeting. I remember when I threw that in his face, once, and told him, "Consider coming to the school meeting!" He didn't like it, and as usual, he took refuge in the fortress of his silence. I added, "Some people think I'm divorced or living apart." From then on, he began to attend our children's annual year-end ceremonies.

This dress still has its tags on it, though a year or maybe two have passed without my wearing it. I don't know where I bought it. Sometimes I'm amazed at how I've bought this dress or that pair of shoes. I'll give it to Jaya: "Please take it."

What seductive, fugitive pleasure do people find in buying new things? In Kuwait, people go out to shopping malls and look at each other; they have nothing to do but shop or go to restaurants.

Sometimes I think, is it reasonable that work is Yaqoub's only pleasure? Recently he seems irritated and alienated all the time, and I feel as if he's avoiding being near me. It crossed my mind to wonder what's troubling him—could there be another woman in his life? But I answered myself immediately that I don't think so; he doesn't even find time for us, for me and the children, and then day and night he's worried about his contracts and the company's affairs on one hand, and about Ahmad's predicament on the other. Sometimes I'm anxious, wondering how any woman can guarantee that she's the only one on her husband's mind, and that he's not betraying her. I'll be with Yaqoub in a mall or on a trip, and I'll see how he looks at passing women; I tell myself that all men look at women. Then I tell myself again that I'm sure there's no other woman who would put up with his silence, his seriousness, his explosions of anger, and his inattention!

Here's another dress that's never been worn. Sahar chose it for me last year; she loves to shop. In recent years she's become obsessed with her body and watching her weight. She wants to keep a figure like a fashion model, so she's brought in her own athletic trainer to work with her, and she's gone through a series of companies that take charge of organizing her meals and advising her on quantities and healthful eating. That's not to mention the dozens of powders to cleanse the complexion, the moisturizing creams, the incense, and the perfumes. I think she buys clothes for me to bring me a bit of cheer, the dear girl!

A thought floats through my head—I wish I had one single, small wardrobe.

When I worked at the ministry, every night I prepared my dress for the next day before I went to sleep. My coworker Tahani said to me once, only half-jokingly, "You spend more on your clothes and your purses than your whole salary!" She laughed and added, "Well, your husband is a millionaire."

What she said alerted me and made me look closely at how my co-workers dressed. I noticed which of them wore the same dress more than a single day. At that point I deliberately began to appear in the same dress more than once.

Yaqoub is generous with his money but stingy with his emotions, not only with me but even with his children. I know full well that he becomes very upset if anything bad happens to any of them. I remember the day when Sahar fell off her bicycle and broke her leg. He had packed his suitcase for a trip, but as soon as he heard her scream in pain, he ran to her. He took us to the hospital, and I saw the panic on his face. Even when we came home and her leg was encased in a plaster cast, he canceled his trip and mumbled, "I'll stay with you."

He's a father who's dedicated to ensuring his children have everything they need, and he's eager for them to succeed in their studies and in their lives. But he practices his love and concern for them at a distance, and with a calm that borders on silence. Once he told me, "Everyone loves in his own fashion." He fell silent, as if swallowing his sorrow, then he added, "I have not been happy in my love for Ahmad."

Oh my God, this dress is still here! "Jaya!"

I'm going to try to organize my dresses according to color.

In recent years both Abrar and Sahar have begun to insist that their father come to our family occasions, so he has started to spend more time with his grandchildren, the children of Du'aij and Abrar. I see him turn into a child again when he plays with them. How it tickles me to hear him laugh when he forgets himself, playing and joking with them!

He and I neglected our relationship, so it has languished. I'm now convinced that a man is interested in his wife to the extent that she shows her concern for him. Maybe the smart wife is the one who calmly inserts herself into her husband's world, because it's so easy for him to slip away, protesting, "I'm busy!"

I shouldn't have listened to him or left him to the demon of work and contracts. For a few weeks now I've been telling myself that I'll embrace him and bring him back to me, but I feel as if he's becoming more distant. I know that recently he's been more concerned about Ahmad than ever before, but I sense that there's something else, besides Ahmad, that's occupying my husband's mind!

8

I can't believe how much I long for her!

My heart trembled when my car stopped in front of the entrance to the company. A single building unites me with her, but I don't know how to reach her. I was troubled by the notion that she might not be here today; it occurred to me to walk through the various departments of the company, but what would the employees think of that? I had never before taken any notice of them, and then on Thursday I summoned them all to my office. If today, Sunday, I inspect the departments, everyone will notice that something has happened. Anyway, what good would it do me to see her?

I sat down behind my desk. Marwan informed me that the Iraqi embassy had organized a dinner party tonight, in honor of the contract concluded with the Baghdad company, and they had called to invite me. I remained silent, so he asked, "Shall I confirm that you will attend?"

"Make my excuses to them. It's enough for Ismail to go."

Farnaz's file is still in my desk drawer; I'd like to know if she's here or not. The company offices take up four floors of the building, and the Department of Programming and Development is not on this floor. I wish I could see her.

Does this make any sense? I've barely arrived in my office,

and everything flies out of my head except the thought of her. I'm no longer capable of explaining my rash feelings, my disordered thoughts, or my burning desire to see her. Nor do I want to sit still any longer!

Yesterday, the moment I got to the beach house Shaikha took one look at my expression and asked, "What's wrong?"

I was surprised by her question, and denied it, as usual. "Nothing at all."

"That's not true." She was hovering over me, and she soon informed me, in a troubled voice, "There's something on your mind, I'm sure of it!"

I pasted a small smile on my face, to hide the image of Farnaz. "I'm tired. This last week has been wearing, because of the Baghdad deal."

She went on looking at me, as if to weigh the truth of my words. Her eyes said, "You're lying." "Yaqoub," she said. "You must rest! How long are you going to keep running after tenders, from one contract to another? You've done enough! We need you more than money."

To escape her pursuit, I got up and asked, "Where are the kids?"

I left Kuwait to study in America in 1971 and lived five years in New York, returning in 1976 after I had finished my university study. The parliament had been dissolved and the political situation was electric, but nonetheless at the time Kuwait was buzzing with social, economic, and intellectual movements, bustling with activity in journalism, theater, and sports. Sometimes I miss those years.

I remember it—a brief telephone call from my father to one of his friends in the National Bank of Kuwait, and I found myself employed. It seems to me that the transformation in social mores began about a decade later, or a little more. At first I was surprised when I saw the hijab beginning to spread among my aunts, one after the other, and I noticed that beards had taken over the faces of many of my friends. Then bright colors withdrew, along with clothes that were filmy or short, and black ruled over women young and old in government institutions, in universities, in shops, and in all public places.

After my return I met Shaikha. She did not wear the hijab, she was eight years younger than I was, and she was a friend of my sister Dalal. I saw her several times, and I began to watch her, discreetly and silently. We exchanged a few passing greetings; she was an attractive, modern young woman. When I asked Dalal about her, she smiled and said, "She's the flower of the women at Kuwait University; she has character, beauty, and culture!" Dalal brought us together several times, sitting with us as we talked. After a time, I told her that I thought Shaikha was an amazing young woman.

We were married in 1983, when Shaikha was in her last year at the university. Yesterday, as I was having breakfast and she was sleeping, the story of our relationship passed before my eyes. I don't remember any major disagreement arising between us, nor does my memory hold any moments of overwhelming desire that carried me to her. After a few months of marriage, I discovered that she is extremely sensitive to any remark affecting her—hours of pleasant companionship can be wiped away by a simple, passing comment. I pointed it out to her, telling her, "You're very sensitive!"

The same scene was repeated dozens of times. We would be invited somewhere, she would be late, and I would call her, with some irritation in my tone. She would come, a clear expression of annoyance on her face, and soon begin criticizing the tone I had taken with her and justifying her delay. I would be surprised by her reaction and her sensitivity. We would leave the house with our spirits burdened by anger, enough to spoil the occasion and drive a wedge between us.

I remember when I told her that the small end tables in the formal living room were not well placed, and that they could be arranged in a way that fit the space better. She was upset and talked to me at great length, trying to convince me that this was the ideal arrangement, that she had been guided by magazines of interior decoration, that no change would be acceptable, that all her friends found her taste exemplary, and, and, and.... I was amazed that she kept after me about it for days, insisting on convincing me. So I changed my mind.

"The tables are placed perfectly," I said. "Let's forget about them."

"You're just saying that to humor me."

"That's right. I hate the tables and I hate the room and I—"

I swallowed the rest of my words and left the house, leaving her sitting where she was.

Any word that carries the slightest whiff of criticism completely upsets Shaikha's mood, which soon shows in her black looks, her voice, her breathing, and her quick steps, so I avoid her. With the passing of time, I've become convinced that I can't shift anything in her nature, and that any remark on my part may start a quarrel and arouse her anger. All I can do is accept everything as it is, swallow my observations, and take refuge in silence. After two years of marriage and the arrival of Abrar, I became convinced that she would be happy and calm as long as

I welcomed whatever she wanted or did and went along with it. But it crossed my mind to wonder how a relationship between a man and his wife could be sound when any moment of disagreement is a moment of conflict.

My friend Dr. Fadil, who has a psychiatric practice, once said to me, "The greatest predicament of any marriage is that the relationship produces itself secretly, with no knowledge or intervention from either the husband or the wife, specifically in the earliest period. It takes shape covertly and out of their sight, accumulating intangibly, like water. In each one's mind a picture is formed of the personality of the other, with his traits of temperament, affection, and respect, but also with his annoyances and his convictions that resist change!" Dr. Fadil visits me in the office or at home from time to time, and I'm always happy to see him and to listen to his explanations. "The true relationship is hidden in the subconscious mind of each spouse; it only reveals its real face in moments of anger, conflict, and dispute."

I'm amazed at what I'm going through. I've spent my life determined to take advantage of every moment: in my office I've surrounded myself with contracts, payments, meetings, mail, phone calls, reports to read, stock exchange indices to check, taped lectures on YouTube, and works of literature to read for pleasure. I enter the office and forget life and its affairs, monopolized and besieged by matters of work, with the sea nearby.

There's a vast difference between love of affection and love in marriage. During the last few days I've realized that nothing happens between Shaikha and me except that we live together in the same house. A husband, a wife, children, grandchildren, money, and a comfortable life, nothing more. It came to me that the veins in the plant of love and marriage are drying up, and the image disturbed me. Then a question reared up before me: how have I lived my life over all these years?

The ringing of my phone demands my attention. "Hello, Ismail."

"Marwan told me that you won't come to the party at the embassy."

"That's right." I was silent for a few second and he was too, waiting for me to justify that. "You know me, I prefer to remain distant."

"That's your nature, Yaqoub." He said it as if alluding to something I did not understand.

I feel confused. Does it make any sense that this Farnaz has destroyed my life?

I'm pained by the thought that I no longer want anything from Shaikha. Another question sinks its fangs into me: what remains of the marital relationship, if one of the two no longer desires the other? Marriage is a sweet longing for the other, ever renewed. If the longing languishes, the joints of the marriage stiffen in paralysis and cannot move.

Our intermittent sexual encounters now happen to satisfy a need, to demonstrate (with some embarrassment) my continued desire for her, to make an unsteady claim of manhood before her. Sometimes I sense that she comes to my room with her desire, but I will hold myself aloof from her, for some reason I can't identify. I'll cover myself with silence, for fear that my breathing will give me away. Then, when she withdraws, I have to face myself: Why, Yaqoub? Shaikha is your beloved! I become lost, searching for answers that don't come. I get up to go to bed, grieved, and the question stretches out beside me: Why has my relationship with my wife been extinguished?

Marwan's call pulls me away from my thoughts. "The mail is ready." He comes in carrying the file, places it before me, and before he leaves, he reminds me, "The trip to Masira is set for Thursday."

"I'm not going. Cancel the tickets. I'll call my friend Sami."

I don't know what's happening to me! Is it Farnaz, or was the dry fruit of my spirit just waiting for someone to shake the branch so it would fall? It's obvious that it was hanging by a thread without my knowledge. That hidden voice, also, continues to whisper to me: Follow the trail, watch where this girl leads!

I'll call Sami and make my excuses. I'll claim I need to be present in Kuwait to finish the contract with the Baghdad company.

I don't remember that Shaikha has ever seen me off for a trip, nor have I seen her face among those waiting for returning travelers. I tell her that I'm leaving on a trip, and she answers with the same phrase always: "Go in God's care!" Sometimes I'm surprised that she doesn't even bother to ask where I'm going. Once I chided her: "Don't you want to know anything about it?"

"I have confidence in you, dear." I continued to look at her, so she clarified, "You taught me." Then, imitating my voice, "'I don't like anyone to interfere with my work!'"

It seems to me now that our marriage was a trip in a comfortable car along a desert road, where only a single scene appears on either side, bringing boredom and drowsiness to our hearts. We have two sons and two daughters. It hurts me that a branch of the family tree has been cut off and is now at the mercy of the wind, fighting with his life in his hands.

The day I left Abdel Shafi in the police station with his identification in my pocket, I received a call from Ahmad as soon as I got to the car. "What you've done is an injustice. It's displeasing to God and his prophet! You've thrown Shaikh Abdel Shafi in jail!" His tone betrayed his anger.

"Come home and we'll discuss it."

"I won't go home until you get Shaikh Abdel Shafi out of jail and apologize to him!"

I detested his pronouncement, but I sucked in my explosion of anger and said again. "Come and we'll talk."

"I won't go!" He ended the call. That may have been the beginning of the end of my relationship with him.

Less than an hour later my telephone rang, and I heard the voice of my friend, the district commander. "Yaqoub, my friend, God give you a good evening."

"Hello!"

He explained to me that one of the important personalities in the district had gone to the police station in the company of a lawyer and asked the officer in charge to release the Egyptian Abdel Shafi, saying that it was not right to hold him without any infraction, misdemeanor, or crime. The man was threatening to contact the interior minister, and the officer had called my friend.

As usual I remained silent, listening to him. When he finished, I told him that I had warned the Egyptian previously, because what he was doing was destructive—he was filling the heads of children with ruinous, dangerous terrorist ideas. I asked, "What does an accountant have to do with stuffing the heads of children with extremist fundamentalist ideas?"

"It's a matter for the Ministry of Religious Endowments," he replied. "We've spoken to them more than once about the necessity of locking the mosque doors immediately after prayer times, but to no avail." The tone of his voice changed. "I can't hold a man without a charge."

"I'll go to the police station to lodge a complaint against him for having fought with me."

"I'll wait for you to arrive."

I immediately threw myself onto my bed and may have dozed for half an hour, the phone beside me in silent mode. But the moment I woke up, I found that I had missed three calls from Ismail. When I called him back he said angrily, "I was about to go to your house."

He informed me that a friend of his in a high position had called him, and he was asking me to please pardon the Egyptian. I was surprised by Ismail's call, and even more surprised that one of the important men in the district had himself gone to get Abdel Shafi out of jail, bringing a lawyer, and that the affair had also led to the intercession of an important person with my cousin, so that Ismail was now begging me to pardon the man, "for my sake!"

"But Ismail, the man is subversive!"

"Yaqoub, for God's sake! He's a man who explains the noble Quran, chapter and verse, to kids, in God's house. How is he a subversive?"

"He's stuffing their heads with rebellion against their families and planting the seeds of violence and terrorism in them!"

"Yaqoub, please don't blow it out of proportion, for my sake!"

My hand was forced; I sent Abdel Shafi's identification to the police station with Bayoumi, my driver. I had been frightened by something hidden in this affair, telling me that it was bigger than Abdel Shafi, much bigger than any one preacher or study circle. For someone had certainly organized all this—someone who used these people, who kept tabs on them, who paid them generously for their work, and who would defend them from any harm that might come to them.

A few days after the event, Shaikha slipped into our conversation that she wanted to retire, saying, "I want to rest!"

I was surprised, and answered, "But work is life!"

"Life is living, not only work, and I've gotten bored. The complaints of the supervisors bother me a lot, they affect my mood."

"How will you spend your time?"

"Like my friends—I'll sleep and wake up when I like, I'll pay attention to myself, to my house, to my daughters and my grandchildren."

Now I can recall what she said with complete clarity. She did not say, "my husband," nor did she refer to our relationship.

The sea seems agitated today—as I am, with the thought turning in my mind that our marital relationship is nearly dead. Ever since I went to America, I've been used to living alone; even after we were married, I remained independent in my thinking and my feelings. But now I yearn to get to know Farnaz. I whispered that to myself, looking at the sea. I don't know where the scent of gardenias came from.

I remember that it was a year ago or a little more when Shaikha asked that we go out to dinner together. I was surprised by the request, but something in my heart welcomed it. The Jumeirah l-Messila hotel had opened recently so we went there. We had barely begun to eat when her question slipped out: "What do you think of the hijab?"

The question struck me like a dagger, so I shortened our discussion. "Do you intend to begin wearing the hijab?"

"My mother and all my sisters wear it, and I've become a grandmother." I shook the crumbs from my hands and entered my silence, so she asked, "What are you thinking about?"

"I'm thinking about Ahmad. I detest the hijab, and I can't imagine looking at you wearing it!"

"I won't wear it with you. I'll wear it when I'm with others."

"Why?"

"It's a duty to wear the hijab."

"Who says so?"

"The Quran and the prophet's sayings."

"That's not true."

She smiled. "How so?"

I was silent, looking at her face. I felt that she had not asked me to dinner to renew the connection between us, or to enjoy time together and some conversation, or to ask for my opinion; rather she invited me to announce her decision. I raised my arm, signaling to the waiter to bring the check for the unpleasant meal.

I remained silent all the way back, and the moment we went in the house, I said to her, "I'm convinced that the hijab is not a religious duty. You can research that." Since she saw how upset I was, I told her frankly, "I can't stand a woman in a hijab. You can do as you like."

Farnaz covers her head with a light cloth, and something moves my heart when I look into her eyes or at her face. What attracts me to her? I became lost thinking about that, but then another question stung me: how long are you going to keep thinking about her? Make a move, meet her, to see what your heart will tell you.

I became aware of the silence of my office. I looked at the chair where she had sat, and her scent suddenly rose to me.

9

"Call in a young woman who works in the Programming and Development Department—I think her name is Farnaz."

I had called Marwan, and I hung up. It was close to noon; it had been a week since I first met her with the employees who came in. I was going crazy, wanting to see her. I could no longer sit in my office when she was in the same building but I couldn't see her, and it had become hard to get her out of my thoughts, hard to control the painful desire to meet her and speak with her. I don't know how our meeting will go. Marwan is calling. "The employee is here."

"Send her in."

I became aware of my heart beating, and I felt as if I wasn't the person I was used to being. There was a light knock on the door and her face appeared. "Good afternoon, sir," she said, waiting at a distance.

I began looking at her as if I were reassuring myself that she was really there. A young woman with a tender face. A mouth with full lips, a small beauty spot. Black eyes, and eyebrows . . . how does a man drink in the woman his heart desires? I wanted to run to embrace her, press her against my heart, smell her perfume, possibly kiss her!

I sensed fear in her eyes, so I began, "I'm going to open an account on Twitter, and I'd like your help."

I had prepared my plan. She resettled the light covering on her head, as it had slipped a little, revealing the front part of her hair. "Now?" It was the same gentle tone I had heard last time, and it calmed my heart.

"Yes."

She came closer and asked, "On your laptop or your desktop computer?"

"On the laptop." I stood up and came from behind my desk, carrying the laptop and moving toward the meeting table. She remained where she was while I sat at the head of the table, then she sat beside me. I was enveloped by her captivating perfume: jasmine flowers, refreshing lemon, and gardenia.

I pushed the laptop toward her. I sensed that she was trying to hide a small tremor in her delicate fingers. I followed her as she went to the Twitter website and requested a new account. Then she asked, "Pardon me, sir—will it be in your name, in the name of the company, or under another name?"

"Let it be under the name 'al-Khayyam.'"

Her eyes flashed oddly. "What image would you like to have for the account?"

Once again the obsession appeared—how can I drink her in? I watched her, her breathing, her fingers trembling slightly. "Choose anything from nature." She lifted her eyes to me in confusion, so I said quickly, "Put in a picture of the sea of Kuwait."

She googled "sea of Kuwait," and the pictures quickly appeared. She calmly pushed the computer toward me and said, "Choose the one you like."

I looked through the pictures and chose one that looked like the shore near my beach house. She placed the picture as I was trying to catch my breath.

"What phrase would you like to have as the header, identifying you?"

"The coming moment is wrapped in a cloak of secrecy."

She set about arranging the page, and she showed me how to follow those whose tweets I liked and to block those I did not want. She said softly, "The first tweet should be a greeting from you."

"You write it." I noticed that she had a smile that started at her lips and rose to her eyes, to light up her face. "Write whatever you like."

The beauty spot guarding her upper lip seemed to watch me. She calmly typed out her sentence: "The sun rises to give light to everyone." She looked at me. "Do you like it?"

"Very much."

I felt my heart beating rapidly. I was taken with her presence, with the scent of gardenias about her, with the slight tremor in her delicate fingers, with the pink polish on her nails, with her small hand marked by dark veins that was nothing like Shaikha's hand. I was taken aback by the annoying comparison that came to mind. She leaned back in the chair and her head covering slipped, revealing shining hair. Again my heart beat fast as I contemplated her without the hijab, her brown hair noticeably curly and short, barely reaching her shoulders, and earrings dangling from her ears.

Once again, the question came to me: how can I keep her for myself? How can she stay near me, how can her scent remain, her beauty mark, the look in her eyes, her curly hair? I thought to stand up, but some weight held me in my chair. I was surprised by my hunger for her, even more by the light trembling of my heart, as if I were not the man I knew.

She quickly replaced her head covering. Our eyes met, and my heart whispered to me that she had sensed my covert glances and had smelled my hunger for her.

Without looking at me, she asked, "Would you like anything else?"

It was as if the tremor in her fingers had moved to me. I said, "I'll call you if I need your help."

"Of course. I'll leave now."

"Thank you very much, Farnaz." I said her name looking into her face, and I enjoyed the taste of her name on my tongue.

A small smile appeared in her eyes, and she responded, "You're very welcome."

She moved toward the door, and I wanted to keep her longer. I called, "Farnaz." I noticed that I was calling her by her name. "May I take your telephone number, in case I need help?"

She hesitated for half a second, enough to tell me that she had doubts about me. Then she said, "Certainly," and dictated to me the number of her cell phone. I recorded it on my own, then I called her, saying "This is my number."

"I'm sorry, I left my phone in the office." She remained where she was, as if she expected some other request; I said, "I'll call you when I need to."

"Please do." She tossed out these words, then quickly opened the door and disappeared, fleeing, the scent of her perfume running fearfully behind her.

She speaks the Kuwaiti dialect! I said that to myself, though I had noticed a slight Persian accent in her words. It was the first time in my life that I imagined liking a Persian accent. The question came to me sharply: What's happening to you, Yaqoub? You're going crazy over a Persian girl?

I went back to my seat and looked out into the distance. I was still under the effect of Farnaz's intoxicating perfume when the phone rang and Marwan informed me, "Mr. Uthaiman would like to see you."

Some instinct told me that he had been sitting with Marwan when Farnaz came into my office. He entered, with his black beard, carrying the employee rosters. He told me that he had recorded the remarks and questions that some had raised. "Do you want to take any administrative measures about them?"

"No." I shook my head, looking at him irritably, showing him that I had discovered his spying and his ugly pretext for coming in.

"I'll leave the rosters on your desk." He set them down and withdrew, while I remained silent until he had gone out and shut the door behind him.

What do I want from this girl? I feel as if there's something more, something beyond sex that pushes me toward her, that leaves me shaken. As I sat thinking the image of Ahmad came to me, followed immediately by the smell of blood, roiling my spirit.

He rebelled and fled my house, throwing himself voluntarily into fighting, blood, and death. Again, the anxious thought returned: is there some connection between Farnaz and Ahmad? I stood up and began to pace in front of the window of my office overlooking the sea, and soon I was upbraiding myself: at this age you've become an adolescent again, your heart delighting in an Iranian girl! I was talking to Yaqoub, as I was split into two halves, one yearning to run after the girl and the adventure, and the other afraid of loss and ruin.

Ahmad was lost to me after the incident at the police station. He began to avoid everyone in the house, fixing his eyes on the floor as he entered or left, as if he hated to see what surrounded him. Trying to draw nearer to him I went to his room one evening and knocked on the door. I found it locked. "You're locking yourself in your room?" I asked, my voice showing how surprised I was.

"Yes," he answered, rejection in his voice.

"May I come in?"

The moment I entered I was greeted by a stale odor. I saw that his room was neglected, the window closed and books piled on his desk. There was a woven palm-leaf mat on the floor.

"What's this?"

"A mat."

"Where's your furniture?"

"I took it out. I don't need it—I sit on the mat, following the example of our lord Muhammad, may the peace and the blessings of God be on him!"

"Where's the television?" His look, his room, and the tone of his voice wounded my heart and filled me with sadness.

"The shocking immorality in television programs and films makes me angry—it's all forbidden. And it's not right to turn people away from thoughts of God and obeying him!"

Silence came to sit with us. I was hurt by my son's isolation and his distance from his mother, his sisters, and all the good things in my house, wounded by his solitude in this room with its stagnant odor. The change in his thinking frightened me.

"Are these your schoolbooks?" I asked, pointing to his desk.

"Schoolbooks, and others."

I knew they were religious books, but I was afraid to anger

him by getting up to examine them. I wished I could take him in my arms and hug him to my breast. "Ahmad." I addressed him gently, my eyes fixed on his face. "I'm your father. Tell me frankly what you're thinking."

Again, silence descended on us. Then he said, "Nothing."

"Who was the person who was with you in the mosque?" I don't know where that question came from.

"Professor Umar."

"A teacher at your school?"

"Yes."

I didn't want to make him feel that I had come to interrogate him, nor did I want to anger him. "Come and have dinner with us."

"I've eaten." I was not expecting him to answer so readily.

"What have you eaten?"

"I have my food here," he said, pointing to a small fridge I hadn't noticed. I got up and opened it to find a bag of bread, a piece of cheese, two cucumbers, and a bottle of juice.

"You eat all alone?" I was overcome by a sudden anxiety. He remained curled in on himself.

Who stole my son from me? The question flew through the window of my office and hovered at a distance over the sea, then settled on the waves, moving with them. I was touched by a faint odor of blood.

I heard a light knock on the door, then Ismail's face appeared. "Peace be upon you." He tossed out the greeting then sat down across from me. "The day after tomorrow we're going to Baghdad, I and the architect Kareem and the new project director, the architect Azmi."

For the first time I felt that I was distant from the company, its projects, its deadlines, its schedules. "You'll process the preliminary bonds and receive the advance payment?"

"Yes. I'll stay maybe three days, and Kareem and Azmi will observe the preparation of the site and the beginning of the work."

"Before you leave, I'll call our ambassador in Baghdad and arrange things with him."

He was looking at me with an odd expression, and he said, "I hope everything is okay—your mind is elsewhere." He was asking a question in the form of a statement; I remained silent. Had Uthaiman told him anything about Ahmad, or had he confided something to him about Farnaz?

"Ahmad's absence keeps me from sleeping."

"God help us! Have you heard anything new?"

"Uthaiman is the one with the news."

I don't know why my response embarrassed him. He rose, prayers on his tongue: "God keep him, wherever he is!"

That night, after I had left Ahmad's room in the grip of pain, I spoke to Shaikha. Her tears flowed as she said, "I was going to tell you." She said that she took food to him but that he left it at the door. Once she stayed outside his room for more than a quarter of an hour, until the door opened. He refused to let her in. When she asked him why he did not take the food, he said to her:

"The cook who prepares the food is a Christian, and she might be an unbeliever!"

Shaikha told me she had been shocked by his answer, then she became confused and did not know what to do. Her voice breaking, she said, "His sister and I have begun to be afraid of him!"

I became aware of the silence of my office. I looked at the chair where Farnaz had sat, and her scent rushed to me, along with the question—when will I see her again?

10

Mr. Yaqoub's stare frightened me.

In winter, dark shadows come early. I saw by my car clock that it was four-thirty when I stopped in front of our building. It takes about half an hour to get to the apartment from the company offices. I love my little car! Before I got it, I had a hard time getting to and from the office.

Poor Baba! His little "one-eight" pickup has become decrepit, and he's begun to dream of buying a new car. After I was hired in the company, I made an agreement with a taxi driver, because I was embarrassed to go in Baba's ancient car. I excused myself by telling him, "Office hours start at eight, and you leave at five A.M."

He nodded and agreed, without enthusiasm. "As you like." I felt as if he realized that I was embarrassed by his car and didn't want to insist. Mr. Yaqoub's salary for one month might be more than the price of the car that Baba dreams of.

The voice of "Uncle" Shinawi, the building watchman, greeted me. "Good evening, my dear Farnaz!" His kind looks remind me of my father. He added, "The maintenance company is working on the elevator."

Our apartment is on the fourth floor. My mother opened the door before I got there. I looked at her in surprise, and she said, "I was watching you from the window." I kissed her and headed for my room, as she called, "I'll heat up lunch for you."

"I'm really hungry."

I greeted Safi, who was looking at me as she walked cradling her baby. She answered my greeting and asked, "How was your day?"

"It was fine, thank God."

I took Husain from her and hugged him to me, kissing the palm of his little hand and smelling his scent. I love the smell of children; it's intoxicating.

I put on my house clothes, went to the living room, washed my hands, and sat down to eat. I love my mother's cooking; all our relatives say how good it is. "Wow, there's *shabzi* today! I love it."

"Enjoy it," my mother responded. I saw there was something unsaid hidden in her eyes, so I asked her, "Did Reza call?"

"Yes." She was silent for a moment, as if preparing the rest. "He needs money."

I smiled at her and asked, "How much does he need?" She did not answer, so I told her, "I can send him fifty dinars, about a hundred and fifty dollars."

The good news made her face light up, and she stood up to give me a kiss. "Thank you, dear one! After lunch, you and I can go to send the sum, before your father gets back."

My dear Reza is in need. When we visited him, he whispered, "Life here is hell, I can't stand it!" I looked at him and he added, in a tone that pained me, "Everyone calls me 'the Kuwaiti,' and they treat me like a foreigner. And they kick me around like a ball; every month I'm in a different province with a different assignment." He laughed bitterly. "I've become an expert! I know every inch of the Iranian Republic."

I have about four hundred dinars in my bank account. Ever since I was hired, I've been saving a small amount every month. Today I felt that the president of the company was using a pretext to see me. When I got back to my office, Mervet stood up and hurried over to me. "What did he want from you?"

I was afraid to lie to her, but I was also afraid to speak frankly. I said, "Something to do with the computer." She seemed to be devouring me with her eyes, so I added, "One of the programs wasn't working."

She didn't care for my answer or find it convincing, sensing I was hiding something from her. The ringing of the phone on my desk saved me, so I stood up, saying, "Mr. Uthaiman wants to see me." She didn't hide her surprise: "How strange, a little while ago it was the president of the company and now it's the deputy director!"

I didn't respond, leaving hurriedly for Mr. Uthaiman's office.

Ever since our eyes met at the elevator, my heart whispers to me things I don't understand about Mr. Yaqoub. Today I felt as if he was concocting any reason at all to be near me. He certainly would have been able to open an account on Twitter.

Uthaiman was annoyed. He asked me, "What did the president want from you?"

"He asked me to open an account for him on Twitter."

"What else?" The way he said these words frightened me.

"Nothing at all."

He continued to examine me, playing with his black beard, as if weighing the truth of my words. I avoided looking at him.

"In the future, you will get my permission before going up to him, and you'll come to me after you leave him."

"Yes, sir." I said that and remained standing, waiting for him to permit me to go back to my office. What would Mr. Yaqoub say if he knew what Uthaiman said to me?

I love *shabzi*, that most savory stew of vegetables, along with white rice and saffron, as well as the mulberries I love, a salad, and a glass of milk.

I was surprised today when I heard Mr. Yaqoub call me by name. Something shook my heart and made me afraid. Even after I finished opening the account for him, I felt that his eyes were nearly devouring me. I had planned on giving him my telephone number, but he asked for it first.

The president likes a young employee like me—could something happen between us? The question took me unawares. He's a married man, older than my father; he can't possibly have designs on me. If he wanted young women, he must have a thousand ways to get them. He likes *me*? I wish I could believe it. A young Iranian woman marrying a Kuwaiti millionaire—he would make me a citizen, I would become a Kuwaiti and live like a queen!

When I got back to my desk, Mervet whispered to me, "You're lucky!" I didn't understand what she meant, so she added, "You're fortunate. The president knows you and he'll take an interest in you."

In order to dispel any suspicion she might have, I said, "It was nothing, just a simple question about a program that wasn't working."

How could he take an interest in me? It's been less than a year since I was hired; I don't think he would make any move to increase my salary or promote me. I don't have a university degree. I wanted to complete my studies, but I can't be accepted in Kuwait University, and I don't have the money to enroll in a private university. Could he help me complete my university education? My mother hopes I'll marry a Kuwaiti.... It's impossible—he's older than my father. Anyway, what would lead him to form a connection with me?

My mother is sitting with Safi, waiting for me so we can go to the exchange office and I can transfer the money to my brother.

My father has worn himself out, but he still hasn't been able to guarantee a visa for Reza to visit. Iranians are forbidden to visit Kuwait, but since Reza was born here and has family in Kuwait, he is allowed to get a visa. It's just that it requires a lot of influence and a sum of money. The president would surely be able to get the visa.

During his last phone call, Reza told me, "If I return to Kuwait, I won't go back to Iran. I'll take any job, and not go back."

I would be lucky if Mr. Yaqoub raised my salary to five hundred. Something in his eyes frightens me. The employees in the company are intimidated by him; most of them had never met him before the recent series of meetings. He usually entrusts his deputy, Ismail, with running the company.

I wish he would call me, on the pretext of asking about the Twitter account. I don't think he does have designs on me. I'm younger than his oldest daughter—does it make any sense that he would want to amuse himself with me? The bite I was eating stuck in my throat. I must be careful; I'd like to be closer to him, but I'm afraid. Muhannadi beat Safi and divorced her, but if Mr. Yaqoub differed with me or got tired of me, he would throw me out of the company and cancel my residence permit, maybe even throw me out of Kuwait. Why did he choose me, and not some other girl? Maybe he does like me.

Mother came out of the room saying, "I asked Safi to come with us, but she refused."

"She doesn't like to go out with her son."

"Possibly." She nodded in agreement, and asked, "Shall I change?"

"Yes. I'll finish now and wash the dishes before we leave."

After I was hired, I never heard a thing about the president of the company. I feel as if my mind is imagining things with no basis in fact. I don't think a man in his position, with his money, and traveling as he does, needs to start a relationship with a minor employee in his company. And then, a man with his status is too busy for that. Hardly a month goes by when he doesn't take a trip—maybe he has girlfriends all over the world. If I did become closer to him, I would ask for his help in getting a visa for my brother to visit us; for the last year, Mother has been weeping, longing to see him. He might also help me a little with my salary.

But it would be a scandal in the company if my salary were the only one raised—people would say, Farnaz is the president's girlfriend! Uthaiman and Ismail would never agree, and they might harm me in some way. I'm certain that Uthaiman doesn't like me.

I've eaten a lot today, God be thanked. I don't want to gain weight. Now I weigh one hundred and thirty pounds, and I'm five feet, five inches tall.

I'll go wash the dishes. Mother asks, "Shall I help you?"

"No, thanks. I'll finish quickly and we can leave."

"Shall I make you tea?"

"Later."

I can't imagine being far away from my family. Our Lebanese neighbor wanted to take me to south Lebanon, and that dog Muhannadi beat Safi the whole time they were married. The president must be happy in his marriage and in his relationship with his wife; they don't lack for anything. After our meeting with him, Mervet said, jokingly, "I would agree to marry him!" I stared at her, so she added, "He's a man in a hundred." I smiled, and that seemed to annoy her. She became very serious and said, with no trace of joking, "A lot of men are men in name only." I didn't understand what she meant, and somehow the atmosphere between us became electric. Then her voice filled with sadness, there was a glimmer of grief in her eyes, and she said, "Very few women are lucky, in this world."

I'd be a lucky woman if the president of the company became my friend! I'd be born again—I'd be a different Farnaz! But playing with a person like him is dangerous. It might even bc fatal. No, no!

I've finished washing the dishes. I'll dry the sink, go to the bathroom, change clothes, and leave with Mother.

11

"I want the sea to be with me always."

I gave my instructions to the architect, Kareem, the moment I bought the land and work began on building our office tower. I wanted my office to face the sea. When it was time to furnish it, I told Abrar and Shaikha, "I love simplicity, and I don't want my office to be crammed with furniture. What matters is that I have a bookcase for the books I enjoy."

Ever since I was little, I've been enchanted with reading and with the sea. My grandfather was a ship's captain who traveled and traded, and my father learned under him and became a captain as well. Some secret yearning attracts me to the sea; perhaps it's my childhood and how simple life was then. Sometimes I feel drawn to the aroma of the past: my grandfather and grandmother, my mother and father, my uncles, their wives, and their children. My grandfather's large house, the familiar warmth of a Friday, with three generations of people no longer to be found.

Many times, and whenever we go to the beach house, the waves call me, and my feet unconsciously take me to the sea. This is why I never tire of taking fishing trips with Sami.

This morning I spent two hours meeting with Ismail and Kareem, going over every clause in the contract, and all the first steps in the project with the Baghdad company. When Kareem left and I was alone with Ismail, I warned him, "I don't want my name to appear in any instrument pertaining to the contract whatsoever!" He looked at me attentively. "Someone might dredge up all that misery from the past and say, 'the company belongs to one of Saddam's henchmen.'"

"Understood."

He went out, and somehow the rank odor of blood returned to my nostrils... where is Ahmad now, with what group? I was preoccupied with the question. The satellite television stations and the newspapers speak of nothing but terrorist operations and combat. To flee from the loneliness and oppressive atmosphere of my office and the thoughts that needled me, I told Marwan, "I have a meeting. I'll be back in an hour."

I found Bayoumi waiting for me at the entrance to the building, but I thanked him and said I would go alone.

I drove with music playing. Traffic was light on Arabian Gulf Road. At the light before the Amiri Hospital I turned left, entering the parking lot for the Souq Sharq Mall. I left the car there and walked toward the shore. A young man with a beard came toward me and brought the image of Ahmad to my mind.

When I visited his school for the first time, the director met me with an expression that was almost a frown. He was a man in his mid-forties, with a thin black beard surrounding his face; he spoke slowly, in an attempt to add gravity to every word. I explained to him that I would like to ask about my son Ahmad, academically and socially. It was as if he had expected my visit and had prepared his answer: "All praise to God, Ahmad is an excellent student." I was watching him in silence, from behind my doubts. "He's a pious, calm young man, with evident leadership abilities, well-liked by his classmates and his teachers." He fell silent, as if he was telling me to move on to another question. I don't know how others interpret my silence, but I do know that most people hate it. Since I continued to look at him, he added, "Mr. Yaqoub, we welcome your visit. Not many businessmen find the time to ask about their sons."

"I want to meet with Professor Umar."

I felt as if my request was a blow to him. Something in his face flinched, and he objected, saying, "I'm here to answer any question."

I avoided irritating him with more silence, so I repeated, "I'll meet with Professor Umar, please."

Professor Umar came in with a short dishdasha robe, a repellent thick beard, dusty sandals, and cracked heels. His eyes spoke clearly of his irritation, never settling on any one thing. I remembered him immediately; he was the man who was with Abdel Shafi in the mosque. At that moment my heart missed a beat, fearing for my son.

"Peace be upon you." He threw his greeting in the director's lap and sat down hostilely. I restrained my wrath and said calmly,

"I've come to implore your help."

He was surprised by my request. I told him how Ahmad stayed in his room constantly, how he no longer sat with us or ate with us, and how he kept to himself entirely, locking the door of his room.

"Thanks be to God, who has guided him. The prophet, upon whom be peace, said: 'There will come a time when one who is steadfast in his religion will be like someone holding a hot coal in his hand.'"

"Meaning?" I asked, trying to project calm.

"May God reward him for his suffering and his forbearance, for he is afflicted with a hard life in your house and among your servants!"

His last sentence was a slap in the face. My eyebrows knotted and my expression became aggrieved. I was certain that he had played an essential role in what had happened to Ahmad. "What do you know of our house?"

"Christians and unbelievers manage its affairs, the food, the drink, driving the cars." He looked at me as he answered, rancor permeating his words. "May God help our son Ahmad, who can't uphold the law of God among the people of his own household!"

I ground my teeth in anger. I looked at the director, but I sensed that he supported what his colleague said. I wished I could pounce on the teacher, fix my hands around his neck, and do away with him. I was certain that he and the Egyptian were behind my son's brainwashing, behind his destruction. The school bell rang and he stood up, telling the director that he had a class.

"We have not finished out talk." I stopped him and rose to block his way. "Who gave you the right to interfere with the life of my son and the affairs of my house?"

"Calling others to uphold God's law and the practice of his prophet, upon whom be peace, is a duty for every Muslim, and no one's permission is needed for that!"

He shook with anger as he said this and tried to step beyond me, but I stopped him, saying, "I advise you to leave my son alone!"

"Are you threatening me? I swear to God that in serving him, I have no fear of anyone!"

He hurled those words at me, and the director's voice came to me: "Mr. Yaqoub, it's not right to threaten a government employee in his workplace!"

The teacher managed to evade me and slip out quickly, so I found myself face to face with the director. Many thoughts churned in my mind, but I was certain that no discussion with him would save Ahmad. My heart burning with anger, I said to him, "God help Kuwait, when you are the ones teaching her sons!"

"Mr. Yaqoub, it's not right!"

I shouted at him in my anger: "It's not right for you to destroy our sons with your reactionary, backward, sick thinking!" Our eyes met and I felt that he was cowering like a mouse, hiding behind the mask of his hateful smile. I left him there and walked out, boiling with anger.

It was peaceful in the mall parking lot, the February sun gentle. Breezes brought the waves to break on the rocks along the shore, the movement and the sound soothing my spirit.

My spirit had been in shreds when I left the school, dragging my feet, not knowing where to go to complain about the evil Umar or his complicit director. I thought about transferring Ahmad to another school, among many other thoughts that came to mind. I have contacts through which I could reach the prime minister, the minister of education, his deputy, but.... A heavy rope of sadness twisted around my neck, nearly choking me; someone was pushing my son toward extremism and violence. My son was slipping through my fingers, and I couldn't do anything about it! I called my friend, Dr. Fadil, wishing him a good evening.

He returned my greeting serenely, but quickly changed his tone. "You seem disturbed."

"Are you at your clinic?"

When I sat before him and explained my dilemma with Ahmad, he remained silent for a few moments before answering. "This is hard. It's clear that you're coming to it very late; they have poisoned your son's mind, and he has become one of them." His words shocked me. There was a heavy silence between us. He added, "Your problem with your son can be found in many homes in Kuwait."

It's unsettling when someone reveals your most private thoughts before your very eyes: "What Kuwait is going through today had its origin at least three decades ago." Dr. Fadil spoke calmly, as if he wanted me to absorb his thoughts. "In the wake of the defeat of the nationalists in 1967 and their dispersal, after the elimination and scattering of the enlightened, modernist movement, and in the absence of any social or humanitarian policy program, some fundamentalist, political Islamists seized the opportunity to infiltrate schools, mosques, and families, under the cloak of religion. They knew that their path to the new generation was through school curricula and mosque study groups. They entered the house claiming piety and good works, performed for the sake of God and for the life to come."

I was watching him, hearing the echo of what reverberated in my own heart: "Many young men became convinced that joining the religious wave would set them on the path of guidance, virtue, and rectitude. Some of the most intelligent realized that it was an easy path to a position and to promotion, maybe to becoming a minister or a member of parliament. Most of the young women saw that the hijab was their path to pleasing God and their families, and to marriage."

I interrupted him, in my agony. "What can Ahmad hope for from them? I can give him what they can't!"

"You're wrong. He hopes for guidance, he wants to live for God alone and to seek martyrdom, to meet the prophet, upon whom be peace, to live in paradise, and to enjoy the beautiful houris there."

My friend's voice laid bare what I had known but feared to face. His words stung every part of my spirit.

"They concentrate on young men, hunting their victims—whom they send off to fight in their place—among the students in schools and universities, among those who frequent the mosques. Meanwhile, families both rich and poor help them finance their activities, drowning them in money, willingly, through contributions, the prescribed *zakat* alms levy, and charitable gifts." He fell silent, catching his breath, before condemning me. "These groups seize the opportunity presented by distracted families to take control of their victims."

I sat with him for nearly two hours and left with one piece of advice: "Embrace your son, all of you, if you can." His voice saddened me as I was leaving, saying, "I hope you have luck on your side!"

The sea itself knows that I was unable to embrace Ahmad, and by the time I drew near to him, his connection to his community was much stronger than any closeness to me or his mother.

The air was refreshing. I decided to walk a little in the mall, and out of nowhere the idea came to me to call Farnaz and ask her to come and have a cup of coffee with me. But I sensed that the waves were asking me, "Who gave you that right? And what's between you and this girl? What if Shaikha saw you, or Abrar or Sahar? What if Du'aij's wife happened to pass by?"

I realized that this was the first time since I returned from America that I had left the company during working hours, just to ease my mind and sit by the shore, the first time I deliberately meandered among the shops. I had the anxious thought that it was as if I had not really lived my life. The phrase wounded me, and I talked to myself calmly: You didn't think of Shaikha? Your wife didn't come to mind? Anyway, what permits you to call a minor employee in your company to come have a cup of coffee with you in a public place?

It's not right! I'm exploiting my position with her.... For nearly four decades I've buried myself in my office and my business. I'm left in a quandary: Shaikha is distracted by her house, her daughters, and her grandchildren; Du'aij is with his family and his companies; Abrar is with her husband, Sahar is in her last year of the university, and Ahmad is fighting in Syria. And here I sit before the waves and my own bewilderment.

It's as if Farnaz has lit a fire in my breast!

How can I see her alone? Should I take her to Sami's apartment? Who says that she'll agree to go, that she'll submit to my wishes? What would I say to her? What would our meeting be like? Anyway, what do I want from a girl the age of my daughters—am I looking for love from her, or am I trying to possess her body? What would Shaikha say if she knew about it? It's true that our relationship is strained, but she would go crazy if she knew I was betraying her, and she would push her brother Uthaiman to take vengeance on Farnaz. Perhaps it was a mistake to agree to hire Uthaiman. Anyway, how can a simple young woman overturn my life and destroy my family? What would Ismail say? That Yaqoub is infatuated with a young Shi'ite, that he's in a relationship with her?

Life is strange. My sorrow over my son's fate seems to be equaled by my entanglement in a relationship that makes my heart tremble.

Maybe I should watch myself from now on and distance myself from this girl. But something in her eyes, her smile, the beauty mark on her lip calls to me, makes me eager to meet her, to follow some secret sign leading to her. I've over sixty—how long will I go on working, like the ox that turns the water wheel? I go in circles, yoked to money, money, money. Don't I deserve a few moments to refresh my heart?

I feel as if the sea is subdued, listening to my dilemma. I won't prolong my time with it. I'll go find my car and go back to my office.

12

Alone in my office, in a calm that's receptive to the whisperings of my spirit.

The first time I saw her with other employees, the second time she came to open a Twitter account for me. The last time I sensed that she was uncomfortable as she came in, when I summoned her on the pretext of finding other Twitter accounts. I've met her three times now. Marwan summoned her and saw her enter, and maybe he kept track of how long she spent with me each time. Never before had I met an employee or been alone with a young woman. He must certainly have told Uthaiman about her and begun to observe her. This could turn into a scandal, if Ismail knew about it or caught any whiff of a relationship between us.

For the first time in my life, I feel as if I'm unbalanced, no longer able to concentrate on the company business. No sooner do I get to the office than I'm gripped by my desire to see her and speak with her, and the question arises—what is this woman's secret?

I'm used to following signs, to thinking over whatever I encounter: dreams, events, people, even news items or film clips. Something secret will whisper to me, telling me to delay, to advance, to refuse, to withdraw, to buy immediately, or, or, or.... Rarely is my impression wrong. Messages from the unseen, from the future, messages of mercy, of secrets—I haven't been able to put a name to them, but I've become addicted to interpreting what happens to me. And ever since I first glimpsed Farnaz, the question keeps coming: what's hiding behind my attraction to her, my longing for her?

During the past week I thought about removing her from her job, in order to be done with obsessive thoughts of her presence in the same building with me and my burning desire to see her.

The internal telephone rang. "Hello."

It was Marwan. "God keep you, have you signed the mail?"

"Not yet." I hung up and reached for the file, but my cell phone rang with a call from Ismail. I answered it with "God keep the Baghdadis!" He was calling to assure me that everything was fine, saying he was at the worksite with the architect Kareem and the project manager, the engineer Azmi, beside him. Those two had met with the engineers and supervisors to choose the most suitable among them. He said that he himself would return the day after tomorrow while Kareem would stay about a week, to make sure that Azmi had the project well in hand and had begun to prepare the site. I asked, "Have you met with the Kuwaiti ambassador?"

"Yes. He was very friendly and said he was ready to give us any help we need. All the steps to start the work are going according to plan."

"Have you received the advance payment?"

He told me he had, and ended the call with "Everything's fine, thanks be to God."

When Marwan came in to take the mail file, I slipped Farnaz's file inside it and handed it to him. I don't want that file to remain with me. Then I turned my back to my desk and allowed my eyes to wander over the horizon of the sea, before asking for Bayoumi and returning to the house.

I had lunch with Shaikha, then went to my room to rest a while. When I woke, around six, I went out to the living room and discovered that I was alone in the house. Visions of Farnaz seized the opportunity to rush toward me and surround me. Since I couldn't get her out of my head, I hesitated a moment then sent her a small message: "Good evening." The message flew as I hung on its letters and waited, dangling on an electronic thread. I felt as if my heartbeat nearly stopped as I waited for her answer. The minutes played an annoying game, barely budging, stuck in their muddy swamp.

After about ten minutes, my phone vibrated with a small alert and a message: "Good evening, sir." I was as happy as a child. For some reason I stood up, holding the phone, not knowing what to answer. At that moment, another message came: "I'm sorry, my phone wasn't with me." Something appeared from behind the message and whispered to me that she had deliberately delayed answering, in order to increase my longing for her. I wrote my question: "Can I call?" The answer came without delay: "Certainly."

"Hello." It was her distinctive tone, which I love.

"Hello, Farnaz." I excused myself, saying I may have called at a bad time, and she answered that she was ready to help in any way. Suddenly I found that I had nothing to talk to her about, and I faltered. My question came without any thought: "Could we meet?" I don't know how that rash question came to me—was I the one who pronounced it, or some other person? It's hard for me to say how many moments passed before she answered with a question:

"Tomorrow in the office?"

"No, outside the office." I noticed that I was still standing, and that a line of perspiration had descended from my armpit to my waist, despite the chill in the air.

"It's hard," she whispered. Once I come home from work, I don' t leave the house."

Something in her voice communicated her confusion, telling me that she might be afraid of me, that I was exerting pressure on a young woman I did not know, with nothing between us to justify my invasion of her world. She might be engaged or in a relationship with a young man of her age. I withdrew: "As you like."

She quickly stopped me: "Go ahead, sir, we can talk now." I was confused, not knowing how to answer her. I took refuge in my silence for a few seconds, and then said goodbye and hung up.

I was angry, disgusted with myself. I sat thinking about what had happened, blaming myself. "Yaqoub, you're behaving like a rash adolescent, running after a girl who's younger than your daughter! What do you want from her?" I was at a loss, not knowing the answer. It had been nearly two weeks, and everyone around me had noticed that something in me had changed.

After Shaikha had failed to get a single word out of me, she sent Sahar to me last night. I was reading an economic report when I heard her voice saying, "Good evening." There was an expression I love in her eyes. She comes to me when she misses me, or when she wants to buy something new.

Smiling slightly, I forestalled her: "What would you like?"

She smiled calmly and answered as she sat down next to me, "Not a thing." I looked at her, and in a strange voice, she asked, "Baba, are you okay?" Suddenly her voice faltered, and tears filled her eyes. "Are you sick?" Fear showed in her eyes and darkened her face.

"My dear!" I hugged her to me and her tears flowed.

"Mother says that you're sick and you're hiding it from us."

"Dear Sahar, my health is excellent, thank God."

"Mama said you're keeping a secret from us."

I averted my eyes and said, "Mama's very sensitive, and she's guessing." I reassured Sahar, swearing to her that I did not have any illness and that I was thinking only of work, as the company had begun a new project in Baghdad. I hugged her to me; her fear had shaken my heart. The question came to me—how long has it been since I hugged my daughter? Since I hugged my wife? What makes a man neglect his wife's nearness, what makes him hold himself aloof from her when he lives with her?

I'm sitting alone in the living room, darkness encircling the garden outside. My telephone sounds with a message alert, and Farnaz's name appears: "I apologize again, sir. My family does not allow me to go out after I come back from work." It occurred to me that I should change the name, as Shaikha or Abrar or Sahar might happen to be near me, or even Uthaiman.

Poor girl—sorry for the one pursuing her, apologizing to the one intruding on her life! It annoyed me to think that by means of my position of power I was imposing myself on a girl I know nothing about. I thought again about hiding the name on my phone, and with no hesitation I changed it to "Al-Khayyam." Some secret in her message that set my heart at rest.

I texted her, "There's no need to apologize." I wrote a second message: "I'm sorry to have bothered you." I read it and was amazed by what I was doing. I whispered to myself again, what's happening to me? It's as if I'm not the person I know, the person everyone knows. I erased the message and threw down the phone. Ahmad's image came to me, I don't know from where. The smell of blood attacked me, and my heart shrank.

I remember the last time I sat with him. That night the servant had prepared dinner, and when I asked Shaikha about Ahmad, she answered, somewhat resentfully, "He's in his room." Since I understood the fraught relationship between them, I stood up to go to him. I knocked on the door and stood waiting. I shouted his name, and the door and a wall of silence stood between us. I called again, "Ahmad!"

The key turned in the lock and the door opened a crack, enough for me to see his face. Something about his eyes and his beard shook my heart, but I swallowed my pain and said, "Come have dinner with us."

"I've already eaten, thanks be to God."

"I miss you, my son, come and sit with us."

He was silent, looking at me, then he said, "I have to study."

"You're running away from sitting with me."

"Not from you."

I understood what he meant, as I knew about his quarrel with his mother and sisters. I had no desire for dinner; I opened the door to his room and went in, and he hurried to close the door behind me. I was annoyed by the stale odor of his room, which was noticeably neglected and dirty, with books strewn on the mat where he sat. I wanted to avoid angering him, so I said, "Come out and sit in the garden."

He walked behind me in his short dishdasha, his head bowed. When we sat down, I began, "What's bothering you?"

He remained enfolded in his silence for several moments, before saying, "There's so much that angers God!" My heart skipped a beat at the expression, but I wanted to let him vent his anger. "My mother and my sisters do not wear Islamic dress, they bare their heads and the flesh of their arms and legs! Wolves in the form of men assault them with their hungry eyes and chew their flesh, and Father, paradise is forbidden to pimps." He was silent for a moment, as if swallowing his anger, before going on. "The servants, the cook, the gardener, and the chauffeur are not Muslims, they're Christians and they're open about it with us. My mother sends them to church and gives them money. We eat and dress at their hands, and that's not permissible." Anger creeping into his tone, he complained, "In our house there's a room for abominations, Father, a room to show brazen, wanton films!"

"Son, it's a room for the family to relax, with a large screen and surround sound, to show movies."

He cut me off angrily. "A screen to show films of unbelievers with scantily clad women, it's wickedness and abomination, may God preserve us! It displeases God and his prophet, and it can't be ignored!"

He raised his face to me and scolded, "And you, Father, God forgive you, you deal with banks that practice usury, and all your income from them is ill-gotten gains, forbidden money! The whole family eats and drinks from what's forbidden, and by God, that's a weighty matter!"

I looked at him, grieved and heartsore. I realized how distant he had become from us as he waded up to his chest into the excesses of fundamentalist thought. He went on, "I grieve for you, Father, and I pray God to overlook your transgressions!" He was silent for a few seconds, then went on, "I know that you pray, but you should pray in the mosque, maybe then God would forgive you. I pray to God that he guide you in your business and your property!"

We each withdrew, stiff in our seats. "Son," I said, "you're restricting yourself needlessly. God tells us in the Quran that religion is ease and not hardship, and God is forgiving and merciful." He went on staring at nothing. "Your mother also prays, and she's hurt by your harshness. It brings her to tears."

"Mother?" His voice was suddenly emotional. "She's careless about praying the prescribed prayers at the proper times, and we find this in the sayings of the prophet, God grant him peace: 'The first of a servant's acts to be examined is his prayer, and if it is sound, he is safe and successful, but if it is spoiled, he fails and is lost.'"

"Ahmad, you're very strict and harsh with yourself, with me, and with your mother!"

He looked at me irritably, and his tone was sharp. "May God richly reward Professor Umar. He's the one who supports me."

I was thunderstruck. "What?"

"He gives me money for my expenses at the beginning of every week, enough for my food."

"And your bank account, where I make monthly deposits?"

"It's a usurious account and the money is ill-gotten. I pray to God on high to help me and keep me away from it."

We spoke of several things, and I discovered that the Ahmad I was sitting with was not my son Ahmad. I became more distressed by his extremist ideas. He said, "This is my last year of high school, and after that I'll move to the university and live there."

There was a moment of silence between us. I looked at him, completely at a loss about what I should do with him.

"Father, please don't be angry with me." He left the phrase hanging between us, before finishing. "Religion is giving counsel, and I must justify myself before God, and tell you that you will be found a sinner."

"In what?"

"You're a strong, powerful man, but you are not guided by God."

The sentence was a slap in the face, but I took it, to allow him to reveal what was going through his mind. "You're strong in your business dealings, but you turn away from applying God's law to the people of your house or among your employees—there's no room set aside for prayer in any of your companies! And you yourself don't go the mosque and you don't pay the *zakat* that's due on your earnings, when it's clearly and incontrovertibly owing!"

Furious, I shouted at him, "Dear Ahmad, do you know what you're saying? They've put a few phrases in your head and you're repeating them to me!" I sensed him shrink back into himself. "I won't allow you, neither you nor your community, to teach me how to live. I was a Muslim before you were born and got religion!" I shouted. "Do you hear me?"

He got up and I pulled with all my might on his hand. "Sit down, I haven't finished speaking!"

He sat down again, and once again shrank within himself. I felt dislike for him. I couldn't stand being near him, his odor and his breath. Seconds of silence passed. Then I left him in his hateful self-absorption and got up to go back into the house.

I don't know how much time had passed in these thoughts when I heard Shaikha's voice wishing me a good evening. She came into the living room with Sahar, who hurried toward me, hugging me and saying, "Baba's going to come watch the film with us tonight."

I smiled at her, and she bent over to take my hand and led me to the movie room.

13

My weeping stayed bottled up inside; I had no wish to break down in front of my coworkers. But the moment I got into my car in the parking lot and closed the door, the urn of my grief shattered and I wept. I hated to go back to our apartment, but I had nowhere else to go.

"What's wrong?" Mother's question attacked me the moment I opened the door.

"Nothing."

She paid no attention to my answer and continued to face me, waiting for me to say something else. I avoided looking at her, but she took both my arms and shook me violently, a mad fear in her eyes. "What happened?"

"I quarreled with the director." Her eyes devoured me. I didn't dare tell her that I had just lost my job.

"You quarreled?" She loosened her grip on my arms. "They fired you?"

Our eyes met. She's my mother, so she understood the shame in my eyes. She left me standing at the door and moved away. She said, bitter weeping coloring her voice, "This is my black fate!"

Alone in my room. A little while ago, Safi took her infant and went to sit with my mother in the living room. It's just after six-forty-five. Ever since I came home I've been torturing myself, hesitating, thinking about contacting Mr. Yaqoub. How would he react to a call from me, what would he say about me? An employee can't contact the president of the company outside of work hours, and anyway there's no relationship between us that would permit that. . . . He's the president of the company, he's in charge of everything. But I'm in trouble and no one else can help me.

Mr. Uthaiman's office manager summoned me five minutes before the end of the day. He must have calculated everything maliciously, intentionally firing me just before the weekend, to cut off any opportunity to appeal to the president. Some Kuwaitis take trips during breaks; maybe Mr. Yaqoub is traveling, or at the least he'll be busy at the beach house with his family. I'll spend the time with my anxious, black thoughts. I had been thinking of taking Mother and Safi to the historic Mubarakiya shops, but now everything has changed. I'll wait till Sunday morning, when the work week begins.

What will I do? I'll begin the humiliating, despairing rounds, looking for a new job. I can't bear to wait until Sunday. There's pressure on my chest. I've done nothing wrong. I'd like to go out on the balcony and shout at the top of my voice, "It's unfair, it's unjust, it's wrong, wrong, wrong!" I'd like to weep loudly. I'll send a little message to Mr. Yaqoub and see how he answers. "Good evening, Mr. Yaqoub." I press the button and the message flies off.

In his last message he asked me to meet him outside of the company. I found it strange and I was afraid, so I refused him right away. Could he be the one who issued the order to end my employment? Did he ask Uthaiman to take care of it? I never told Mother about what happened between us. She would have condemned his rudeness and harassment of me and demanded that I leave the company immediately. She would not allow her daughter to meet a man alone.

How will I meet my car payments? I've just begun to breathe a little freely, even happily. I've been at the company less than a year.... I nearly fainted when I read the letter firing me. Mervet could not believe what happened. I asked to see Mr. Uthaiman, holding the tears in my throat, but he refused to see me.

"Hello, good evening." My telephone vibrated with the answering message from Mr. Yaqoub.

My heart skipped a beat—maybe he thinks that I've agreed to meet him. I don't know how to give him the news. It would be best to talk to him. I'll ask, "May I speak with you, sir?"

"I'll call you shortly." The answer came quickly. That despicable Uthaiman must not have told him what happened. What angers and confuses me is that I haven't been at fault. I haven't had conflicts with anyone, I haven't been late with any work assigned to me, and I arrive at work early every day.

Maybe I shouldn't have asked to speak with Mr. Yaqoub while I'm home—what if Mother heard my voice and came to see who it is I'm talking to? I'll tell her that I called the president of the company to ask for his help. My telephone is set on vibrate, and I'll speak softly. I can't find any reason for the company to terminate me, except that Uthaiman was upset by my visit to the president, and maybe he suspects that a relationship has begun to form between us. The last time I met him I told him, "I don't go to the president's office unless he summons me." Ever since I was hired in the company, I've noticed the look of hatred he directs toward me.

The phone vibrates. "Hello!"

"Hello, Farnaz." His voice is calm. I don't know how to begin. I'm afraid, and I begin to sweat.

"I'm sorry to bother you, Mr. Yaqoub."

"Your voice is trembling; what is it?"

"Mr. Yaqoub, before the end of the day I received a termination letter."

"What?" As if he was surprised by the news.

"My. Yaqoub, please help me! My situation. . . ." Suddenly my voice dissolved into tears. "Please!"

"Without tears, please, who made the decision?"

"I don't know. The letter was signed by Mr. Uthaiman."

A moment of silence passed. I'm afraid my mother will come in.

"After the weekend, come to my office." He was speaking calmly.

"I'm sorry to bother you."

"It's no bother." I thought about asking him what he was going to do, but he confirmed, "Sunday at ten-thirty I'll be waiting for you." I was confused, unsure of how to answer, but he withdrew, saying goodbye and hanging up. I still clung to my phone, shaking with repressed sobs and wondering, is that it?

"Where does he get all his calm?" Mervet said to me. "He's a fascinating personality!" I couldn't sense any emotion or intention to help me in his voice. What will he do? Will he oppose Uthaiman, and possibly Mr. Ismail, to bring me back to the company? Could he have been the one who plotted this, to make me give in to his wishes? I don't think he's that devious. He asked me to meet him outside of the company. I'm younger than his daughters—could he be thinking about sex? He's a powerful man and could easily have many women, so why would he choose me?

When I asked Mervet about the reason for my termination, she was silent for a few moments and then asked, "Did they terminate anyone else with you, in the same decision?"

"No."

When I asked Abdallah, the head of the department and Uthaiman's friend, he answered brusquely, "Instructions from higher up."

What will Mr. Yaqoub do? He asked me to come to his office, perfectly calmly, then he hung up. How can a man decide the fate of another, throwing him to perdition or taking him by the hand and helping him?

The evening I sent money to Reza, Mother kissed me, clearly moved. "Dear, can you help your brother every month?"

I had smiled at her, and said, "Certainly."

Now it's no longer certain. How will I help Reza? How will I make my car payments? Where will I get money to spend on myself? Safi's return to the house with her infant has added to my father's burden—what will he say when he hears about it? I'll ask Mother not to tell him, to wait until Sunday. I'll tell her I'm going back to the company to meet the president, maybe he can help me. I won't tell her about anything that's happened between us.

What moves a man to pursue a girl? Is it sex alone that governs human relations? I was frightened when he asked to see me outside of the company; I couldn't imagine being with him alone. I remembered what Faris had said: "In the apartment we can be at ease." Does the president want to be at ease and enjoy me? Perhaps he chose me after learning that I'm Iranian and Shi'ite, thinking he could have a temporary marriage with me.

When I gave him the news of my termination, his voice showed no affect or emotion; rather, he remained calm. Why would he help me? No one does anything out of the goodness of his heart anymore. He asked me to set up an account for him on Twitter when he could have opened the account himself—from talking with him, it was clear to me that he knows a lot about computers, and it wouldn't have been hard for him to do it. I've gone to his account more than once, without seeing any tweets or the addition of anyone to those he follows. He must have something in mind.

What will I do on Sunday if he bargains with me, if he says he'll give me my job back if I sleep with him? He can go to hell, and his company with him! If I discover that that he's harboring sordid thoughts, I'll leave his office and not go back. But what if the company cancels my residence permit and refuses to turn it over to another Kuwaiti sponsor?

My father would go crazy if he found out that I was expelled to Iran. I should have told Mr. Yaqoub about my residence permit; the personnel department will certainly see to canceling my permit. My poor father, he'll go and beg any of his Kuwaiti friends to create a permit for me. He rejoiced when I was hired and said, "What's important is the residency permit." Then after a few seconds, he added, "It's hard to find a company that will agree to employ an Iranian these days."

Why is this happening, and why did that blow fall on Safi? My poor mother, her face lost all color when she saw me come in crying. Recently she's been crying with Safi, and now it's my turn to bring more disasters down on this family. How, where can a person find good fortune to get him through life? I was dreaming that the president would increase my salary! I should ask Mother to wash her face, to greet Father with a smile.

The poor man comes home exhausted. He's spent every day

of his life in work, toil, and pain, thirty years of it here. He came as a young man. He told me that first he worked as a porter in the Mubarakiya market, then as a deliveryman in a brick factory. Then he worked for years in a garage, then as a driver for a company, then at last he decided to buy a small pickup where he toils away. He's lived for thirty years in Kuwait, and he doesn't have a thousand dinars to his name! He's spent his life working, supporting his father and his family in Iran, and then after he married, he's divided himself between his family here and his large family there. How cheap his days were, and how hard on him! What has my father gotten from Kuwait? A bent back, weak sight, and a wrinkled face—and still he's running after his daily bread!

I mustn't be blind. Yaqoub alone could be a golden key, opening to me the doors of riches and happiness, changing my life and that of my family. I possess my youth and my body and nothing else. Muhannadi toyed with my sister's body and trampled her youth, and I'm afraid that someone will come who will toy with me and destroy my life.

If he bargains to meet me as the price of returning to work, I'll accept. Why shouldn't I meet him? I won't be afraid of him, and I won't allow him to impose anything on me against my will. Many women, many girls wish they had the opportunity to come close to a rich, important man. He owns more than one company and he's a millionaire; he could move me to any of his companies. He's also handsome, and his personality is fascinating.

Perhaps God has willed him to save me and my family and has sent him to me. We're a poor family, the situation of Iranians in Kuwait is hard, and it's much harder in Iran. Fortune has sent me a valuable gift—I won't be stupid and waste it. If I married him, he would give me citizenship and I would be a Kuwaiti. He would open a palace for me and my family to live in; my father could rest and give up his little one-eight. I would have money to play with, to travel, to shop.

Should I wait for a husband like Muhannadi? Yaqoub is my first step toward a different life, and I'll hold fast to him. How long should I be miserable? Maybe I was stupid to refuse his request the first time. Everything that's happened tells me that he admires me. Mervet said frankly, "I'd like to marry him." Then her voice changed and she winked at me, laughing and saying, "Or be his friend."

My father has lived a life of injustice, pain, and humiliation, and my sister Safi married and lived at the mercy of a man who was despicable and harsh.

I'll see what he says on Sunday, and if he mentions meeting him, I'll agree.

I need a strong man to lean on so I can live securely, and I won't find anyone stronger than him. It's a lucky girl who finds a strong man to lean on, one who will stand beside her and remove obstacles from her path; and if the man has the power and wealth of Mr. Yaqoub, then any woman he shelters is lucky a thousand times over!

If anything happened to my father, how would we live in Kuwait? We can't go live in Iran; Reza says that life there is unbearable. He says, "The Iranians humiliate us constantly," and he tells me over and over, "Kuwait is a paradise in spite of everything!"

Maybe I should send another message to Mr. Yaqoub, asking him to stop Uthaiman from canceling my residence permit.

14

Thanks be to God. Again, thanks be to God! My good fortune and my protection come only from God, upon him do I rely and to him do I return, repentant.... In the name of God, with whose name nothing on earth or in heaven is harmed, he is the All-Hearing, the All-Knowing. O God, I have accepted God as lord and Islam as my religion and Muhammad (God bless him and give him peace) as messenger and prophet.

"Yaa-Siin" when it is recited to him! I will take refuge with God from Satan the accursed and recite the chapter "Yaa-Siin," so that God most high may bless this night and may bless my marriage to my new wife, and so that he may ordain for us righteous descendants.

Thanks be to God, there is no power or might save with God. Whenever I'm settled in one place, I have the habit of spending the time between the sunset and evening prayers alone. No one interrupts me then; it's my time of solitude. I sit on my prayer mat directing my face to the qibla, observing the gathering night with my worship and my prayers. I give my face to God, I wash my heart by asking pardon, by repentance, until my tears flow. I take refuge in reciting the Quran, in contemplating its commentaries, in memorizing more of its verses, in learning more about the life of the prophet (God bless him and give him peace) and the lives of his pious companions and our righteous forebears, in going deeply into books of exegesis and classical fatwas interpretating of points of religious law. *"Now hath come unto you a Messenger from amongst yourselves: it grieves him that ye should perish: ardently anxious is he over you: to the Believers is he most kind and merciful. But if they turn away, Say: 'Allah sufficeth me: there is no god but He: On Him is my trust, He the Lord of the Throne (of Glory) Supreme!'"*

A little while ago, I told Ibrahim, "I'm going into my time of solitude now. We will hold the marriage after the evening prayer."

God had decreed that I would meet Ibrahim in Istanbul when I arrived there from Amman. My instructions said, "You will arrive in Istanbul and go to the house of the Hajj Abu Uthaiman." I had the address with me. I was met by a man with a white beard, a friendly face, a warm embrace, and a hoarse voice that cried, "Welcome, welcome to the Kuwaitis!"

He made me feel as if he knew me. He told me that he loves Kuwait and that he has a cousin who works there. After a short pause, he whispered, "We've heard many good things about you." I learned that his two-story house had many rooms, and that he took refuge in Turkey in 2012, after his brother and two of his sons had been martyred. His house is one of the stops for jihadi fighters when they first come to Istanbul. He took me to a small room, where I met Ibrahim. He introduced us, saying, "Ibrahim is a brother for you, a jihadi who arrived yesterday from Saudi Arabia." He smiled, adding, "You're both from the Gulf."

The next morning, Ibrahim and I toured the mosques of Istanbul. I remember how amazed I was by the Hagia Sophia mosque, and by the Mosque of Sultan Ayyub; I remembered what God, the Great and Almighty, says in the Quran*: Allah does not change a people's lot unless they change what is in their hearts.* I was pained by the state of the community of Islam and what it has come to.... Abu Uthaiman smiled and told us, "Turkish kabobs are famous." We had lunch in a large restaurant noisy with customers, and when Abu Uthaiman paid the bill, he smiled and said to us, "I'm not being kind to anyone—the community's financial office reimburses me for everything I spend on you and the other jihadis."

The third morning he handed us over to a Turkish man who spoke Arabic and who had a Volkswagen Passat. As I was saying goodbye to our host, he whispered, "Your uncle, Sheikh Uthaiman, is a personal friend of mine." I was surprised and looked sharply at him, so he added, "Every time he comes to Istanbul he stays in my house, and I remain by his side the whole time."

That's when I began to understand my uncle's relationship with the jihadis. I learned that they have a network of helpers whose task it is to meet new jihadis and to coordinate with the smugglers who will take them across the Syrian border, and that all this takes place in full view of the Turkish authorities and with their consent.

The Turkish man's task was to take us to the province of Idlib via one of the Turkish border crossings, where a Syrian smuggler who worked with the community picked us up to take us to houses and inns in the strip along the border. From then on Ibrahim has been by my side, as close as my shadow. He's a trustworthy, ferocious fighter, unshakable in God's cause, morning and night seeking martyrdom. He's my brother in God, my truest friend, a well to safeguard my secrets.

Glory be to God, and praise, to God most great be glory! About five months ago, when by God's power and might our position in this city was secured, I asked Ibrahim to look for a home for me that would be in an underground cellar. "God bless you," I said, "the deeper the cellar the better, far from any eye or voice!" I added, "Let there be three different places for me to spend the night, by turns—I shouldn't be observed in any one place." When the builder came, I told him, "A simple room with an earthen floor, and for furniture only a palm-leaf matt and a prayer carpet." I told him I must have a wooden bookcase and a simple, undecorated table, so I can read and review battle plans on my computer.

Thanks be to God, there is no power save in God, I seek your forgiveness, O God, and repent to you. This is my room and my blessed home. My uncle Uthaiman sent me incense from Kuwait, and my wife, Umm Umar (may God reward her) has learned how to sweep the floor and spray it with water, how to perfume the room with incense and arrange the mats, and how to orient my prayer carpet toward the qibla. Thanks be to God, who gives and whose gifts no one can turn away! My spirit becomes calm when I seek my prayer carpet, when I stand to pray, with the sentence of the beloved, the chosen prophet (God bless him and give him peace) like perfume in my ears: "Give us rest with it, O Bilal, announce the prayer!" I face the qibla, far from the world and its passing pleasures. I ponder the creation of God, may he be glorified and magnified, and all he has bestowed on me of his great goodness, and how he has honored me by making me a sword hanging over the heads of his enemies and the enemies of religion, to uphold his law on his earth and to apply his prescribed punishments to his servants.

O God, to you belong thanks until you are satisfied, when you are satisfied, and after you have been satisfied.

Yesterday, Hajj Abu Bilal surprised me by arriving with his neighbor and the neighbor's daughter, the bride. Along with the leaders and commanders of the jihadis, I was busy with arrangements for our anticipated battle with the devil's own Daesh fighters—we won't patiently bear their arrogance anymore, as they live in luxury from oil exports! We won't stay at the mercy of their grudging gifts and meager financing. We're preparing something for them that with God's help will shake the ground under their feet and break their back.

May God guide Abu Bilal, he backed me into a corner by his arrival. The first time he brought up the topic, he had said, "Sheikh Ahmad, I have a bride for you who's so beautiful she can tell the moon to stand up so she can take its place!" I only smiled without answering him, so he continued, "A girl like a houri, she's not yet eighteen, still ashamed of her shadow." He told me that her father was one of his neighbors and had been his friend for over thirty years, and that he was a believer—pious and trustworthy. The first time I sent him off without an answer, but as usual, God bless him, he didn't give up on what he wanted. He brought it up again.

"The jihadis fighting for the sake of God need to rest their hearts. The prophet, may God bless him and give him peace, said, 'Marry, for I will multiply the nations through you. Do not be like Christian monks.' And God, may he be glorified and exalted, made woman a repose for her husband, where his limbs can find peace and the flares of his body be calmed."

That day, I answered, "Thanks be to God, I have a righteous wife, a good woman."

"Why shouldn't you have two? And then you'll bring relief to a needy Muslim family, and maybe to other families as well. The prophet, may God bless him and give him peace, said, 'If anyone relieves the cares of a Muslim, then God will relieve him of one of his cares on the Day of Judgment, and if anyone shields a Muslim, God will shield him on that Day.'"

He explained to me that his friend Abu Khalil was destitute, and that the monthly subsidy that I would provide to him and his family, from the community's treasury, would be aid for his wives and his children, as well as a new link between the community and still more young followers and jihadi supporters. He paused briefly, then he added, "If God has decreed marriage for you, your father-in-law would have the right to no less than two hundred dollars a month. It's amazing how God has filled the treasury with good things!"

I wanted to explain that things have changed in the treasury, but I didn't say a word. I brought it up with my wife, Umm Umar. "It's true that this is the religious law, but I won't marry a second wife without your consent and your permission."

She whispered timidly, "O sheikh, obedience is due to you. I will not oppose the word of God, that a man may marry *two, three, or four!*"

"God bless you! You will remain my dear Umm Umar. Also, she may be two years younger than you."

"She'll be a sister to me, God willing, and we'll work together to serve you and make you happy."

I told her that Abu Bilal had arranged the matter, and that the girl was from Deraa like her. Her face lit up with joy, and she said that she might know her, as everyone in Deraa knows everyone else. She said, "May God reward you and bless you richly, sheikh! You'll bring together two girls, lawfully, in one house."

"There is no god but thou: glory to thee: I was indeed wrong! ... O my Lord! Let my entry be by the Gate of Truth and Honor, and likewise my exit by the Gate of Truth and Honor; and grant me from Thy Presence an authority to aid me. Oh Lord, make my marriage something good for me in this world and the next, and help me, by your grace and kindness, to help my wife's family in ways that please you. There is no god but thou: glory to thee: I was indeed wrong!"

During our meeting yesterday, we discussed the circumstances surrounding the timing of our raid on the barracks of God's enemies, the devil's Daesh fighters. Perhaps tomorrow we'll go over the detailed arrangements for the attack for the last time, and agree on the specific time, keeping it a secret. As usual right before each attack, I've noticed that my brother jihadis have increased the pace of their worship, and some of them have begun fasting, to draw near to God, wishing for martyrdom, and preparing to meet the beloved prophet of God. God bless him and give him peace, preparing for a paradise as vast as the heavens and the earth.

For the second time I'm going to marry in secret, far from my country, with none of my family to witness my marriage. Sometimes I long to see my father. My uncle Uthaiman is constantly in touch with me. May God reward him richly on our behalf! He's one of those financing us, sending us sums from charitable people, from more than one account in more than one country.

I can never forget his kindness. He was the one who first took me by the hand and walked with me to the mosque near our house, introduced me to Sheikh Abel Shafi, and commended me to him. I still remember his words: "Ahmad is my son. God made him both brilliant and steady, and we've placed high hopes in him!" He warned me, "Don't mention this to your father." When I asked him why, he said, "Your father has no love for Islamist groups and doesn't sympathize with their views. He might be angry with both of us."

Sheikh Abdel Shafi, may God amply reward him, was the first one to form me. He began with Quran recitation and having me memorize some of the shorter verses, together with their explanations, then he moved me on to books of the prophet's hadith sayings. Little by little he steered me toward the state of my life and of my family. He was the first one to draw my attention to the noble hadith, which says, "There will come a time when the one who is steadfast in his religion is like one who's holding a hot coal!" I remember the saying he often repeated: "Some people live like animals, making no distinction between what's permitted and what's forbidden."

Ustaz Umar took me under his wing at school. How surprised I was to discover that he and Sheikh Abdel Shafi were friends, and that both of them were friends of my uncle Uthaiman. I remember the day my uncle told me, "You are the pride of the family in this generation!"

"What about Hamad?" I asked him. His son Hamad and I were studying at the same school, and he was also an outstanding student. But he replied, "God, may he be praised and exalted, sends his guidance to whom he pleases." He gave me to understand that God had opened my heart to his commands and his love, to walking on the path of prayer, of righteousness, and of guidance. At the time my heart was attached to the two books of Sayyid Qutb: *In the Shade of the Quran* and *Milestones*, to his views and commentaries, which Sheikh Abdel Shafi explained to me.

I entrust myself to God, for God is discerning with his servants. O God, bestow on me righteousness and guidance from you and help me against your enemies, the enemies of religion! O merciful, O compassionate!

I don't know how my mother will take the news that I have married two wives. May God forgive her and be good to her. How it hurt me to see her and my sister Sahar flaunt their beauty. There is no power or might save in God! I complained to Sheikh Abdel Shafi, and he quoted the Quran: "Invite to the Way of thy Lord with wisdom and beautiful preaching; and argue with them in ways that are best and most gracious," adding his favorite saying: "Be patient, my son, the reward is hereafter." My mother, may God forgive her, was not about to accept preaching or counsel; she went on displaying herself without any hijab. When I went to my father and told him bluntly, "Paradise is forbidden to pimps," he fumed in anger and did not uphold God's law in his own house. I was greatly afflicted by the people in my family: my mother, my father, my two sisters. I hated my father when he refused to uphold God's law in his house. I hated him when he humiliated Sheikh Abdel Shafi, and I hated him more when Uncle Uthaiman told me, "He's a tyrannical man, everyone in the company is afraid of confronting him." But as God is my witness, I summoned him with beautiful preaching. I wished that God would open his heart to guidance. I prayed for him, but.... I seek your forgiveness, O God, and I turn to you in repentance. May God be glorified and thanked, glory to almighty God. My God, you have bestowed great goodness on me. My Lord, may it be my lot to thank you for your blessing. My Lord, pardon me and my parents and all the believers on the Day of Judgment.

Ustaz Umar is the one who opened my eyes to true Islamic life. He invited me to visit him at home. I sat in his gatherings, I ate his food, I saw his children, his wife and his daughters, and how God had protected their faces with the niqab veil. Even the Philippine servant had become a Muslim under his guidance and had adopted the niqab. I saw how there was no television in his house, how their pleasure was to study the book of God and the ways of his prophet and to study hadith together.

May God reward him, he is the one who lit my way and told me to avoid eating in my house from the hands of Christians and Magians. He advised me to buy a small refrigerator, which would supply my needs and keep me from having to eat with my family. When I confided in him that I did not have the money for the refrigerator—as I had stopped taking any of my father's money, which came from usury—he earned my thanks by offering to buy it for me. He brought me to tears when he recited to me the hadith that says, "Seven will be shaded by God on the Day of Judgment when there is no shade but his own," and among them will be, "two men who love each other in God."

A few months ago he contacted me, by means of Abu Bilal. He greeted me and congratulated me on the victories of the jihadis over their enemies, which our people and our companions in Kuwait had heard about. He gave me the good news of several young Kuwaitis whose hearts had been opened to faith and the love of jihad, and who were on their way to us.

I take refuge with God from Satan the accursed! My thoughts have run away with me and I have not recited the "Yaa-Siin" chapter. O God, marry us and suffice us with what you have permitted and keep us from what you have forbidden, O God, O generous, O noble lord of the throne.... My father, may God forgive him, has wronged himself, neither making his family live according to Islamic morals nor refraining himself from dealing in usury and consuming ill-gotten gains! He obstructed me and kept me from upholding God's law in my house and among my family. How I cried over my weakness and insignificance and turned myself over to God. Finally I held to my teacher Umar's advice: "Bear up, for the believer is tested. Live alone in your room, for you are not of them, nor do they belong to you." He consoled me, saying, "Soon God in his grace will bless you and you will emigrate. You will leave them for the path of preaching, of paradise, and of the houris!"

O God, I ask as the prophet did, I ask you for constant faith, for a humble heart, for beneficial learning, for true conviction, for upright religion, for protection from all trials.

This morning I met Hajj Abu Bilal, and he introduced me to his friend Hajj Abu Khalil. He kissed me and told me that he was honored to give me one of his daughters, and that the family's connection to me was a cause for celebration for them. He had told his daughter to obey blindly, and to dedicate her life to serving me. I welcomed him and thanked him; I told him that I had sent orders to the community's treasurer to send him a monthly stipend of two hundred dollars, and that I would give my wife the initial dowry payment: a sum of one thousand dollars.

I expected to see my bride, if only behind her niqab. I like a short, full-figured woman, and I do not care for one who's tall and thin. But he anticipated me. "You'll see the bride tonight, and her beauty will dazzle your eyes!" At the time I expected that Abu Bilal would ask for her to come, so I could see her appearance, her body, and something of the look in her eyes—for all of this is within the limits of the law—but he did not.

May God be praised! He makes the Night overlap the Day, and the Day overlap the Night. He has subjected the sun and the moon. Each one follows a course for a time appointed. Is not He the Exalted in Power—He Who forgives again and again? The years are passing by so quickly. I remember how I left Kuwait, emigrating, fleeing, despised, humiliated, having just enough to get to Jordan. In Amman I was met by Abu Maan, who put me up in his house with his family. I was his guest for three days, until he arranged my travel to Istanbul and my meeting with the kind Abu Uthaiman, from where I traveled to Idlib with Ibrahim, my brother in God, and we entered Syrian territory.

When I first arrived at the camp at the front, I was met by a masked man who asked for my passport and then asked me detailed questions about how I had left Kuwait and made my way to them, and about the names of those who helped me in Jordan and in Istanbul. I sensed that he was speaking in a Saudi dialect. He asked me about those I studied with in Kuwait, and in what neighborhood that was and in what mosque. He asked me about my view of religious commitment and about my family situation, falling silent when I told him that my father is a millionaire. Finally he asked me about my view of jihad, who had encouraged me to join them, and if I knew any jihadi in the community.

After that, an elderly Tunisian sheikh taught us for two weeks. There were about ten of us, Arabs and foreign brothers. He went over with us the provisions of monotheism, belief, and charges of unbelief, and what we had to know about fighting apostates. He spent time considering the sect of rejectionists, those who refuse to uphold one of the clear laws of Islam, and who will not return to their senses and abide by that law unless they are forced to. He also taught us that the law of war since the creation of humanity is kill or be killed! I had to repeat, "I hear and obey you." After that I transferred to the training camp, along with my brother Ibrahim, for about a month. There they drilled us on how to use weapons and disassemble them, and there for the first time I saw a variety of weapons: pistols and Kalashnikovs, all the way to RPGs. Before the end of the session, the leader met with us and asked us which of us preferred jihad in battles, and who wanted to join the battalion of those seeking martyrdom, those heroes who hurry toward paradise, toward meeting the beloved prophet of God, may God bless him and give him peace. After we completed the training course, they gave each jihadi two hundred and fifty dollars.

As soon as we graduated from the course, I realized what a blessing God had bestowed on me, and I began to dream of martyrdom, of paradise, and of joining the righteous and the martyrs among the companions of the prophet.

In Istanbul I learned that my uncle Uthaiman was one of those financing the community. I reproached him later for not telling me, and he answered, "God orders everything in good time!" He told me, "I was afraid for you, afraid of what your father might do." Then he predicted, "You will be important, and everyone will treat you as you deserve." I think he's the one who used his connections so that I was appointed as an emir, commanding a group; he was delighted when I told him the news, and answered saying, “Maa shaa Allah, look what God has willed! May God bless you and bless us in you! You are our pride, Abu l-Fath!”

“Sheikh Ahmad, sheikh....” It was the voice of my brother Ibrahim behind the door. “We’re waiting for you, I’m about to give the call for the evening prayer.”

O Living, O Everlasting, from you do we seek help, O God, on you do we rely...I will lead the group in the prayer, and afterwards we will perform the marriage. Tonight I’ll sleep in my new wife’s bed. All praise to the one who has allowed the permissible and who has forbidden the unlawful!

15

It's as if I've left myself, as if I've left my life! It's been nearly an hour since I arrived in my office. I've enjoyed my coffee, and I sit facing the broad surface of the sea.

For more than thirty years I've been far away, running after transactions, banks, meetings, travel. I've been marked by a way of life I can't undo; I've developed a taste for it and enjoyed living it. Part of the blame falls on Shaikha; she shares in the coldness of our relationship, in its illness. She let me distance myself from her, and when I returned I would find her indifferent, the same as always.

I feel as if I never knew love, never experienced it! I once read that someone who lives without love has died without knowing the pleasure of life. Now I realize that I liked Shaikha and married her without feeling any tremor in my heart, without experiencing any overwhelming desire. As soon as we were together, Shaikha was content with me as a husband, and I was satisfied with her as a mother for my children and mistress of the house. She went one way and I went another, and we were brought together only by infrequent occasions of joy or grief, on a trip, in a birthday party, or during an illness. Afterwards each returned to his own path, leading away from the other.

Do you love Farnaz? The question came to me through the broad window of my office. I'm becoming entangled in a love story with a young woman who uses captivating perfume! A young woman I've seen only in passing.

"Peace be upon you." I was surprised by Ismail, who had returned from Baghdad.

I stood up to meet him. "Welcome, welcome, you've returned safely, thank God." I greeted him and kissed him. "Sit down and tell me everything."

"Thanks be to God, everything went as well as we could hope." He paused, then continued in a sad tone, "Baghdad is not what you knew in the seventies and eighties."

I looked up at him, recalling the most beautiful images of Baghdad in my mind—Baghdad of the Tigris, Baghdad of Abu Nuwas, Baghdad deeply rooted in history and beauty. Baghdad of Al-Mutanabbi Street, of books, fragrant with scholars, where friends met in generous and noble homes, at overflowing tables, in companionable cafés, Baghdad....

"The project is in the Green Zone and the security measures are extremely strong. It's hard to enter of leave the zone, you pass through five or six checkpoints." As I listened to him my heart bled for Baghdad. I had not visited it since 1990, the day when Saddam destroyed our faith in everything, baring his face as a ferocious dictator. The day he occupied Kuwait and took possession of it with an almost unprecedented, rash bloodiness. "I went out just once, in the Kuwaiti ambassador's car, to accept a dinner invitation from the director of the company."

He added, cautioning me, "The project might be delayed. The engineer Kareem will remain a week with the project director, the engineer Azmi, but...." His face took on a strange expression. "The Iranians have a tangible presence and strong influence everywhere. Their followers and militias control Baghdad's utilities! We should have chosen a Shi'ite project director." His next sentence struck me: "He would be acceptable to them, he'd know how to come to an understanding with them, and it would be easier to manage dealings with the government. The Shi'ite militias alone govern Baghdad!"

I looked at him for a moment before picking up my phone and calling Kareem. "Good morning, Chief!" I told him about my meeting with Ismail, and I instructed him concerning the necessity of naming an assistant project director who was Shi'ite. I specified, "He must come to Kuwait as soon as he's appointed. I want to meet him here and come to an understanding with him."

I hung up, then I looked at Ismail. "Please follow up on this with Kareem. Have him send me a copy of the Shi'ite engineer's passport as soon as he's appointed so I can secure a visa for his visit."

He seemed surprised by my decision. I told myself that when the engineer arrived, I would come to an agreement with him. I would open an account for him in a foreign bank and transfer to it sums in dollars, in the measure he cooperated with us.

Ismail commented, "It will be very hard to get a visa for an Iraqi."

"I'll speak to someone who will have one for him in an hour."

"Then we're agreed," he said, rising to leave the office and bidding me farewell.

Farnaz was coming at ten-thirty. I lifted the phone and asked Marwan to have Uthaiman come.

The day of my meeting with the employees, I noticed that the largest group were Egyptians, and that most of them came in with beards and prayer calluses on their foreheads, speaking with a pretentious language that I hate. It was clear that Uthaiman had filled the company with his followers.

There's a knock on the door, followed by Uthaiman's face. "Peace be upon you."

"And upon you." He came in and sat down. As usual, I remained silent for a few seconds, then I asked him, "Why did you terminate the Iranian employee?"

His face showed a sudden surprise. "The computer department has enough people. The company doesn't need her services."

"Did she make any mistake or fall short in anything?"

"No."

"How long ago was she hired?"

"Less than a year ago, as I remember."

"Who hired her, and why? And how can we terminate an employee without any notice?" He faltered, not knowing how to answer. "Immediately, issue an order to return the employee to her work, and increase her salary by fifty dinars. Issue a second administrative order that the hiring of any employee in the company, of whatever rank, will not be effective without my approval and my signature, nor will the firing of any employee take effect unless I personally sign the papers." His expression showed his anger. "Circulate the second order to all the directors."

"But Yaqoub . . . "

"Bring me the two orders immediately so I can sign them." I fell silent, looking at him, then I added, "It's not acceptable to attack people through their livelihoods or to expose them to psychological harm. Give this employee three days' paid vacation." I felt that he was boiling and wanted to speak, but I said "I'll expect the two orders" and ended the meeting.

He rose to leave, but I stopped him, asking, "Has having a beard become a condition of employment in my company?"

The question disturbed him. A look of constraint flashed across his face, and he withdrew in embarrassment.

The moment he left I summoned Marwan. When he came in, I said, "Uthaiman will be coming with two orders. There's no call for him to bring them to me himself; you take them and bring them to me to sign."

Will this simple girl change my life? By means of her, what's going on in my company has started to reveal itself to me. I whispered to myself that I'm now certain that some secret lies hidden behind her. Uthaiman did not realize that he was bringing her close to me the day he terminated her! The One who makes all things easy brings them where they were destined to go. This isn't the first time for me to work hard, and then find help coming from where I least expect it. I'd like to see Farnaz now, to smell the scent of her perfume.

My telephone rings and a strange number appears on the screen. I hesitate for a few seconds, then answer.

"Peace be upon you."

My heart trembles to hear Ahmad's voice. "Son! Where are you?"

"I'm fine, thanks be to God."

"God be kind to you, I don't know what to say. When will you come back—haven't you had enough of fighting?"

"Baba, I had a dream about you yesterday, a dream that was a vision."

"Where are you, Son? In what country? I'm so upset about you."

"I told you, I'm fine, thanks be to God. I want to say..."

“Before you say anything, please, Son, come back to Kuwait. Please, have mercy on me!”

“Baba. I ask God to receive me graciously, and to grant me martyrdom.”

“My son, my beloved!” I felt my heart beating fast, and my mouth had gone dry. “Are you in Syria now?”

“Listen to me, Father. God has blessed me with his all-encompassing grace. I have married two righteous women, and I have a child who’s almost a year old. His name is Umar.”

“What? You’ve married two women, and you have a son?” A sudden attack of weeping seized me by the throat.

“Father, I’m calling to beg you—repent, turn back to God sincerely, draw near to him, and pray for martyrdom for me!”

“Ahmad, I beg you to come back to Kuwait. You can have anything you want.”

“Father, through God’s gifts I don’t need your generosity. I pray to him night and day, may he be praised and glorified, that he will guide you and my mother!”

“Son, your mother and I need you. Where are you now?”

“I’m in God’s country. May he guide you to the straight path and bestow upon me either the blessing of victory or the blessing of martyrdom!”

“My son, I. . . .”

“Peace be upon you!”

The connection was cut. I felt as if I couldn’t catch my breath. I called back to the same number, but each time there was only static on the other end. His voice had stirred up a painful longing for him. He had married twice. He had named his son Umar, for his wretched teacher! I turned to face the sea with my distress, and the odor of blood rushed to meet me.

Marwan came in with a folder. “The two orders.”

I turned back to the desk and took the folder. I read the first administrative order, rehiring Farnaz Sadegh Qurmuzi to her position with a raise of fifty dinars per month. I signed it with the word “authorized.” I looked over the second order and signed it as well, telling Marwan, “Copy both of them. The employee will come, and you will give her the original. Then she should go to Uthaiman to sign her new contract. She has three days of leave.”

He picked up the file and left, and Ahmad’s voice came back to me, with its tone of farewell. His call had not put my heart at ease; he had told me of his marriage and demanded that I repent and pray for him to be martyred. I wonder what Shaikha will say when she finds out that he has married two women.

I remember when she told me that he had left the house—I didn’t know what to do. He had finished high school less than a month earlier. My son’s disappearance enveloped me in a strange feeling. I was very disturbed when I saw Shaikha crying in agony, as if she were lamenting his death.

I contacted my friend the district commander and informed him of Ahmad’s absence from the house. I hesitated a little when he asked, “Do you suspect that he’s with anyone?”

“The teacher, Umar.” I realized that I didn’t know anything about him other than the address of the school, and schools were closed for the summer vacation.

“Do you know his full name?”

“Umar Abdallah, or Umar Ubaid, I think.”

He took down the name of the school and its address, and he asked me not to do anything without consulting him. “I’ll follow it up myself, and I’ll call you as soon as there is any information.”

The next day, a little after eight in the evening, I had a call from him. "Yaqoub, my friend, come to the police station right away."

He was waiting for me in a police car when I arrived at the station. He got out to greet me, then said, "Come with me. We'll talk on the way." He told me that we would go to the police station in the Salibiya district, and from there an armed force would accompany us, to raid one of the farms in the Kabd district.

The police cars surrounded the farm, and he warned me, "Our experiences have been bitter. You stay in the car, there could be shots fired and you must be careful." I stayed in my seat, while six armed men advanced to open the gate of the farm.

In the interrogation, Professor Umar said that he was helping Ahmad by sheltering him on his farm, moved by brotherhood in God. He said that God, may he be glorified and exalted, had bestowed guidance upon Ahmad, so he could no longer bear the sight of the people in his house who had strayed and still keep silent about it.

Ahmad confirmed that to the commander. "I went of my own free will to live on the farm of my brother, Professor Umar, and he honored me with his help, may God reward him richly for that." He embarrassed me when he turned to me and informed me in front of everyone that he was free to make his own decisions, that he would not return to live in my house, that he had presented his papers to enroll in the College of Religious Law, and that he would live in university housing.

I asked the commander for time alone with Ahmad. Everything about him had changed—the look in his eyes, his speech, the expression on his face, his body, the hair on his head, his clothing, his smell. I said, "My son, we are your family." He remained silent, listening only. I don't know if he heard me or ignored what I said; when I finished, he answered in a decisive tone:

"I know the way to our house, and I detest everything it leads to. I know the way of God, and he, may he be glorified and exalted, has bestowed on me the blessing of seeking him."

I was alerted by the sound of a phone message. I saw the name "al-Khayyam," and read, "Thank you very much, sir! I don't know how to return your favor!" I was at a loss about how to respond, so I let it go. I don't know why my heart felt a touch of happiness. Ahmad is fighting and hoping for martyrdom, and here I am preoccupied with love notes!

Less than a year after he left, Shaikha had stopped mentioning his name. She cleaned his room and threw out everything in it. She repainted the walls and bought new curtains and furniture for it. Ahmad had disappeared from our life, and everyone became used to his absence; perhaps they were even relieved by it. A number of times I asked myself whether everyone had forgotten him.

I don't remember that Du'aij, Abrar, or Sahar ever mentioned him. They had deliberately forgotten him or were avoiding mentioning him in front of me, perhaps afraid of stirring up anger and pain in me. Everyone knows how attached to him I am. Only Farnaz has distracted my mind from him during the last few days. I must see her and sit with her.

I picked up my phone to call one of my friends who's among the owners of the Sheraton Hotel. He welcomed me warmly, but I said immediately, "Could you please speak to the hotel and have them reserve a suite for me for a month?"

He was silent for a few seconds, surprised by my request. Then, "The director of reservations will call you right away."

"Have him call me on my cell phone, not my office phone."

I long for Farnaz. I must meet her. I can no longer simply sit and think about her, and I won't take her to Sami's apartment. I want what's between us to remain a secret; I don't want a single word to touch my reputation.

My telephone rang. "Good evening, Mr. Yaqoub. This is the director of reservations for the Sheraton. Excuse me, please—will you be taking a royal suite or an ordinary one?"

"An ordinary one. Put the bill in my name, and I'll pay it at the hotel."

"Certainly, Mr. Yaqoub. I'll need an hour for the suite to be ready to receive you."

I hung up, and the thought occurred to me that I would not take Farnaz to any suspicious place. The Sheraton is near the company offices. I'll write her a message: "If you are in the company, call me on my internal number, 1111." I think she's still here.

The internal phone rang, and I answered, saying, "Don't mention my name."

"Of course."

"I want to see you."

She shrank behind the receiver, breathing audibly. "When?" Before I could answer, she added, "I can't, after working hours." She spoke in a whisper, as the sweetness of her fearful words flowed straight to my heart. I remained silent. "I can't thank you enough, sir, I received the order reinstating me . . . "

She swallowed my name, and my heart throbbed. I said, "I've arranged things. I asked the company to give you three days of paid leave, and we can meet in the morning." I heard a sound near her that I thought might be Uthaiman's voice, and the call was cut off.

I'll meet her during working hours, at the hotel. So that no one will notice that we're both gone. I'll tell Marwan that I'll be attending some meetings at a bank during the coming days.

"I'm sorry for hanging up." It was a message from her. I wrote, "Arrange your time, and we'll meet during the morning hours." The answer came immediately: "I'll try."

What will Farnaz say about me? Will she tell her coworkers that I've harassed her? Will she keep my messages and show them to some attorney to prove harassment? I rushed to write, "You can be sure that I have no ill intentions." I wanted to add another word, but I held off. I spent a few seconds talking to myself: "You're acting like an adolescent, Yaqoub! Chasing a young girl who works in your company and imposing your will on her. You're exploiting the fact that she's an employee."

I wrote to her, "I hope no one learns of what passes between us." My message had barely gone when the reply came: "I promise you that." She must certainly have agreed because I returned her to the company and raised her pay. Uthaiman brought her close to me by his deed—I couldn't have thought of a better plan than what happened. Things have become easier!

I don't know how much time had passed when my phone rang and Shaikha's name appeared on the screen. "Hello."

"Where are you?"

"At the office."

"Lunch today is something you like, butterfish, so when are you coming?"

I hesitated, not knowing how to answer her. "I'll finish what I'm doing and then come."

I hung up, and it crossed my mind to wonder what's happening to me. I'm arranging a meeting with Farnaz while Shaikha is thinking of me, enticing me with my favorite dish!

16

Mervet is looking at me suspiciously. I can barely believe that I have my job back; it's as if I'm dreaming!

I woke up this morning at the usual time, and as I began to dress I was annoyed by the thought that I might wake up the next day only to stay in bed, eaten up by emptiness.

"Where are you going?" Mother asked me.

"I'm meeting with the president of the company." I turned my face away, afraid that she would see what my eyes tried to conceal. I delayed leaving, since my appointment with Mr. Yaqoub was for ten-thirty. Mother hovered over me, suspecting that I was planning something I did not want her to know about. Safi was absorbed in her baby and in worry about her situation, a constant look of pain in her eyes.

I left as late as I could, and as I drove the road seemed calm, unlike most days. I felt as if there was less traffic and it was flowing smoothly. The traffic light at the Northern Nuqra Mall usually stops me with an irritating red color, but today it welcomed me with green. I took that as a good omen, foreshadowing a green light for the rest of the day.

Since I had left early, I wondered what I would do to fill the time until ten-thirty. Where would I go? I wished I could reach out and hurry the hands of the clock. It occurred to me to pity people—we rush the passage of time, the hours of our lives, so the moments of bitterness we're living will give way sooner to better times to come.

Mr. Yaqoub is too smart to waste the moments of his life. I don't know how he thinks, nor what bargain he will offer me when we meet. I don't know where he will take me, or what face he'll show me, or what he'll say to me or ask of me, or if he will be the same person I've met before. He alone returned me to my job, and it's certain that he could throw me out.

Ever since I walked into my office and sat down at my place, Mervet has been staring at me in a way I don't understand.

I had many nightmares over the weekend. Mother and Safi were sad for me, and I came in today with fear and hope in my heart. I went to the president's office, taking care that neither Uthaiman nor Mervet nor any of my coworkers would see me. I was greeted by Marwan, the office manager, who asked me to sit down. He gave me a copy of my new contract, signed by Mr. Yaqoub, with a raise of fifty dinars. I didn't believe my eyes when I read the contract; my body trembled slightly, and I was careful that no tear of joy betray me. He told me, "Go to Mr. Uthaiman to receive your copy of the new contract. Those are the president's instructions."

Mervet said, "What a stroke of luck!" She looked up inquiringly. "Mr. Yaqoub himself signed your work contract?" She smiled. "Our lord has opened the gates of good fortune for you!"

I've been unsettled ever since I came back to the office. I've been careful not to mention his name or to refer to him as "the president." I glimpsed a look I don't care for on Mervet's face when she learned that he had signed my contract.

Since I received my new contract, a voice inside of me has been whispering, "Be flexible with the man, don't add to your father's burdens or bring more trouble to your mother's heart. Be flexible with him because you need him, be flexible with him because he's the president and you're an insignificant employee." But another voice scares me: "What if he asked me. . . ."

I was hoping to have a loving relationship with a young man, and now the president of the company is blocking my path. What if he asked me. . . I won't submit to him, I'll run away. Maybe he's thinking about a temporary contract marriage; he learned I'm Shi'ite, so he wanted a secret marriage for his own pleasure. I might be a passing whim, one that appeared in the midst of his preoccupations, a girl he saw who appealed to him for some reason, and like any man, he wanted to approach her, to experience the touch of her body, its taste. A person in his position won't sacrifice anything for me. Each of us wants something from the other: he wants pleasure and entertainment from me, and I want him so that I can live!

The moment Marwan gave me the order, a small tremor shook my arm. Some hidden sense whispered to me, "Nothing in this world is free. This is the beginning of your adventure with the president." And when I learned that he had given me three days' leave at company expense, at a time when he wanted to meet me, my heart trembled in fear. It occurred to me that he might be behind everything.

I know that he has the power to do whatever he wants. My fate is in his hands, and with the stroke of a pen he returned me to my job with a higher salary. For the first time, I've realized that nothing stands in the way of people with power, and they decide other people's fate effortlessly. I've lived my life poor, and here one of the richest men of Kuwait wants to meet with me.

Sometimes it occurs to me to wonder what secret signal a woman's body sends to excite men, to whet their appetite so they follow the illusion submissively.

What's wrong with a relationship between us? What's the most that can happen between a woman and a man? I will be his friend, and he will coddle me. Many young women all over the world wish for a relationship with a rich older man, one who will lavish money and gifts on them. Something in that gave me a strange feeling of pleasure. I repeated, what's wrong with it? But apprehension settled over me, saying, "You might pay a high price!"

Before I left this morning, Mother stopped me and said, "God provides sustenance, Farnaz." As if she had noticed I was dressed differently than usual, she inspected me with a look whose meaning I knew well. "Be careful! Don't demean yourself to anyone."

I won't demean myself, Mother. The man helped me voluntarily more than I expected—he returned me to my job and raised my pay, and he gave me three days of paid leave.

Mother, Yaqoub is a gift sent by God, and I won't waste it. Big opportunities only come once, Mother, and lucky is the one who takes advantage of them! How many times have you repeated to me, "My wish is to see you a bride." But what good did marriage do Safi? Once she bared her arm to me and I saw a circle of reddish blue.

I gasped, "What's that?"

She choked on her hidden tears and answered, "Muhannadi pinched me so hard I nearly died."

Mother, Yaqoub is older than my father; anyway, everything in him suggests that he's calm and courteous, perhaps wily. But what price will he ask for bringing me back to the company? He must have something in mind. Where could he meet me? Maybe he has several places for companionship and pleasure. Is he accustomed to choosing one of the girls or the women who work for him, or has my own good luck brought him to me? Men are strange—nothing breaks their tyranny but a woman's body. In exchange for their pleasure in it, they give up their pride and power and become children again!

What does he like about me? How will I meet him? I told him that I couldn't meet him after work, so he gave me time off from the company. I feel a question move in me—what hidden adventure awaits me with him? My sister Safi is more beautiful than I am, and many young men ran after her. I remember that she said to me, grinding her teeth, "Men are dogs, they sniff out a woman's readiness then watch for the chance to pounce on her!"

She was talking about Nidal, the son of our Palestinian neighbors, with whom she shared a love story for two years. He made a date with her for one evening, and when she went to meet him in his apartment, she was surprised to find that his family weren't there, and that he meant to rape her. She saw her chance when he went to the bathroom, and fled in spite of a nearly paralyzing fear. I remember her words: "When their instinct is awakened they don't see anything else, and then they turn into mad beasts."

I had intended to get a sense of the president's intentions this morning. I paid attention to my hair and used a touch of makeup, but he did not meet me, and simply directed his office manager to give me the contract.

I didn't sleep well last night. I woke up from one hour to the next, as if I was hurrying the arrival of daylight. But nothing changes the turning of time.

I'm alone now, my anxieties roiling inside. Maybe I should leave the company, since I have today off. I must communicate with him, to learn what he wants from me. Everyone knew I was fired, but I've come back to work, and everyone will know that he brought me back and increased my salary. I don't know what the others will say about me; they will certainly whisper and wink, "the president's lover!" What will Mervet say when she finds out that he gave me a raise of fifty dinars? I won't tell her anything, I won't tell anyone what passes between us. I'll contact him and assure him that I haven't said a word. Even my sister Safi, I won't confide anything in her.

When I left Marwan's office, I took my fear with me to meet Uthaiman. "Good morning."

"Good morning." It was his office manager who answered me. "I'll inform Mr. Uthaiman that you've arrived." The phrase suggested that Uthaiman knew about the matter, and that he was waiting for me. After a few moments the door opened, and the office manager invited me to enter. Fear clung to me.

"Good morning, Mr. Uthaiman."

"And upon you be peace." He seemed irritated with me. "There was an administrative error with respect to your termination. Consider that nothing happened."

I would have liked to shout for joy. I asked, "Shall I return to work now?"

"The company has given you paid leave for three days."

"Thank you very much, sir."

"You're welcome."

I stepped away calmly and carefully, leaving his office.

I don't know what Mervet will think if I were to leave the company now. Maybe I should wait until everyone leaves, and then go out with the others. I must show nothing. I won't give anyone the opportunity to sniff out my relationship with Mr. Yaqoub!

17

I woke up from my siesta terrified, as if I had forgotten an important appointment that was pending. I usually turn off my phone when I take a nap. I took a sip of water from the glass near my head and opened the phone. The screen lit up and two messages from al-Khayyam appeared. I opened the first: "Mr. Yaqoub, thank you, thank you, thank you." I hesitated a bit before I opened the second: "I'm sorry if I bothered you."

I sat for a while on the edge of my bed, then I left my room and met Shaikha, who was walking ahead of a woman carrying a suitcase and saying, "Come along, this way."

She took the woman to Ahmad's room, then hurried back to me. "Sahar and I are invited to a wedding tonight, and this is a salon employee who will do our hair and makeup." Something bothered me, and I looked at her in silence. "The chauffeur will take us to the hotel at eight." She hurried off to catch up with the woman from the salon, while I remained standing where I was.

All during my slumber I had been hovering around the image of Ahmad, which kept appearing to me from afar, and the moment I woke up, the image of Farnaz appeared. The question came—what is the relationship between Ahmad and Farnaz?

Shaikha and Sahar will leave the house at eight; I'll try to call her. I sat on the living-room sofa and summoned a servant, asking for coffee. Then I wrote a message to Farnaz: "I'll call you after eight, if you can talk then."

The reply came without delay: "I'll wait for you."

My heart fluttered like a child's! I reached out to turn on the television, searching for a station broadcasting songs. But as soon as the image of a singer appeared, with her swaying dancing, I reduced the volume to nothing. Shaikha had taken the woman from the salon to Ahmad's room! That bothered me, and I wanted to get up and throw the woman out of the house. I should have been firm when Ahmad left, so his room would remain clean and furnished until he came back. I'll go sit in the garden until my coffee comes.

As I stepped out of the house, I became anxious. It occurred to me to go to the mosque, to see if Abdel Shafi and Umar were still enlisting green Kuwaiti youths to be firewood for terror, killing, and blood.

I sat in my place in the garden, well out of sight. After a few moments I saw the servant coming with the cup of coffee.

Something has touched my spirit recently; I've begun to feel that I'm no longer myself. Images of Ahmad assail me, when I'm awake and in my dreams. Something hidden in his call today frightened me, as well as the fact that it coincided with the beginning of work on the Baghdad contract.

I hear the call to the evening prayer surrounding me on all sides; there's a group of mosques near our house. If Ahmad comes back, will he return to live in his room? He has married two women; I'll have to buy a house for him, his wives, and his children. I'll buy him a house or a piece of land in any area he chooses, then leave him to set up his house and family. Just as with Du'aij, I'll do the same for him.

I'll walk in the garden . . . I love the *barhi* date palm. When we moved in, I asked the gardener to bring me a *barhi* date palm from Basra, as the taste of its fruit is like honey. Shaikha adores gardening; she chooses plants and trees, cares for them, and rejoices childishly when they bloom. I love the scent of night-blooming jasmine, so I asked her to include it among the other plants. I don't know why the scent exhilarates me, along with common jasmine. Maybe that's what attracted me to Farnaz.

Many days I come back from work to find some white jasmine in a small crystal vase in my room. Shaikha will soon ask, "Do you like the flowers?"

"Very much. The scent is captivating."

She smiles for a few seconds and then asks, "Why don't you say anything? Why don't you express your pleasure in anything?"

I don't know what to tell her. Once I answered sadly, "Because I don't know how." I added, "Because I'm not used to it." I did not say frankly that joy is a human skill, and that only those who practice it are good at it, and I. . . . At that moment I wanted to take the flowers out of my room.

I see Shaikha and Sahar leaving the house, though it's only seven-fifteen. My phone rings with a call from Shaikha: "Sahar and I are going to pick up Abrar from her house before we go to the wedding."

"Enjoy yourselves."

She answered quickly, "Goodbye."

The car drove off. I'll write a message to Farnaz: "Can I call?" The message flew off and the phone rang immediately with a call from al-Khayyam. "Hello."

"Hello, Mr. Yaqoub." She was whispering, and my heart felt sudden happiness. "I'm sorry I sent you two messages."

"Not at all, I was sleeping."

"Sound sleep, I hope!" She said the usual phrase spontaneously, then fell silent, as if she felt she had infringed on my privacy. She changed the subject, asking, "Sir, I'm on leave tomorrow and should not go to the office?"

"That's right. You're on leave for three days." She said nothing, so I told her, "I just rented a suite at the Sheraton so we can meet." There was a moment of silence between us. "It's close to the company offices, and you can park your car in the lot for the Watiya Mall behind the hotel and enter through the rear door."

"Sir, please don't go on. I've begun to tremble!" She was whispering in a weak voice.

I was irritated with myself and at a loss over how to respond. I got out "Goodbye!" and hung up.

What I was doing surprised me. The phone rang and the name al-Khayyam appeared. I hesitated before answering.

"Please, sir, don't be angry." I had the impression that she was being hard on me with her kindness.

"Farnaz, please believe that I don't want anything from you."

"Sir . . . " she began, then clung to her silence.

We talked for a long time. She described herself as a simple person from a small family, who had never been alone with a strange man. I was determined to reassure her that I did not mean to bother her. "Farnaz, I myself don't know what I want from you," I confided.

"Sir, that frightens me more." Silence stretched between us again. Then she said "Alright, we can meet tomorrow."

My heart fluttered, almost leaving my breast. I gave her all the details she needed to get to the hotel and the suite. I suggested we met at ten, but she objected, saying, "I'll leave home at the normal time, as if I'm going to work." So we agreed to meet at eight-thirty.

The call ended with our agreement; I was like a happy child... and confused in my thinking. What was happening to me? Did it make any sense for me to have an adventure loving a young girl? I realized that I had come some distance—I had written messages, made phone calls, rented a suite to meet her, and made a date! I yearned to see her right then.

Some time ago Sami gave me a small box, and laughed as he told me, "They're sure, and they have no complications. One pill and you'll be a young man again!" I put a small smile on my face, and he urged me, "Try them!"

Tomorrow I'll meet Farnaz. We'll be alone in a respectable place that's clean and secure. What can happen between us? Is it possible that I could become young again, by means of her? She's delicate. When she was working on the computer that day in my office, I noticed the dark vein in her arm, the beauty of her hands, and her soft fingers. But nothing in the world can take a man back in time, even by a day! Being a young man again, that's meaningless talk—there's no power on earth that can take any person backward, man or woman, not even by an hour. The mechanism of time does not work as we wish; it moves in one direction only, and every step we take cuts us off from the path behind us. There's no going back on the path of life, and only those born under a lucky star are happy on the way.

When did you become an old man, Yaqoub? The question frightened me. How has the water of your days soaked into the sandy path of making deals and earning profits? Has fate sent you Farnaz to make your heart beat again in your breast? There are men who marry at seventy, but I'm not one of them. Ever since I was an adolescent, I've calculated every step I've taken. Anyway, it's a miserable justification for marriage between an old man and a young woman in the flower of her youth to say that he will enjoy her warmth and the nearness of her body, and she will enjoy the pleasures of his money!

A little while ago, Farnaz agreed to meet me. She did seem reluctant when I broached the idea, but then she agreed. Maybe she's dreaming of getting close to me and harming me? They say women's ruses are great! I'm afraid this Iranian will entangle me! But she knows who I am, she knows she can't stand in my way.

Wait a moment. I stopped myself and told the Yaqoub I know: You are the one who became attached to her, you are the one who ran after her, who yearned and dreamed of going to her, of meeting her! And you are the one who put her back in her job and increased her salary, the one who planned everything in this relationship. You, Yaqoub. But a strange voice inside shook me, saying, "Get up, be generous, find a gift for your beloved, for the first meeting between you."

Is Farnaz my beloved? The word shook me, and the scent of gardenias spread around me. I got up and looked at the peace of the garden. Then, as if hypnotized, I decided to take my car and go quickly to the Salihiya Mall.

18

"To Abrar's house," I directed Dadu. Sahar and Abrar and I will go together to the wedding in the Hotel Al-Raya.

Yaqoub's annoyance was clear as he watched the girl from the salon follow me on our way to Ahmad's room. I know him; I know that my use of Ahmad's room for makeup pained him. He would like to keep it clean, neat, and ready for Ahmad when he returns.

The last time I saw my brother Uthaiman, he remarked casually, "I don't think that Ahmad's going to come back."

What he said scared me, and I raised my voice to him. "Why not? Where did you get this information?"

I felt his expression change, as if he had let something slip. His answer seemed like a dodge: "It's not information, just what I expect. All our boys, when God blesses them with the resolve to engage in jihad, they go to fight in Syria or Iraq or Afghanistan, and not a one of them has come back."

"Have they all died?"

"No, no, some of them have gotten married and settled down, some have traveled from the battlefields to other countries, and some have been blessed by God with martyrdom."

"You know something about Ahmad, and you don't want to say it."

I confronted him, and he fell silent briefly before confirming my suspicion: "I have some good friends in Syria, and they call me whenever they hear anything about him."

"Have you told Yaqoub about that?"

My question surprised him and annoyed him. He rushed to say, "Please don't tell him anything! He can barely talk to anyone; all he does is scowl angrily or give orders!" He was obviously exasperated with my husband. "He remains silent, looking at me as if I'm a thief, and if I bring up anything like this with him, I'll never get away from his questions and criticism!"

It occurred to me to wonder how my brother could push my son toward jihad, when he had sent his own two sons to America for their higher education after they had completed high school. His son Hamad was a close friend of Ahmad's. "Why didn't Hamad go with Ahmad to join the jihad?"

My question seemed to surprise him. "God did not decree that he would find the resolve to become a jihadi. God, may he be praised and exalted, chooses those he wills for his path." I stared at him, and he got up to leave. "Peace be upon you."

He veiled his wife and daughters, and he had leaned on me more than once. "You're no longer young, Umm Du'aij. It's not right for you to go out without a hijab." He only stopped when I told him,

"Don't talk to me about the hijab. If you insist, then talk to Yaqoub. He's the man responsible for me."

"My makeup is bad tonight." Sahar's voice pulled me back. Ever since we got in the car, she's been playing with her phone and taking pictures of herself.

"My dear, your makeup is very pretty, and it's perfect for your hairstyle and your dress."

"When we get to Abrar's, you'll see that she won't like it."

"The makeup, the hairstyle, and the dress—it's all beautiful, and Abrar will tell you so."

"I won't sit with you at the party. My friend Muneera is coming, and I'll sit with her."

"As you like."

Sahar has spent six years at the university, and last year, just as she was about to graduate, she withdrew. When her father asked her about it, she said, "I'm in no hurry to graduate. I'd like to take a year off to relax before I begin to work."

He responded with silence, as he usually does, then he asked her sharply, "Relax? You'll dic from so much relaxation!" He became agitated and his voice rose. "It's not right for a person to waste his life sleeping, playing, and shopping, to waste it in trifles! You should have informed me before making an important decision. It doesn't only affect you."

She recoiled into herself and swallowed her words. He looked at me reproachfully. "Shouldn't you have told me about what's going on in my house?"

"She didn't ask for my opinion, and I was as surprised as you by her decision."

Sometimes I feel as if he treats me like an employee of one of his companies, as if our family were a business. He finances it and I alone am responsible for running it, and for presenting him with detailed reports about every aspect of it. I remember an incident when I was going to accompany a delegation from the ministry on an official trip, and I asked him to try to stay with the children. At the time, Abrar and Du'aij were in middle school and Sahar and Ahmad were in elementary grades. He responded calmly, "It's hard."

"What's hard?"

"It's all hard—staying in the house with the children is hard, talking to them is hard, going over their lessons and solving their homework problems is hard, playing with them is hard, entertaining them is hard." He looked up at me seriously. "Do you know why it's hard?"

"No."

"It's hard because I'm not used to it, it's hard because it doesn't sprout overnight, it's hard because it's a lifelong skill which needs to be learned and practiced, and I have not learned it and not practiced it. Last of all it's hard because it takes time, and I don't have time." He stood up in annoyance. Before he left, he added, "Raising children is a sacrifice, and you have devoted yourself to it, caring for nothing but your children." His last sentence made me happy, but he was washing his hands of raising his children, and that frightened me.

"I love *samiri* and *khimari* singing. If they have it tonight, I'm going to dance."

I smiled at Sahar's remark. "You know me, I have no objection. All the girls will dance."

I no longer care much about parties and celebrations; they lost their luster in my eyes years ago. Now I go to parties for Sahar's sake, since any mother might be charmed by her and see her as a wife for her son. I hope Sahar gets married.

Some time ago a young man presented himself, an engineer from a well-known Kuwaiti family, but when I broached the subject with her, she objected strongly. "I don't want to get married now!" I just stared at her. "First I'll graduate from the university and begin working, and after that I'll think about getting married."

I didn't like her response. I advised her, "Give yourself the chance to see the young man and sit with him before you refuse him."

"There's no need for that. I refuse marriage on principle, including marriage by way of a matchmaker."

"It's not a matter of a matchmaker. His mother saw you with your friend Muneera and asked about you, then she called me."

Sometimes I criticize her. "How will you ever manage with a husband, children, and a house? You don't even get a glass of water for yourself, let alone cleaning, straightening, or cooking. Even your wardrobe is organized by a servant!"

She will listen to me, playing with her phone the whole time, and when I fall silent she looks up, smiles, and says, "Mama, don't worry. I'll have a nanny for each child, a cook, and someone to clean and iron the clothes."

Ever since we got in the car, Sahar has been busy with her phone. Dadu drives silently, I've been at ease with him since he first arrived from the Philippines, and I thank the lord that he brought me a calm, peaceable man. He has spent more than ten years with us; he may be over fifty. Ahmad never rode with him, saying, "He's a Christian!" He insisted on taking Bayoumi for his errands.

I don't know how I've failed Ahmad. He's the youngest of my children, and when he was coming along, I was in the thick of my work at the ministry. I would be tired when I got home, and more concerned about Abrar and Sahar. Du'aij had come to depend on himself from the time he started high school; he's like his father, planning everything, not wasting a moment of his time. I never had any problems in raising him or helping him with his lessons; even when he got married, he met his wife on his own and brought her to meet me.

Ahmad liked to be alone ever since he was a child, and he was often silent. I was frequently puzzled about what clothes to choose for him, as I didn't know his taste, and he never said a word, positive or negative. I realized early on how attached Yaqoub was to him. Whenever he came back from a trip, the gifts for Ahmad were more numerous, more beautiful, and more expensive. I remember once when he came back from one of his trips and he had bought Ahmad his own camera. Sahar asked him, "Where's my camera?"

He smiled and said, "I brought you a watch. Next time I'll bring you a camera."

Sahar was eleven at the time, and she burst into tears. Ahmad, who was a child of no more than ten, immediately stood up and held out his camera to Sahar. She refused to take it, looking at her father, so Ahmad set it down beside her and went off to his room.

I don't know what makes one child different from his siblings. My brother Uthaiman loved Ahmad, and he's the one who took him to the mosque for the first time. Unusually, Ahmad came to me and pled with me: "Mama, don't tell Father that Uncle Uthaiman is taking me to the mosque." I was surprised by his words and by his pleading tone. "Father doesn't like Uncle Uthaiman, and he might get angry and beat him or fire him from the company."

At the time I promised him not to reveal his secret and to protect my brother, but I was left wondering what Uthaiman wanted and what he was planning for my boy. Did it make sense that my brother would harm my son? Now, after Ahmad has turned into a jihadi, and Uthaiman's son has returned from America after completing his education there, my conscience often hurts for having kept a secret from my husband. It wasn't right to hide it. My heart tells me that my brother is the one who guided my son to the path of extremism, violence, and killing. It's certain that if Yaqoub had known about it, he would have intervened and stopped it.

Some time ago Yaqoub was angry with Uthaiman, and he told me, "I can't stand the sight of him! But I keep him in the company because of his relations with the Islamist groups. He brings us tenders through them and gets major discounts from them, without guarantees or collateral."

At this point, I can't tell Yaqoub what my brother did to my son—God only knows what he would do to me and to Uthaiman. Especially since he's been going through some psychological phase lately. He goes to bed angry and wakes up angrier still.

During the last few days, I've asked him more than once what was bothering him. "Nothing," he says, and mentions the Baghdad tender. Or he says, "Ahmad." But the last time, I told him, "There's something else on your mind, not the Baghdad tender and not Ahmad—something I don't know about, something you don't want to tell me about or share with me."

He looked up at me as if just discovering my presence next to him, and asked, "Do I know everything you think?"

I smiled. "No."

"And do you tell me everything you're going to do?"

"No."

"Shaikha, everyone has anxieties and secrets they don't reveal to anyone else, and I'm like that."

This frightened me. "You're hiding things from me, after all these years?"

"Naturally. There's no husband who doesn't hide things from his wife, and no wife who reveals everything to her husband." I looked at him as if I were weighing the truth of what he said, and he added, "It's a great mercy that we don't know everything about each other."

I don't know how the question popped out of my mouth, but I responded, "Is there some woman who's on your mind?"

My question seemed to electrify his facial expression. But I know my husband; he swallowed his surprise and answered, "You." Something in his tone kept me from believing him. He added, "We've spent our lives together, Shaikha."

"That's why I'm asking."

"What do you mean?"

"I mean, some men go back to being adolescents when they're in their sixties."

He nodded, smiling. "Many do." Then he got up suddenly. "Since you're reproaching me with my sixties, I'll look for a good gym where I can regain some of my fitness." Then he withdrew, leaving me to my confusion and my thoughts.

"Abrar, we'll be at your door in one minute."

Sahar's voice, talking to her sister, brought me back. I wish I could go back home. I feel pressure on my chest, and I want to cry.

19

This has never happened to me before, to be in this situation or to go through moments like these!

I've been here half an hour, alone. I sit for a while, then I stand up and walk around the room, then I go back to sitting. A little while ago I stood in front of the mirror, with my careworn face, the lost look in my eyes, my tightly pressed lips—my whole person, with my headcloth and cords, my dishdasha, and my shiny shoes. I stood contemplating myself for a time, as if I was making sure that I was indeed Yaqoub, the man I have been, the man I know.

Ah, Yaqoub! Ahmad is the one who has broken your back. Ahmad, the one you thought would be the heir to your business empire, has left Kuwait and become a jihadi fighting in Syria, or maybe Iraq. When Du'aij graduated from the university, he told me frankly, "I want to start my own company."

"Don't you want to help me, or work for me for a while until you found your own?"

"No," he spat out, like a shot to my face.

"I wish you the best of luck!" I then resolved that I would not talk to him about anything related to his work unless he came to ask me about it, and I made a vow that Ahmad alone would be at my side, and that I would arrange for everything to come under his direction.

Oh, my boy! Here I am remembering Ahmad, while I'm burning with desire to see a girl I'm meeting for the first time. A girl who has led me down an unknown street.

I left the house before my usual time. Bayoumi met me, and I told him that I would drive myself to a private meeting. I left him standing, surprise written on his face, as I obeyed my fluttering heart and flew off to come here.

Yesterday, as soon as I hung up, I took the car and went to the Salihiya Mall. I bought a Chanel purse for Farnaz and hid it in the trunk, keeping the car keys with me. All the way back I upbraided myself: "You aren't Yaqoub! Something like magic has affected you and is still dragging you after it, pushing you to do things no one would believe you've done. You weren't as impetuous as this when you were an adolescent! You never took your car to a shop to buy a purse for Shaikha or any of your sisters or your daughters, and here you are, going to Salihiya, going into a shop without a thought for anyone you might meet, buying a woman's purse, picking it up and carrying it out of the mall. What's changed you in the course of a few days and made you so thoughtless, Yaqoub? And what's motivating you to still more folly than you've already committed?"

When I came into the hotel, carrying the bag with the purse in it, I was trying to hide from myself. It was early, and the halls were nearly empty. I went to the desk to get the key to the suite, being careful that none of the hotel directors who knew me would see me. I took the key like a thief and hurried to the elevator, fleeing to the suite.

I'd like to have a coffee. I'll wait for Farnaz, so we can drink it together. I smile at myself in the mirror: "You're talking about her as if you knew her! You can't remember being so eager for a date with Shaikha, your wife, or looking forward to meeting her with such yearning!" It occurs to me to wonder what stirs up a fresh longing in a person's heart and makes it seethe, and what extinguishes another. Where does my longing to meet her come from, and what is she hiding behind her? How long will I follow the trail that leads to her?

I stood up. How have I become attached to her when I don't know a thing about her? Why her, and not someone else? What do I want from her? A tangle of questions is piled on my head, and I've gotten lost in corridors of anxiety, unable to find an exit. I sat down again.

In many situations in the past I've let my mind roam, trying to imagine what will happen, in order to prepare myself for it. But I can't do that with Farnaz.

It's almost eight-thirty when my phone rings.

"Good morning, Mr. Yaqoub." Her voice is weak; maybe she'll make her apologies. "I've arrived at the parking lot, but I don't know where to go."

"Go down to the ground floor and turn left, then leave the mall. On your right you'll find the rear entrance to the hotel. I'll stay with you on the phone."

"I'm scared!"

"There's no reason to be scared. The hotel is quiet." There was a moment of silence; I could hear her breathing.

"Mr. Yaqoub, I've left the mall and I'm about to go through the door to the hotel."

"Good. In a few steps you'll find the elevator on your left."

"One moment, one moment." I'm following the sound of her breath on the phone, and the sound of her steps. "I'm at the elevator."

"Go in. I'll leave the door to the room ajar for you."

I rush to the door and stick out my head, to be sure that the hall is empty. What am I doing? I'm not Yaqoub! I feel my heart beating rapidly. I leave the door very slightly ajar and hurry back to my place. I'll try to be calm until she comes. Something inside tells me, "You're not yourself."

I hear steps, and the sound of the door closing quietly. At last, Farnaz is standing before me, she... she's the girl I glimpsed by the elevator, but embarrassment or fear clings to her face.

"Good morning," I begin.

"Good morning," she answers, her voice shaking.

"I'll sit here. Please, sit anywhere you like."

She's wearing a light blue dress figured with shining white flowers, a narrow belt around her waist, and a light golden shawl over her head. The perfume that lives in my imagination came in with her, and the scent of gardenia fills the room. A subtle question leaped into mind—how can a girl be a flowering branch? It also occurred to me to wonder how she saw me, and what she would say about me.

I said, "I'm sorry to have bothered you." She sank into the farthest part of the sofa facing me and remained silent. "Farnaz." She looked up at me. "What's frightening you?"

"No, I'm not frightened."

I felt as if I had ensnared myself by inviting her, as I had nothing to say. A miserable silence came to sit with us. She seemed to be avoiding looking at me, so I asked her, "Did you receive your new contract?"

"Yes, thank you very much, by God...."

"There's no need for thanks." For the first time, I noticed that my mouth was dry. "I haven't had coffee yet, I was waiting for you. Would you like to join me?"

She lifted her head and our eyes met; a touch of hidden happiness refreshed my spirit. She said, "I take my coffee with just a touch of sugar," and a sweet joy flowed into my heart because we would have coffee together. I pressed buttons on my phone and ordered the coffee.

I encroached on her silence. "Tell me a little about yourself."

In a shaky voice, she said, "Mr. Yaqoub, I don't know how I've gotten here!" It was clear that she was confused, and I wanted to tell her honestly that I was as confused as she was. "It's the first time I've made an appointment with a man and met him in a place I don't know. I don't know how my feet brought me here, or how I've done what I've done!" She avoided looking at me as she spoke. "I felt as if everything was watching me, pursuing me." Her voice still shook, and she clung to the end of the sofa. "Mr. Yaqoub, I'm a simple person. What would you like to know about me?"

"Talk about anything you like."

As I looked at her, I was certain now that something in her eyes, something in her face and the tone of her voice had captivated my heart. Clearly, she had groomed herself with great care; I was pleased by her understated lipstick, by the small beauty mark at the left side of her upper lip. I felt as if a reckless breath stirred in my breast, while her captivating perfume danced in the air of the room.

She sat up a little, displacing the shawl over her head, which she hurried to put back. She began speaking in a soft voice. "I was born in Kuwait, and I attended Kuwaiti schools from first grade through the fourth year of high school. When I graduated, I finished my studies in an institute, where I earned a diploma in computer sciences."

"Do you live with your family?"

"Yes."

"What does your father do?" She lifted her eyes to me, touching me with a sharp glance, as if to say, what do you want to know? "Excuse the question, I was just curious."

"My father drives a one-eight pickup."

It's strange—this is the first time I've felt my mouth so dry. Never before have I arranged to meet a girl who's frightened, crumpled over herself and her perfume. She's so delicate that I feel as if I have to be careful not to touch her so she won't break. But she alone can take my breath away.

"Mr. Yaqoub, I have one brother who's in Iran. He was also born in Kuwait; he finished his studies here, but he couldn't enroll in the university, so he went to Tehran."

"Is he studying there?"

"No, he enrolled in the military college and graduated from there, and now he's an officer."

The doorbell rang and she jumped to her feet, a sudden fear on her face, but I motioned to her to move out of sight of the door opening. I opened the door partway and took the tray from the waiter, without allowing him to enter the room, then I closed the door and went back to my place. As I was carrying the coffee to her, I noticed that the shawl had slipped off her head. I smiled and said, "That's better."

She made no response, once again returning the shawl to its place. She rose to take the coffee and the glass of water; I felt as if she was losing some of her fear. "Do you have coffee every morning?" I asked, reaching for the water to wet my dry mouth.

"I'm addicted to coffee. I can't start my day until I have had some."

I smiled. "That means your day has yet to begin." A timid smile came to her eyes and face and touched my heart.

I savored the coffee. A young girl covered in flowers sits before me, breathing fearfully, in her long blue dress, her intoxicating perfume, her dark golden hair, with her small beauty mark, her slender fingers, and her polished nails. Something inside me is calmed simply by sitting with her. What has she done to touch my spirit and settle my eagerness? It occurred to me to wonder what one spirit offers to another. A poor, weak girl—how long will I remain sitting and looking at her? What can happen between us? I wished the moment would freeze and I would stay near her. I had a sudden anxious thought: what would Shaikha say, or any of your children or even your friends, if they knew about what you're doing?

"Mr. Yaqoub, why did you choose me out of all the women who work at the company?"

I responded, as if I were talking to myself, "I don't know. Anyway I don't know all of the women in the company, and I haven't seen them."

A cold silence reigned after I spoke. I saw the gift bag on the table, so I rose to pick it up and placed it before her. "This is a small gift for you."

Her eyes moved over the bag and she lifted her face to me. I felt as if there was sweetness lurking behind her glance. That reckless breath stirred again in my chest, as she said, "Thank you, sir, but I can't take it."

"Why not?"

She smiled as she turned her face away. "Why would I take it?"

"It's a small gift of thanks for you, and an apology from the company for the mistake it made that led to troubling you."

"I'm sorry, sir, excuse me."

"There's no reason to be sorry; it's a small gift."

A wisp of a smile showed on her face as she whispered, without looking at me, "It might cost more than my salary for four or five months—what would I say to my family?"

I was surprised to hear this. I had paid for the purse with one of my bank cards, and I had been in a hurry to leave the shop. Maybe it was a thousand five hundred dinars, or a thousand seven hundred. A moment of silence settled over us.

Suddenly my phone rang. It was Shaikha.

"Where are you? You left early, without Bayoumi, and you're not in your office. What's going on?"

"I have a meeting. I'll call you when it's over." I hung up without waiting for her response.

What would Farnaz think of me, now that she's heard this call from my wife? I felt my chest tightening in constraint. My mind spoke to me: "Here you are alone in a room with a girl you've longed for, and you're unnerved and don't know what to say to her. You longed to see her and your longing has grown while she's sitting next to you!"

"Farnaz, do you know any members of my family?"

She hastened to say no, in a weak voice. Then she emended her response. "I know that you have a family relationship to Mr. Ismail, and that Mr. Uthaiman is your wife's brother."

"What about my children?"

"No, I don't know anything about them." Sounding fearful, she added, "Have you heard anything about me, sir? Or that I said anything about your children?"

"No."

Peacefulness returned to sit with us. She picked up her glass of water and took a sip. "Excuse me, sir, may I have permission to leave?"

Her request came as an awful surprise. We had only been together for mere minutes, and I had not yet had my fill of seeing her. I didn't know what to say at first, then I came out with, "You just got here!"

Silence and the purse remained between us. I wanted nothing more than to get up and hug her to my chest so that I would feel her next to my heart, that I would drink in her perfume. I wished to kiss her, taste her lips. I wished... I wanted her to stay with me.

"You haven't finished your coffee."

"I have finished, thank you."

She fell silent and I said to myself, "What a loser! You can't think of anything to talk about."

As much as I want her to stay, I have no idea how to keep her. I surely don't want to annoy her. Where does my need for her spring from? As I gaze at her in her shyness, her withdrawal into herself, her delicacy, her fear... everything about this bundle of flowers and perfume enchants me. She's so delicate that I dread touching her.

She stood up suddenly. "Please, sir, allow me to leave."

"As you wish."

She replaced the shawl on her head.

"Take the purse." She looked at me. "It's yours. If anyone asks you about it, tell them it's an imitation."

"Please, sir, don't put pressure on me."

"I don't want to annoy you ever. But take the purse so that something from me will remain with you." I was amazed at myself as I said that.

A small smile brought color to her face. She bent to take the purse and looked at me. "Thank you very much, sir. You can be sure that I won't tell anyone about our meeting."

She remained standing for a few seconds, as if she expected me to say something more. I thought about going to her and embracing her, as everything within me cried out to her. That breath in my chest stirred again, and then the image of Ahmad attacked me came from I don't know where.

She made a small motion with her hand, whispering, "Goodbye."

"Perhaps we'll meet tomorrow," I said. Her face took on an expression I did not understand.

"Fine."

"One moment." I walked to the table and picked up the key card. "Take this," I said. "I took two cards so you can have one. You might get here before I do, but you won't have to wait outside."

"I won't arrive before you do."

"Don't be so sure," I said, holding out the card. She came closer to take it from me, and I was touched by her breath and her perfume of gardenias. She turned to leave.

Once the door closed, my urgent need for her descended on me. I wanted to run after her and call out to her. The question rose in me with the force of a gale: "What's happening to you, Yaqoub?"

20

God protect us, Ahmad has been captured! Yaqoub would go crazy if he knew.

Have mercy on us, O lord, O merciful! O God who saved Jonah from the belly of the whale, save Ahmad!

Moments ago Abu Bilal called me and gave me the news. A tremor ran through my whole body and paralyzed my tongue. I couldn't answer him. On the other end of the line he kept repeating, "Sheikh Ahmad is alive, alive. . . ." Then his voice broke and he wept as he told me, "My son, my oldest son, Mazin, was martyred."

I'm alone in my office. I ended the call with, "Later, I'll talk to you later." I needed to catch my breath, to take in the news. I began pacing in my office, repeating, "O God, O protector, give us your protection. Oh God, Allahumma, we don't ask that you turn away what's decreed, but we ask for your mercy in it. . . ." I began pacing in circles in my office, not knowing what I was doing, pursued by Yaqoub's eyes.

Oh my God! I never thought, not even once, about the possibility that Ahmad would be captured or martyred. Ahmad has become a commander of a group, a field commander, and he and his group plunge into almost ceaseless combat for the sake of God. . . . One thing dominates my thinking and frightens me:

how will I give the news to Yaqoub? What will I tell him? I tell myself that I won't say a word. I'll keep silent as if I don't know a thing, until God brings to pass what has been decreed. He'll surely learn about it from the news channels, or the newspapers, or somewhere else.

O God, there is no god but you, have mercy on us, O most merciful of all! Turn away from us what our enemies and yours have brought down on us, O lord of the worlds, you who have power over all things. Help us O God, help us, help us O God!

I don't know how long it was until I received a second call from Abu Bilal. He told me he had nearly gone crazy since he heard of his son's martyrdom, and that he was calling out of duty, for the sake of Shaikh Ahmad, and because of his own connection to the jihadis. His voice hardened as he said, "The group holding Sheikh Ahmad belongs to Daesh, or maybe to al-Qaeda, and they've taken him to some unknown place." He repeated to me, "His fellow jihadis assure me that he's alive and was not killed in the battle."

Without thinking, I asked him, "What will they do with him?"

"They'll torture him to extract the information they need. They might bargain with us to free him."

"Bargain with us?"

"Yes. They might exchange him for prisoners we hold or ask for a ransom. Their financial situation has been bad lately."

The idea that they might ask me for financial assistance sprang into my mind, so I shrank back, concealing the thought. Silence stretched between us, then he ended the call, saying sadly, "By God, if it weren't for my love for Sheikh Ahmad and the demands of duty, I wouldn't have called. He burst out sobbing once more, like a child. Through his weeping I heard him say,

"My beloved Mazin is gone—he's gone!"

Before he hung up, I told him I needed Ibrahim's new number, and he raised his voice.

"Shaikh Ibrahim was martyred too!"

"Oh my God!" I shouted, completely forgetting that I was in the office and could be overheard. The tremor seized me again. Ibrahim was my one connection to Ahmad. For more than a year Ahmad had not carried a phone, as a precaution against any surveillance, so whenever I needed him I called Ibrahim and he connected us. May God have mercy on you, Ibrahim, and resurrect you among the martyrs and the righteous!

Where have they taken Ahmad? May God help him when they torture him in their barbaric ways!

I sit at my desk, unsure of what to do. A sudden terror scatters my thoughts and paralyzes me, a strange fear gripping my heart. I won't tell Yaqoub, and I certainly won't tell Shaikha, but I can't keep silent. Maybe I should inform the Kuwaiti Foreign Ministry, so they could intervene to bring Ahmad back. But how can I give them the news? I won't act alone; I must tell Ismail, and he will tell the community. Anyway the Foreign Ministry would ask questions and investigate our relationship with Ahmad and with his group; that would be awkward—very awkward.

I ask forgiveness from God Almighty. There is no power or strength save in God; *I complain of my anguish and sorrow only to Allah.* Some of our friends in the community have good relations with leaders in Daesh or even al-Qaeda. Maybe they should be informed so they can try to free Ahmad.

I was startled by the ringing of my telephone. The name of Abu Ubaidallah, the official responsible for the treasury appeared on the screen. "Shaikh Uthaiman, the Daesh fighters who have taken Shaikh Ahmad are demanding a ransom."

I answered quickly, "You are responsible for ransoming your commander. Sheikh Ahmad is your dutiful son, and one of your commanders!"

He said nothing and I remained silent, then he clarified. "After our dispute with Daesh blew up and they stopped funding us, there's only a paltry sum left in the treasury. It barely covers the salaries of our brother jihadis and our daily expenses."

"How much did they ask for?"

"They haven't specified yet." He surprised me by saying, "I don't know how to tell you this, but they want their ransom from Mr. Yaqoub, Sheikh Ahmad's father, and they asked for his phone number."

"Impossible!" I was shouting, disturbed and frenzied. "Yaqoub wouldn't give them a single penny, even if they killed Sheikh Ahmad and all the jihadis."

He said nothing for a few seconds, then justified himself. "I swear to God, that's what they asked for."

I was at a loss. "I can't give Yaqoub's number to anyone!" I shouted. "Anyway, Sheikh Ahmad is their prisoner. Why don't they get the number from him?"

He said nothing, as if taken by surprise by my question. Then he said calmly, "Sheikh Ahmad hasn't used a telephone for a long time, and he surely hasn't memorized the number."

"This is a catastrophe."

"Please, Sheikh Uthaiman, work out something. They might kill Sheikh Ahmad if we make problems for them."

The call ended there. I came out from behind my desk and began pacing in my office, repeating the prophet's words: "There is no power or strength save in God Most High, the Almighty! Allahumma, I hope for your mercy. Do not entrust me to myself for the blink of an eye, O Living and Everlasting. Allahumma, we take refuge in you from the strain of trial, from misery coming, from ill fate overtaking us, from our enemies' rejoicing. Allahumma, we take refuge in you from your blessings diminishing, from our health changing, from your sudden vengeance arriving, from all your wrath descending, O God!"

What will I say to Shaikha if anything happens to her son? She knows that I'm the one who led him on this path. I've begun to read criticism in the look in her eyes. I've loved Ahmad since he was a child, his silence, his reflectiveness, his manliness. I placed my bets on him, took him by the hand, stood with him, and he did not disappoint me, but became a jihadi devoted to the word of God. By God, everyone in Kuwait should be proud of him if they knew of his deeds. He's a pious child of the religion of God and of the Sunna of his prophet, one of the swords of God.

May God help you, Ahmad! *There is no God but thou: glory to thee: I was indeed wrong.*

I must tell Yaqoub, for if anything bad happened to Ahmad—may God not allow it!—he won't forgive me, and I won't forgive myself. Let him explode however he likes, let him yell out everything he thinks, even if he throws me out of the company. What matters is that he know about it, that he solve the problem in his own way.

He's a strong man, with connections all over the world, and now is the time to be serious. I can't bear the responsibility for what will happen. I'll leave it to Ismail to inform the community; we'll certainly have to call a meeting to discuss the subject. This is a real slap in the face for me.

Recently I've had the feeling that Yaqoub can no longer bear the sight of me. When he receives me his very breathing speaks of his annoyance, his exasperation, and his dislike of me. Yaqoub would not hesitate to harm me in any way that he could if he knew about what I've done with his son, and about my membership in the community. God protect me! "Allahumma, we take refuge in you from the strain of trial, from misery coming, from ill fate overtaking us, from our enemies' rejoicing."

I don't know if Yaqoub is in his office or if he's gone out. I must face him. I'll go to his office and ask to go in, and I will give him the news, however much I hate it. I'll say, "I've heard that Ahmad has been taken captive." I have no idea how he will react or how he'll face the situation.

I remember that he asked me one day, "Do you know a professor who teaches Ahmad, whose name is Umar?"

I hurried to say no, to defend myself. I denied having any relationship or interaction with Ahmad's school.

"Unfortunately this teacher is a destructive man, filling the boys' heads with things that will make their families upset with them and drive a wedge between them."

I was barely breathing as I listened to him. That day when I called Umar, he told me that Yaqoub had visited them at the school and had argued with him and threatened him.

What will Yaqoub do to me? I'm afraid something bad will happen to Ahmad. I have to forget myself and go to Yaqoub and tell him—whatever happens. I place my trust in God. *And We have put a bar in front of them and a bar behind them, and further, We have covered them up; so that they cannot see.*

21

Meeting Farnaz has inflamed my longing for her even more.

I was upset when I left the hotel. I got into the car not knowing where to go; I didn't want to go home, nor did I have any wish to go to the office. My friend Dr. Fadil came to mind, but I quickly dismissed the thought. What would I say to him?

The moment I moved out of the Watiya Mall parking lot, I realized that it's located close to the site of our old house, my grandfather's house, where I was born and grew up. In those days the walls of the houses were made of kindly clay and they clung together, with narrow, dirt-topped lanes between them, and children's games were restricted to the open squares between the houses or swimming in the sea. I had brought Farnaz to my own birthplace.

I drove to Arabian Gulf Street, wearing dark sunglasses to conceal my face. I don't know why; I had never in my life simply gone for a drive, not in Kuwait or elsewhere. I have no extra time, and I never allowed myself to drive, enjoying soft music while I looked around me—that was an extravagance I've never experienced, a waste of time I can't accept.

All my life I've kept track of time to the minute. Nothing irritates me or gets on my nerves as much as waiting for something to happen. I'm always running with the fiend of time panting behind me, carrying a club to strike my neck whenever I stop or lose a passing moment.

For years I've been like the beast of burden who knows its track. I wake in the morning to pray, then for nearly an hour I meditate, a practice I hold to wherever I am. After that I look through the headlines in the newspaper, and at precisely six forty-five the servant comes with my breakfast tray: my cup of coffee, a small plate with a spoonful of Dawani honey from Yemen, another plate with almonds, walnuts, and a banana, and a glass of water. As soon as I finish, I shave and trim my mustache, I wash in hot water, I put on my freshly ironed clothes and my scent, then I go out to work. I go out to life, as work alone is the smiling face of life in my opinion!

Only Farnaz has made me take stock of myself. For more than four decades I have worked, worked, and worked, daily, unaffected by summer or winter, discontent or happiness, through vacations, in health or illness. In my hours of leisure my companions are books, reports, and documentary films. Du'aij even teased me once in front of his mother and sisters by saying, "Baba's week doesn't have a Friday in it!"

Everyone fell silent out of fear of my reaction, but I corrected Du'aij jokingly, saying, "Neither Friday nor Saturday." Then laughter rang out, and everyone took the opportunity to criticize me and say that I buried myself in my work, that I didn't know how to rest or enjoy a vacation, and that I was constantly busy.

Now I see that every deal took a day from my life, or a month. Every contract pulled me away from my family; every increase in my bank balance corresponded to a loss in closeness to my wife and children. My work took me far away, and lately

I've realized that I've become accustomed to a desolate loneliness that surrounds me always.

I remember how Shaikha always chided me when we traveled: "Enjoy yourself—we're on vacation!" Once, when our quarrel had escalated to the point where she was in tears, she cried out, "May God curse work and its father!"

I've often asked myself where I acquired this way of life. Now that I'm taken by Farnaz's magic, by longing for Farnaz, by meeting Farnaz, by Farnaz's eyes and perfume, I see that she alone has pulled me away from the concerns of my work, that she alone—without my realizing it—has touched my heart and taken me on a path that's new to me, to a strange yearning that nearly drives me crazy.

I don't like to keep driving aimlessly. I called the office and Marwan's voice came to me: "Greetings, Abu Du'aij."

"Has anyone asked for me?"

"Mr. Ismail."

"Is there any urgent mail?"

"Not a thing."

"Thank you. I won't be in today."

I hung up on him without waiting for a response. As I did, I remembered the words of a friend who had criticized this longstanding habit of mine.

Farnaz was trembling throughout our meeting. She came on time. I had not expected that she would have coffee with me, but she said, "I don't begin my day without coffee." She was open, speaking about her family, not ashamed to tell me that her father drives a one-eight. Her brother is an officer in Tehran, and my son is fighting Iran in Syria and Iraq.

The Dasman Palace is on my right and the Kuwait Towers and the sea on my left. I'll sit by the sea for a while.

After Farnaz left, I felt as if I could not stay in the place alone. I began looking at where she sat, her glass of water and coffee cup still showing traces of her lipstick. I went to the place on the couch where she had sat and leaned over to smell her perfume, the cords falling from my headcloth. I was not myself. What are you doing, Yaqoub? I stood up, holding the cords in my hand, and I sensed hundreds of ghosts of Farnaz in the room. I fled, leaving everything as it was.

The meeting with her had passed swiftly. I did not have my fill of her, nor did I tell her anything about my infatuation with her. Now I feel as if I want to see her. My telephone rings, and Sahar's number appears.

"Greetings, Baba. Are you going to come to have lunch with us?"

I remained silent for a few seconds, not knowing how to answer. "I'll be with you in an hour."

The last few days Shaikha has been hovering over me, as if she guesses how preoccupied I am. She's asked me more than once, "What's on your mind?" I always give her the same answer: "Not a thing."

Shaikha has been my companion all along my way. It's true that she has passed fifty, that my desire for her has grown old, and that we each sleep in our own rooms; but something in her eyes, her gaze, her presence near me whispers to me constantly, "Shaikha loves you." I'm the one who has passed through the stages of life without ever stopping at a station of love or even of a passing pleasure.

I remember one incident. I was in Malaysia to sign a large construction contract for a commercial complex and the associated services. After my session ended with a working dinner, I went to my royal suite. No sooner had I gone in and taken off my shoes than the doorbell rang. When I answered, I was surprised by two girls standing before me, looking as if they were models.

"Yes?" I asked.

One of them answered, smiling. "Good evening," she said, speaking clear Arabic.

Our eyes met, and I repeated my question: "Yes?"

With a melting smile on her face, she asked, "Would you like us to spend the evening together?" I looked at her for a few seconds, then I stepped back and closed the door without saying another word to them.

Sami laughed and said, "You're a peaceable man who doesn't have any relations with women." Then he added, "Abu Du'aij, a lover enthralled with the dinar!"

I parked the car in the lot facing the Kuwait Towers and got out to walk near the seashore. Something in my heart still wished I were sitting and talking with Farnaz; I wished I were still listening to her stories; I wished I could hug her and smell the scent of her neck, that I could go on looking at the secret in her eyes. I wished I could hold her hand as we walked together. When she left the suite, I yearned to run after her and go with her, letting her take me wherever she wanted, as long as I was near her.... Yaqoub, what are you saying?

Suddenly I received a message alert, and my heart skipped a beat when I saw "Al-Khayyam" and read "I was very happy to meet you." I hesitated. Then a second message came: "It is my honor to know you. I'm sorry I left quickly and left you alone in the suite."

It occurred to me to send a message asking her to come back to the suite again, but I wrote, "I still miss you." The answer came immediately, a picture of a flower and of two hands, palms together, apologizing. I thought about sending the picture of a kiss that I usually send to my daughter Sahar, along with a flower, but something stopped me, and my phone rang, showing Uthaiman's number. I was not expecting to hear from him; he only calls me if there's something important. A hidden anxiety shook my heart, and the form of Ahmad appeared before me as I answered.

"Abu Du'aij, where are you?"

"Has anything happened?"

"I absolutely must see you."

"Where are you?" I asked, frightened by the terror in his voice.

"At the office."

"I'm on my way. I'll be there in less than ten minutes."

I said that looking at the sea. The odor of blood leaped to my nose, from where, I didn't know.

22

As I got into my car and drove away from the Watiya parking lot, I couldn't believe what had just happened! I couldn't explain my conduct to myself. I reviewed the tape of my short acquaintance with him, from when he came across me at the elevator until the time of our meeting. I had not thought of anything, nor had I arranged anything; I had not dreamed of meeting with him or speaking to him, and I don't know how to describe my relationship with him.

I'm driving on my usual route. I can't go home now because it's earlier than when I usually get home, and I have nowhere else to go.

My meeting with him was different from what I had imagined. I was scared and preparing for the worst when I first went to him. I sat looking at him surreptitiously: he's about sixty, and he seems much older than me. He looked very large to me, with his height, his dishdasha, and his way of sitting. He was calm and kind and reassured me that he didn't want anything from me, but he scared me when he asked about his children and whether I knew them. I didn't understand why he was asking. I kept waiting to find out what he wanted from me, but he never said anything. His words were kind, but I kept waiting for him to come out and say something about what was hovering over our heads.

The moment I got into my car, I opened the bag with the purse and my heart fluttered as I touched the leather. It was an authentic Chanel purse! Safi will be sure to recognize it—it's obviously not an imitation. For a moment I thought about returning it to receive the price in cash, which I need badly. But Mr. Yaqoub did not leave the receipt in the bag, and I don't know which shop he bought it from. This is the first present I've received from him; I won't begrudge it to myself. I'll carry it proudly on my shoulder.

What can I call Mr. Yaqoub—an admirer, a friend, a beloved? It occurred to me that I'm the lover of the president of the company, but I don't know how to act with him.

Faris wanted to meet me in his small apartment, and Mr. Yaqoub rented a suite in the Sheraton to meet me—what a difference. I looked at his watch and his gleaming shoes. If I told my mother or Safi about what happened between us, I know my mother would slap my face and then dissolve in tears and laments; she would never believe me even if I swore every oath there is that he never touched me, and even Safi's eyes would have that look. A man who returns a girl to his company after the assistant director has fired her, who increases her salary and sends her affectionate messages, who arranges to meet her for coffee in a five-star hotel, who gives her a designer purse, and then when she asks to leave, says goodbye without even....

Farnaz! I'm talking to myself now. No one will believe your story. What does he want from you? Is he as kind as he seems, or is he a womanizer who plans everything? Your first meeting with him went well: admiration first, kindness first, a first gift, a first deception...and possibly you'll find another man in your next meeting.

We sat in the living room. I didn't see the rest of the place, but it must have had a bedroom. I'm afraid he's still there. Is this his usual place, a hunter's blind for girls? I wish I had the courage to tell him to give me the money next time, and I'll buy something for myself. A thousand dinars would be enough for ten installments on my car.

I don't know where to go. I'm confused now. If he had just asked me, I would have known what he wants, but he kept looking at me in a way I didn't understand. I'll be lucky if he goes on liking me. Mr. Yaqoub al-Shiraa: millionaire, owner of companies, strong man. I'd like to believe he admires me. If he does, then where will his admiration take me? What's being asked of me?

After what I saw today, I'll be free of my fear and dread. Next time I'll sit with him without a hijab. Perhaps we'll have breakfast together, and I'll pass him a glass of juice...Today we did not shake hands, nor did he touch my hand, but what's wrong with shaking his hand, or even kissing him? He's taller than I am. I'll be lucky if he becomes attached to me and showers gifts on me. My relationship with him will definitely change my life and my family's life; we'll leave our small apartment, my father will buy a new car, Reza will come back to Kuwait, and maybe he'll employ him in one of his companies.

Farnaz, if what you're imagining comes true, then Yaqoub is a gift from heaven!

Ever since I came out of the hotel and got into my car, I've been talking to myself: You barely sat with the man—you are the one who ran away. He's an old man, but he's still handsome; there's still a freshness in his face and his body. I don't know what I want from him. I would live like a queen with him. If only he would love me and be pleased with me. He's better for me than

Faris or any young man who's just taking his first steps to making his way.... Oh my God, if I told Mervet that the president met me in a suite in the Sheraton and gave me a Chanel handbag, she would never believe me!

When my mother was watching over my relationship with Faris, I revealed to her that he had asked to meet me in his apartment, and she shouted in dismay, "How awful, what a catastrophe!" The look in her eyes and on her face changed, and her tone altered. "Farnaz, don't get involved in this and shame us." I was afraid of her anxiety and pained by her worry over me. I got up and hugged her, and I swore to her that I could not meet a man in an apartment or any private place. She went on watching me for days, with fear in her heart and her eyes pleading. She was reassured only when I swore to her that I had broken off with Faris and had erased his number from my phone. I told her again that I did not have any relationship with any young man.

How wretched girls are, and especially poor ones! Perhaps Mr. Yaqoub wouldn't dare communicate with a Kuwaiti girl or hunt down someone from an influential family; he would think differently about it, he would be afraid of a scandal. But Farnaz Qurmuzi, a poor Iranian, is someone he can exploit without being subject to any questioning.

Maybe I should make my excuses next time, since I wouldn't dare stand up to him if any dispute arose between us. He might attack me and then leave me in the hotel room and go out as if nothing had happened. Then where would I turn? Who would stand with me when I had gone to see him in his place? He can depend on his name, his companies, his wealth, and his relationships, and I can depend on the wind. Who will stand with me when he throws me into hell? He'll end my employment in his company and cancel my residency, and then I'll have to leave Kuwait for Iran. I feel my heart beating fast. It's almost one o'clock.

I have three hours to go before it's time for me to return home. I'm just driving around aimlessly. I'll go home and tell Mother that I have a terrible headache and that I asked for permission to leave work.

Today's headache is unlike any other I've ever had—my God, I don't know what to do! I long to contact him and find out what his impression of me was, what's going through his mind. I'd like to say to him, "Please don't play with me. Please be honest. Please don't torment me." Before we met I was afraid, but now I feel lost, swimming in an endless, dark sea that's both attractive and frightening. I don't know where he's taking me, and I don't know what to do. I don't want to turn him away and lose him.

At times when we were together that day, I got the feeling that he loves me and that he believed I was seeking his protection. Maybe I could test his intentions by asking him for a large sum, say five thousand dinars; then if he gave it to me, I would win, and if he excused himself and refused, our relationship would end. No, I'll ask for ten thousand; he's a millionaire. But what would I offer him for his money? The equation always seems shameless: money for a body, money for sex, money for pleasure. In sum: money for life.

Does it make sense for me to prepare my body and perfume it, then go to him in his lair, strip in front of him, and sleep with him? A man who's older than my father. My poor father, there's nothing in him that would attract any young woman to him, or even any old woman. A poor driver of a one-eight, weary, his breath short. God help you, Father. And God help me too, I also need his help.

The telephone is ringing, Mother is calling. “Hello, Mama.”

“How did things go for you today?” Any problems at the company send Mother into panic.

“Alhamdulillah, everything’s fine.”

“When are you coming home?”

“I’m on the way. My head hurts and I asked to leave. I’m coming home.”

I won’t say a word about anything. What happened in the hotel concerns only me. I’ll keep it in my heart and in my head.

23

As I expected, Uthaiman was waiting for me with Marwan. He stood up the moment I entered.

"Please come in," I said, as I went into the office. I know him—a major catastrophe has occurred, his face is flushed with fear. I sat across from him and hurried to ask, "What happened?"

"Ahmad." He said a single word and fell silent, looking at me.

My heart missed a beat, and the odor of blood assailed my nose! Some premonition had told me that the matter concerned Ahmad. I swallowed my confusion, trying to remain calm and listen to him.

"Ahmad has been taken prisoner by a jihadi group."

I had expected him to inform me of my son's death. For a moment I was silent, looking at him as I absorbed the news. "What else?"

"I don't know much more than that. A kind friend in Syria contacted me and told me, 'Your son, the group commander Sheikh Ahmad, has been taken prisoner.'"

The memory of Ahmad's last call ran through my mind. Had he been a captive when he called me? I tried to hold myself together. I looked at Uthaiman and asked, "What else did your friend tell you?"

"He said that Sheikh Ahmad and his group fought a fierce

battle with a jihadi contingent they're at war with, and he was taken prisoner in a coordinated operation. No one knows anything more about him now."

"Does that mean they've killed him?"

"If they had wanted to kill him, they would have done that on the battleground and left his body there like those of the other martyrs, but they were planning to capture him."

I leaned back in my chair, trying to conceal how shaken I was. I looked at him from my silence, trying to decipher the look on his face. What was he hiding from me? "Did your friend explain anything else?"

"No."

"Is he Kuwaiti?"

"No, Syrian."

"How did he learn the news?"

"His two sons are fighters in Sheikh Ahmad's group. The older one was martyred."

It's clear that Uthaiman knows a lot and that he's in contact with his kind friends. For that reason I won't call him to account now, but I'll get as much as possible out of him. "Did your friend tell you anything about the faction that captured Ahmad?"

"He believes that it's working under the umbrella of Daesh, and that it might be coordinating operations with al-Qaeda." He went on talking, while the smell of blood stopped my breath. "The battle happened in the area of al-Bukamal—it's a border region on the northeastern front, near the Iraqi border."

"Who was Ahmad working with?"

His confidence was shaken, and his Adam's apple moved as he looked at me. He was silent for a few seconds, before he managed, "I don't know."

"Uthaiman, why aren't you telling me everything you know?" I threw the question in his face.

Looking confused, he defended himself. "By God, Abu Du'aij, I don't have any more information! All I know is what the man told me."

I ground my teeth. I don't think it's a coincidence that my son was taken on the day of my first meeting with Farnaz.

"What should we do now?" I asked him. "Should we inform the Foreign Ministry or wait? Or go to Syria?" He had no response. I called to mind all my acquaintances and contacts in Kuwait, Syria, and Lebanon, regretting the relationships I once had with influential friends in Iraq.

"We must wait. I don't want to risk doing something that would harm Ahmad."

"Wait for what?" I felt my mouth going dry; my son was the captive of a terrorist group, and God only knew what he was going through. "Is the faction that captured Ahmad working in Syria?"

"The whole world is working in Syria!" he shot out irritably. Then, as if rectifying his rashness, he said in a tone he tried to make calm, "As you know, Daesh operates between Iraq and Syria, and they have a relationship with al-Qaeda. But the man who gave me the news doesn't know if Sheikh Ahmad is still in Syrian territory or if they've taken him someplace else."

"Where would that be?"

"Any place in Syria, or in Iraq, or even in Turkey or Iran. These groups work over broad areas of rough territory, and relations between them fluctuate."

"Can you get in touch with your Syrian friend?"

"No." I found his answer unconvincing, but he gave it decisively.

"Why not?"

"He has no phone. He calls by means of a computer connected to a satellite. I've tried to call him many times, but he doesn't answer."

An hour ago I was engaged in a romantic encounter, and now I'm facing my son's kidnapping. As I returned my gaze to Uthaiman, I had never felt such rancor toward him as as I did then. But I was the weaker party, something I had never been before. "What do you advise?"

"The man said to wait; he'll contact us again."

"Where do you know this man from?"

"He used to work in Kuwait."

"Did he work with us?"

"No, he worked as an accountant in a financial firm."

"Is he sure that Ahmad was captured?"

"Yes. Both his sons were part of Sheikh Ahmad's group, and one of them was martyred in the battle."

A moment of calm passed between us and I reached for my glass of water. My mouth and throat were dry. I had seen no one come in with water and coffee. I was utterly disoriented—what could be happening to Ahmad? In his last call he had informed me that he had married two women, that he had a son named Umar, and that he was hoping for martyrdom.

Something seemed to be pressing on my chest. I spoke calmly to Uthaiman, saying, "You know me, I could contact dozens of influential people in high places right now, but I'm afraid for Ahmad. What do you think?"

"As I said, I don't know anything other than what the man told me. He will call us—all we can do is wait."

He fell silent but I sensed that he wanted to say something, so I urged him. "Speak... speak."

"The man's son is in the ranks of the jihadis. It's certain that any news will reach him and then reach us." He sat up in his seat, and I noticed a strange look on his face. "He asked me for your phone number, but I refused."

His words hit me like a slap in the face. The matter concerned me, too; someone wanted to involve me in this dirty war. "Why did he want my number?"

"I don't know. Maybe to reassure you about Sheikh Ahmad personally."

"Does he know me?"

"He lived in Kuwait for years, so he knows you as a businessman, and he knows that you are Ahmad's father."

It was obvious that Uthaiman knew more than he was saying. It was clear that he's in contact with the community, that something is going on, and that he wants to involve me in it.

Suddenly the door opened and Marwan appeared. "God keep you. What orders do you have for me?"

The workday had ended without my noticing the time. "Nothing, thank you."

To Uthaiman, I said, "I'm thinking of contacting the foreign minister to inform him of what's happened, for fear that we'll be questioned later on."

"It's your decision. You know that these groups don't operate under the umbrella of a state, and don't take instructions from anyone but their commanders. I'm afraid that contacting the ministry would complicate matters, and that it might affect Ahmad." I continued to listen, and he added, "We don't know if he's in Syria or Iraq or any other place."

"You don't want me to do anything other than to wait for a call from your Syrian friend?"

"Please, Abu Du'aij, I won't accept any responsibility. Do as you please. I'm giving you my advice, but the final decision is yours."

I felt a pain in my head. Now I was weak before Uthaiman, very weak—he had seized my very heartbeat. "Who besides you knows about this?"

"No one. I haven't said a word to anyone. As soon as the man called me, I got in touch with you."

My son is between life and death, and I'm supposed to sit still, to tell no one, to do nothing, I who detest waiting! My entire life I've been the one to take the initiative. I've been the stronger party. But now I'm experiencing a weakness I've never known.

"Abu Du'aij, I suggest you go home and keep your phone beside you. I'll contact you as soon as I hear anything new."

I went on looking at him in silence. He was asking me to live my life with my usual calm, as if nothing had happened, when my son could be undergoing torture or could have been killed by now. The pain in my chest returned. He was asking, "If he asks me for your phone number, will you give me permission to give it to him?"

My son has been ensnared, and here's Uthaiman wanting to embroil me as well. "The man is your friend and he'll call to let you know about any developments, so why does he want my number?"

"I don't know. He asked me for it when he called."

Fearing for my son, I agreed to go along with his wishes. I said, "Give him the number."

He stood up abruptly. "Please, Abu Du'aij, don't tell my sister Shaikha anything."

"I don't tell Shaikha anything. You are the only one who gives anyone any news." I spoke sharply, and he left, saying,

"I'll call you as soon as I hear anything."

He withdrew and I turned to face the sea, the pain thrusting at my chest. An anxious thought rose in my mind. It was a strange coincidence that the news of my son's kidnapping coincided with my meeting with Farnaz. Was there a link between them? The loathsome odor of blood came to my nose, spreading to everything around me.

24

I had no appetite for lunch. Everything around me was unsettled. Shaikha asked me, "What's wrong?" and as usual I answered, "Nothing."

I went to my room and placed the phone by my head. I stretched out on my bed, and pictures of Ahmad in his childhood and youth rained down on me, memories of being with him, and scenes with his mother and sisters and brother. It occurred to me to call my friend the district commander, to inform him and hear his opinion, and to ask him to keep the matter confidential. By virtue of the office he holds, he would have a different opinion about this, but Uthaiman had advised me to delay doing anything until I received an answer.

I kept tossing on my bed, unable to chase away the images of Ahmad and my terrifying visions of what he might be undergoing at the hands of Daesh terrorists. I thought about calling Uthaiman, since he might have had some news, but I decided not to; he would call me if he'd heard anything. It occurred to me to seek out Ismail, since I know he has close relations with figures affiliated with religious currents; they certainly know each other and have connections abroad as well. It's not right for me to simply remain silent and wait, while my son is on the verge of death.

Where could he be? Uthaiman said that they deliberately planned to capture him. Should I contact my friend the editor in chief? The newspaper certainly has connections with individuals and groups who work in Syria, and they might have received the news of the capture of Abu l-Fath al-Kuwaiti.

The pain in my chest was still there, with the addition of a headache. I called to Shaikha and asked for two Panadol pills. I saw her concern for me. "What's wrong, Yaqoub?"

"Nothing, I just have a headache." She remained where she was, fear in her eyes. I offered, "Maybe it's the pressure of work."

"God forgive you." She exhaled her grief and hurried to bring me the pills and a glass of water. I took them, and she sat down near me. Sounding dispirited, she said, "Please tell me what's wrong."

I wondered what she would do if I said, "Your son is a captive held by a terrorist group." Would she collapse as I had, or would she take the news coldly, given their wretched relationship?

"I have a headache. The pressure of work."

"Fine, Yaqoub—how long are you going to put yourself through this grind? You'll die working!" Tears were in her eyes.

My telephone signaled a message, and my heart raced. It was from al-Khayyam, so I left it. I said to Shaikha, "Just a colleague at the bank. I won't answer."

"I'm going to shut off the phone and leave you to rest." She reached for it, but I was ahead of her.

"I'm expecting an important call."

"I thought so. Your heart is tied up in your work, in deals and payments."

"Shaikha, my dear, I'm tired. Let me sleep."

Studying me closely, she said, "Should we go to the doctor?

You look pale. You hardly ate a thing at lunch."

"Please, leave me alone to sleep." I spoke rather sharply, and she rose to leave, looking discouraged.

Oh, Shaikha! What can I tell you? More than one headache is raging in my head. Shall I tell you about the one arising from Farnaz, or the one from my fear for Ahmad, or the one coming from how lost and shattered I am? Shaikha, Yaqoub today is not the one you've lived with all your life. I realized that I had not read Farnaz's message; I picked up the phone and read, "Good evening, Mr. Yaqoub. I'm sorry to bother you, but I wanted to ask if you would like us to meet tomorrow."

Really? Is she actually asking if I'd like to see her? Maybe I should go to the Sheraton; I'll be calm there, and if Uthaiman calls, I'll be able to answer him freely, unfettered by Shaikha's looks and her worry. I'll even be able to talk to Farnaz.

Something took my mind away from Farnaz the moment Uthaiman told me about Ahmad, blocking her off from my heart. I was beset with the notion that something connects the two of them—has she come to make up for my loss of my son? But that's impossible, I whispered to myself. No one replaces anyone else; no one can take another's place. How shall I answer Farnaz? I'm waiting for Uthaiman's call, hanging on desperately for the ringing of the phone and a word from him.

O my son, why? Why, Ahmad? How I wished I could go to the mosque and look for Abdel Shafi, to take revenge on him for my son's loss, and also on the evil Umar.... Ever since Uthaiman gave me the news, I've been pushing away the thought of Ahmad's death. I don't want to believe it. I've lived my whole life with nothing more than my own instincts to guide me, so why has the mirror of my heart become clouded over?

After lunch I searched online for any news of him, but I got nowhere. I searched for "Ahmad al-Kuwaiti," "Abu l-Fath al-Kuwaiti," "fighting among terrorist groups in Syria," and "Daesh groups operating in Syria," and found myself in a sea of reports, news, images, and terrifying videos. I was very frightened by what I saw: explosions, killing, miserable prisons stuffed with children, chanting. I found nothing about Ahmad other than pictures here and there and a reference to his appointment as commander of a jihadi group in Syria. The question continued to weigh on my heart: how had my son come to this?

I'll go into the garden; I can't go on lying in bed.

As I was going out of my room, I met Shaikha. "You haven't slept, how are you feeling?"

"Alhamdulillah, better. I'll take today's newspaper and go to the garden."

"Can I get you something to drink?"

"Tea." The word came out like a shot as I rushed to pick up the paper from the table, then fled to my retreat in the garden to wait for Uthaiman's call.

25

Farnaz's perfume seemed to come and sit beside me.

Uthaiman's call came to me in the garden, and I tried to conceal how disturbed I was. "The man called me and asked for your number, so I gave it to him." I listened while my heart fluttered. "The man assured me that the group holding Shaikh Ahmad asked to contact you personally."

"They asked to contact me?" I shot a question at him in disbelief: "Who's the one speaking to them?"

"The young man whose brother was martyred in the confrontation. There's an intermediary from their side who's talking to him."

I felt irritated, unconvinced by Uthaiman's words; there was a lot that wasn't clear, and what was happening filled me with aversion. I asked him again, "They asked for my telephone number?"

"Yes, they asked for the number, and they asked..."

He suddenly fell silent, and I yelled, "Go on!"

"They cautioned me against contacting any authority. As soon as they learn that you have made any movement or contacted any state or régime or group, they will kill Ahmad, and they will film the operation and broadcast the video."

There was a weight pressing on my chest, and I was unsure of how much I could trust Uthaiman. I had no response to his words, which struck me as a complaint. "There is no power or strength save in God! This is a trial, Abu Du'aij."

"Okay, you gave them my number. What's next?"

"The intermediary was told that you can expect their call at any moment."

"But what do they want from me?"

"I don't know. It's hard to guess how those people think. They have their own ways of reckoning."

When he finished the call, I hurried to leave the garden. I had decided to go to the Sheraton; I needed to be alone, to ponder the catastrophe that had overcome me. I needed a moment of calm so I could think, so I could act without looking around me.

I met Shaikha as I was entering the house. I informed her, "I'm going to see my friend Dr. Fadil."

"When will you be back?"

"I don't know." I moved away from her without waiting for her answer.

I entered the suite, and Farnaz's scent still suffused the room. It rose up to greet me. The place was immaculate, as if the housekeepers had just finished tidying up and made their exit. I hung the "Do not disturb" sign on the door handle and pulled the door shut.

I tossed off my headcloth and cords, took off my shoes, and threw my full-length onto the sofa. I turned on the television and began surfing the news channels, Arabic and foreign, on the chance that I might see something about my son.

Uthaiman said, "They will call you immediately." It's been more than an hour and a half that I've been staring at my phone, examining it every minute.

I returned to Farnaz's message suggesting that we meet

tomorrow. Since I didn't have an answer and did not know what my tomorrow would be like, I was at a loss. I wrote only, "Good evening."

I felt the silence and the waiting closing in, as if interrogating me. Sighing in pain, I spoke to myself: Now you're besieged by loss, Yaqoub, and you've lost your compass. Now you've passed sixty, and your son has been captured by a terrorist group, and you feel drawn to a girl who's younger than your daughters. Now, Yaqoub....

A message arrived from al-Khayyam: "A very good evening, sir." I read it twice, and her concern and interest in me seemed clear. I wished I could hear her voice, could speak to her, but what would I say? I can't tell her about my son's situation, and anyway, what could she do? The telephone signaled another message: "Mr. Yaqoub, are you still angry with me for leaving you alone?"

I felt as if I needed no one so much as I needed her to be beside me now. I don't want anything from her, just for her to be beside me. But it's after eight, and she has told me many times that she can't go out after she gets back from work.

Why have they taken so long to call me? What can they be doing to my son? What's his condition right now? My thoughts frightened me, and there was still a heavy weight on my chest. I thought about calling Farnaz to hear her voice, to tell her that I'm not angry with her, and maybe to tell her that I'm going through hard times. But she might think that I'm having differences with my wife. A new message: "Can I call?"

"Please do."

"Hello."

"Good evening, sir." Her voice was somewhat hoarse, disappointed or disturbed.

"And to you."

"Sir, I sincerely apologize."

"Farnaz, don't apologize for anything; you've done nothing wrong." I changed the subject. "I'm in the suite and the scent of your perfume is sitting with me."

"Really?"

"Yes. I came here because I'm upset, and because I'm waiting for a call."

"Excuse me. If you're upset, I'll call another time."

"No, wait . . . " I said, rushing my answer. "I wish you were with me now."

She was silent, and I also said nothing, breathing rapidly. Suddenly a number with many digits appeared on the screen of my telephone, so I quickly ended the call to her and answered it.

I heard static, and then a weak voice, saying "Baba."

"Ahmad??"

"Pay the ransom and submit, you enemy of God!" The man's voice had an accent. He added, "We'll keep this dog under our feet until you pay the ransom."

"What?"

"Beware of contacting any authorities. We'll cut up this heretic enemy of God with a saw and broadcast that on video if you dare inform any person or any authority!"

Beads of sweat started running down my forehead as I asked again, "What?"

The call was cut off as suddenly as it had come. I found myself standing, my heart beating fast, a cold chill running through me. My mouth had gone dry, and I was overcome by the rancid odor of blood.

26

I'm utterly confused and disturbed. I left the hotel not knowing where I was going.

"We'll keep this dog under our feet!" The words pursued me. Should I go to Uthaiman? Should I call him? He's the only one who knows about the matter. The man who called me told me, in his broken Arabic, "We'll cut up this heretic enemy of God." Where can I go? I feel my heart beating hard, my mouth is dry, and my tongue is like a piece of wood. Never once did I dream of such a nightmare. Where can I turn? Who can I call on for counsel? The caller warned me, but. . . . They are demanding a ransom, so it was important for them to get my number; it was important for me to hear my son's voice. A group that claims they're engaged in jihad—what kind of jihad is it to frighten people, to terrify them, to cut them into pieces and make examples of them?

It's after ten at night, and I'm driving my car to nowhere. I should go home.

Calm down, Yaqoub! I lectured myself. You've lived through many difficult situations before, and you should know how to deal with this. I tried to take a deep breath and then cough hard to jolt my chest; there's a medical opinion that says that if you fear a heart attack you should cough hard, so your heart and your chest move. Cough, cough. I began coughing hard.

Enough, that's enough, I whispered to myself. Your son is the prisoner of a terrorist group, they're demanding a ransom, you have to figure out how to get him out of their hands. I thought how strange the situation was: Daesh or al-Qaeda captures the Kuwaiti commander of a jihadi group and then demands a ransom to free him!

The amount doesn't matter. There's nothing as valuable as my son. I would pay everything I have to get him back. But what guarantee do I have of their honesty? What if I pay the ransom and then they won't release him? They're threatening to cut him into pieces with a saw—how can I be sure of getting him out of their hands safely? My heart fluttered; they'll take the ransom and then kill him. I must go myself. I asked myself, are you going to travel to meet with a terrorist group from Daesh or al-Qaeda? How will you get to northern Syria, or northern Iraq? How will you get in touch with them?

A blinding headache is gripping my head. I must meet Uthaiman and tell him what happened and listen to his opinion. Maybe he'll make contact with the group in Syria and we'll hear instructions from them.

A thought whispers in my heart—Uthaiman knows a lot about Ahmad's group, perhaps he's in touch with them. But he doesn't want to reveal anything to me. Any scandal will fall on me. People will say, "His son is a terrorist! His son is a murderer!" They'll say...I don't know what they'll say about me if I go to meet the group, or what those people could do to me.

Just then, a message came in from Uthaiman: "Peace be upon you, Abu Du'aij. Did they call you?" He's asking; does he know about the call? And does he want to learn more from me? Or is he asking because he's worried, like me? I know that Ahmad is his favorite among my children. Should I go to meet him, or call him, and decide about him? I pressed the button to call him, and in a few seconds I heard him say, "Peace be upon you, Abu Du'aij!" I hesitated; I know that any call can be recorded. So I asked him to call me back on WhatsApp.

As soon as the phone rang, I told him, "They called me, they're asking for a ransom."

"Did you expect that?" After a few seconds, he went on. "It's certain that they know you, and for that reason they intentionally took Ahmad."

Why am I not at ease with Uthaiman? I wondered, and remained silent until the question exploded in my heart: is it conceivable that this is a game and that Uthaiman is part of it?

"Did they tell you anything?" he asked.

"They warned me about contacting anyone, and they said they would cut Ahmad into pieces with a saw."

"Good God! That's how they operate; curses on it!"

"Have they imprisoned any other Kuwaitis?"

"No, but when there's a battle, if they win, they choose one or more people as prisoners to bargain for them."

"What do you advise now?" I asked him out of weakness, and I heard him sigh on the other end.

"Did they specify an amount and a time?"

I suddenly was shocked to realize that I had not given a single thought to the amount being demanded or how it would be handed over. Yaqoub, you aren't yourself! I whispered. I told Uthaiman, "It wasn't a long call. They just said a few words and hung up."

"They will certainly contact you again and transmit their demands."

I felt as if Uthaiman was taking me by the hand, as if I was incapable of thinking or making any decision. I asked myself what had thrown my thoughts into such disarray. "I'll go home to rest," I said. "If they call me, I'll get in touch with you again."

"You must rest. Keep the telephone near you, since they might call at any moment."

"Will you contact your friends in Syria?"

"I don't know. I'm inclined not to say anything to anyone, since we don't know how they're thinking. Anyway I can't reach them. Let's keep this a secret between us. If they contact me, I'll tell them that I don't know anything."

"As you wish. Do you have any advice for me?"

"Yaqoub, my brother, you're nervous and autocratic. I hope you'll remain calm during all the calls, and not make any promises. Always give yourself a chance to think, tell them you'll think it over, don't listen to their threats. They might send you a film showing them torturing Ahmad; do not react. Be careful not to make any decision Ahmad could suffer from!"

"Thank you." I hung up, shattered by my anger, my weakness, my futility.

I headed home. God forgive you, Ahmad! The image of Abdel Shafi came to me, and of the evil professor Umar. The rancid odor of blood seeped into the car, filling it and nearly choking me.

27

"Yaqoub, Yaqoub..." Shaikha's voice woke me. "You were talking in your sleep!"

I looked at her face and rushed to pick up my phone, as if I'd been stung. I made sure that there were no calls, no messages. It was almost nine in the morning, and Shaikha was saying, "You don't usually sleep late!"

"I didn't sleep at all. Maybe I dozed off at five-thirty or six."

"Uthaiman called to remind you of your meeting today."

Suddenly I was attacked by images of Ahmad. I don't remember the details of my dream, but all through my sleep I had been running, shouting, trying to catch up to him. Every time I reached him, he went farther away, while the form of Farnaz appeared, each time with a different head covering.

I didn't have any meeting scheduled with Uthaiman. Had they called him, or had he learned something new? I sat up and told Shaika, "Have Jaya prepare my breakfast. I have to hurry to the meeting."

I headed for the bathroom as she left the room, then I hurried back to pick up my phone and call Uthaiman, who answered, "Peace be upon you."

"Is there any news?"

"Nothing at all, I just wanted to check on you."

"I'm on my way."

I ended the call, bathed quickly, and had my coffee. I left with my heart hanging on the screen of my cellphone.

Bayoumi was waiting for me. "Good morning!"

"And to you. To the office."

How strange this all is—it's been many years since I slept as late as I did today! I'm possessed by an odd feeling, as if I'm walking on loose, shifting ground. What's the meaning of my dream of Ahmad and Farnaz?

I became aware of the road and saw that it was not crowded.

Why haven't they called me? Have they maybe killed Ahmad? If they've decided on a ransom, how much will it be, and how will I get it to them, and where? They captured him after the battle. O my son, what miserable battles have you gotten yourself into? It's certain that they know I'm a millionaire. That's why they communicated with me—to extort money. God forgive you, my son!

"Please." Bayoumi was opening the car door for me.

The moment I entered my office, I summoned Uthaiman. His face was calm as he gave me his usual greeting.

"They haven't called me!"

He looked at me, then answered, "I don't know anything."

"Has anyone called you?"

"No."

My phone rang and I grabbed it and looked at the screen, which showed a long number. "Hello."

"Baba." It was Ahmad's voice, very weak.

"My child!"

"Baba, please pay them."

"Ten million American dollars, you infidel!" It was the same repulsive voice speaking in broken Arabic. "You will receive the account number, you'll transfer the amount, then we'll free your dog of a son!"

Without thinking, I yelled back, "I won't transfer a single dollar to you. You can do whatever you want!" I hung up before I heard the answer.

I was trembling all over and saw that a wave of fear had descended on Uthaiman's face. He begged me, "Please don't react in anger!" I stared at him and he went on, "The situation is different now. Ahmad's life is in the hands of these wretches!"

"They can go to hell, and Ahmad with them! He's a terrorist and a murderer like them, and he has to bear the consequences of his choices. He turned away from all that's good and pleasant in the world and went off to fight in the jihad to free Syria!"

"I'll leave you," Uthaiman managed. He stood up cautiously and left my office, dragging his feet.

Perhaps he didn't like my criticism of Ahmad—could he be one of them? The questions shook me. My telephone alerted me to a message; I picked it up and saw al-Khayyam's name. "Good morning, Mr. Yaqoub. Today is the last day of my vacation, so I did not go to the office." I left the message unanswered; I had no heart for it. The voice rang in my ears: "Ten million American dollars!" I said to myself, that's the price of my son! His life equals ten million dollars.

He's destroyed his future and himself; maybe he's killed innocent people, and now he's destroying me with him. But what guarantee is there that they'll let him go if I transfer the sum to them? And if they did, would he return to Syria and to the internecine fights between jihadi groups? How long will Syria be mired in this swamp of killing and blood? All the terrorists, murderers, and mercenaries of the world are fighting each other on Syrian territory! If he came back to Kuwait, he would come stuffed with terrorist ideas! Then I would have to inform on him and hand him over to the Ministry of Internal Affairs for reeducation.

God forgive you, Ahmad! And may God take vengeance on you, Abdel Shafi, and on you, Umar, and on all those who work with you and stand with you!

Was I angry and maybe too hasty in my answer? Will they put Ahmad to torture? As I pictured Ahmad screaming for help, my telephone sounded with another message from Farnaz: "I'm sorry to bother you, Mr. Yaqoub, but I feel as if you're angry, and I hope I'm not the reason."

I was irritated by her message and her pursuit. It occurred to me to wonder what connected me to her, and what thread stretched between her and Ahmad. I'm used to following signs—I meditate, I read messages from the secrets a moment holds, then I act as I think best, and my instinct does not deceive me. No one knows God's inscrutable secrets, but these are the lessons of my life, my silence, my study.

Something in my heart draws me towards Farnaz. I sent her a message: "Farnaz, I am angry, but you are not the reason."

The reply came immediately: "I hope you can rest."

I should have been calmer while I was negotiating with them. They aren't contractors, or owners, or members of a chamber of commerce, or officers of foreign banks. What if they killed my son as they promised? I felt a pain squeezing my heart, and reached for a drink of water to moisten my dry mouth.

I turned my chair to face the sea and found myself strangely choked with tears, wanting to weep, to find relief in crying. I don't remember the last time I cried; it might have been the day my mother died.

Never before have I lived through moments of pain and loss like this one. I thought of going to the suite at the Sheraton, but I remained where I was; maybe it was better to keep close to Uthaiman. I called Marwan and asked him to have Uthaiman come see me.

I tried to remain calm when he entered, saying, "Peace be upon you." He came to sit before me.

"I don't know what to do!"

"Keep God before you, Abu Du'aij. Ahmad's life is more precious than anything else."

"I'm not talking about the money; I'm talking about getting him away from them. How can I guarantee his release? I'm afraid they'll take the money and kill him."

"There are no guarantees."

"Then I'll go to them—I won't transfer the money to them until I have my son!"

A look of astonishment came over his face. "Please, Yaqoub, don't risk yourself! Don't confront murderers who take no account of any state or government. You're not up to them!" I listened to him in the hope he would say something that would save my son. "You have to ask them about how they'll hand him over. Maybe a group of jihadis will agree to go get him."

"They're all murderers. And even if they did get him, they would take him back to battles and blood, and I want to bring him back to Kuwait."

Another message came through on my phone. It contained a link, which took me to a YouTube video. Ahmad appeared, with his beard and unkempt hair; he was almost naked, his body covered with bruises and wounds. He sat cross-legged in the corner of a room with mud walls and a dirt floor, trembling and repeating, "I testify that there is no god but God and that Muhammad is the prophet of God!" I replayed the video several times. Uthaiman watched with me, saying "Dear God Almighty!"

A moment of silence passed between us and then the phone rang, the screen showing the same strange number.

Static reached me first, then I heard a voice with a clear Arabic accent, possibly from the Maghreb. "You will listen to what we say, you despicable usurer. We are the ones doing the talking and you will listen meekly!" I controlled myself and remained silent, my heart fluttering as the man's voice thundered, "This is our last call to you. We will not budge from the ten million. Next time we'll send you a video that will show you who we are!"

"Who will guarantee the release of my son?"

"We'll take care of getting him back to his group of infidels."

"I want to be the one to get him myself."

"You will come to get him?"

"Yes. I'll deliver the ransom to you and take my son."

"Don't even think about playing games with us, or else we'll kill you and your infidel son both."

"I won't go back on my word. Tell me specifically where you are, and I'll go to you."

He fell silent, my heart was throbbing, and my breathing was rapid. His voice returned. "We'll see." He cut off the call and irritating static came over the line.

I had intended to ask him about their location. I looked up at Uthaiman and found that his face had lost all color. In a barely audible voice, he said, "It's impossible for you to go alone!"

"Come with me." It was as if I had slapped him. He lowered his head and said nothing further. I asked, "Are they in Syria?"

"The battle occurred near the Syrian-Iraqi border, possibly in the region of al-Bukamal."

"I'm prepared to go to Iraq or to Syria. I lost my son when he was little; I won't abandon him now that he's grown."

I sensed his weakness, his cowardice, and his malice. I couldn't stand the sight of him. I got up to face the sea and told him, "Please go to your office."

28

Where can a girl find sleep? I went to bed more than an hour ago, but I'm still awake.

Safi finished nursing her infant. She put him in his bed, whispered "Goodnight" to me and went to her own bed. Soon I heard the sound of her regular breathing. I wonder what's ahead for her—what man would agree to marry her, divorced and with a child who's not yet a year old? Her height, her figure, her fresh face, the way she styles her crazy hair, her laugh—all of that attracts attention wherever she goes. She's ablaze with movement, activity, joy. But her miserable marriage and its failure have broken her spirit and extinguished her interest in doing anything. There's a look of sadness on her face.

The day we went out to buy some things she needed for her infant, she refused to put on the least bit of makeup. "Who for? If it's for those dogs, then I no longer care about any of them, and if it's for myself, then I'm happy with the way I am." As we were coming home, she told me, "When Husain turns two then I'll leave him with Mother and look for a job, any job. I don't want to live as a dependent on the family."

Tomorrow I'll go back to work after three days of leave. I'll have to be very careful; none of the employees must have any idea of what's between me and the president.

When he asked me to open an account for him on Twitter and took my phone number, and then began to send me messages, I found it strange. What did he want from me? He didn't mean anything to me, I didn't know what he looked like, and it never occurred to me to speak to him or meet him. But within days he was sending me messages, he gave me back my job and increased my salary, he made a date with me and met me alone in a hotel suite, and he gave me a present!

The day I came out of his office with the others in my department, Mervet whispered to me, "He's a man!" Her tone of admiration was unmistakable.

"A man, certainly," I answered her. But she looked at me strangely and hissed, "A man's man!"

That day I was quiet when we got back to the office. Something in what she said annoyed me, and I kept looking at her stealthily, trying to figure out what she meant.

Now I feel that his meetings with the company employees were only an excuse to meet me, and even his ploy of setting up a Twitter account for him was transparent. For some reason he wanted to come close to me—what drew him towards me? Many times I felt that he was interested in me, and once I forgot myself enough to think that maybe the man loves me. Then there were all his messages, his requests, his impatience to meet me, added to his personal signature on reemploying me in the company, the increase in my salary, his meeting with me, and his present!

I haven't said anything to my family about my salary increase. I don't know how Mother would interpret it, or Safi, or even my father. I'll keep it for myself. Safi noticed the purse; I was ready with an answer for her, but she didn't say anything. Only Mother commented, happily, "Congratulations on your new handbag! It's beautiful." So the purse went over more easily than I had imagined.

When we met at the Sheraton I was shaking and afraid, but I concealed it. Many thoughts went through my mind—I was sitting alone with the president of a Kuwaiti company. I stole glances at him, and I sensed that he was examining every part of my body. At one point I imagined that he was going to get up, take my hand, say "Come with me," and lead me to the bedroom. I remembered what happened to Safi with the neighbors' son, and I was seized by a tremor. Right then I decided I would flee.

I had been sitting in a heap, clinging to the arm of the sofa. But once I got in my car and closed the door, I wished I had stayed with him longer; I blamed myself for rushing away, without finding out what he wanted from me. It crossed my mind to wonder what would have happened if he had embraced me or kissed me. Never before had I stood before a strange man. But he's a married man, with daughters older than I am. What would he say if I resisted him, or refused to embrace him, or refused to respond?

I must abandon these imaginings and sleep! I don't want to look tired the day I return, and I must pay attention to my work and to every word, every letter I write. Uthaiman will certainly be watching for any slip, to punish me for it. He must have learned of my visits to Mr. Yaqoub and wondered about what's between us.

I'd like to send a quick message to Mr. Yaqoub. I'll put my phone on silent and send the message; if he ignores it, that will be enough for me to move out of his way. "Good night, Mr. Yaqoub." I sent the message; I don't know why my heart is beating fast.

It's as if something is pushing me towards him. My message arrived and he's read it, but he hasn't responded. It's possible that he's with his wife and that I'm intruding on him; I should have respected his privacy. It's not right to send a message at night, to be so hasty. I wonder why I'm pursuing him; I wonder what he thinks of me.

I would have liked him to talk to me about himself, about what he wants from me. Should I take him a present when he invites me next time? What present would be suitable? What would light up his eyes? A man like him won't care about a small present from me.

Why isn't he answering me? Has he taken against me since we met? Maybe he's looking for a flirt, and when he discovered that I'm not like that, he turned away. Or perhaps he was waiting for any sign of a response or initiative from me, and when that didn't happen, he understood that I'm not... but should I have been cheap? When the shawl fell from my head, I noticed a smile on his face that scared me, so I hurried to cover my head again.

Something in my heart tells me that what's between us has yet to begin, and that he will keep after me. The screen on my phone lights up with a message from him: "Good night. Perhaps we'll meet tomorrow."

My heart rejoices! But something about him still frightens me.

How will I be able to see him tomorrow? On my first day back the department head won't agree to give me permission to leave. He can go out whenever he wants.... How should I answer him? I want to write, "My friend!" I whispered that to myself, and my heart beat faster. I told myself to stop, "Know your limits, Farnaz!" I lifted my head a little, to be sure Safi was sleeping, before I wrote: "I'll be happy to meet you."

I'll wait to see how he answers. He arranges everything, and he must have a plan to meet. He is my good luck, and I will not resist it. I hope he doesn't come tomorrow with another present for me. Maybe I can convince Mother that I need to buy a few things, then go to meet him after I come back from the company. Meeting at night will be different. I've learned the way to the hotel and I have the room key, so I can go at any time. Even during the lunch break—half an hour would be enough to visit him at the hotel and get back to the office, as if I went down to get a cup of coffee.

He did not respond to my message. I feel my rapid heartbeat. Friendship is strange; how it pumps the pulse of life into our spirits!

I hear my own voice saying, "Farnaz! Don't get carried away. What kind of friendship can there be between you and the president of the company? A man older than your father! Don't forget who you are, don't forget your situation, your family's small apartment, your father's job, your brother's exile in Tehran!"

Reza called yesterday afternoon and said that he's gotten a vacation of two weeks after three years of service. He said that he dreams of visiting Kuwait, that he misses the atmosphere of Kuwait, he misses our house and Mother's cooking, the streets of Hawalli and al-Nuqra, and meeting his friends.

Where will Reza sleep if he comes back to the house? There's no place but the small living room. He spoke to my father and mother and said hello to Safi, and last of all he spoke to me for more than half an hour. We talked about a lot of things, and he told me that he wishes he could come back to Kuwait tomorrow. He said, "They're playing with me. Every so often I have a different place, a different assignment. I've spent the last three months near the snow in northern Iran, and they awarded me a vacation of two weeks. It's seven years since I joined the military service, and they toss me from one station to another, from one job to another."

I asked him if he was thinking about getting married, and his answer surprised me. He said he wanted to marry an Iranian girl who was born and grew up in Kuwait. He told me that Iranian girls are very different in temperament from the girls in Kuwait. He said he must come back to Kuwait and live here, that even after all these years he hasn't been able to get used to living in Tehran. At the end of the call he begged me, repeating his favorite endearment, "*jounam*, my heart." He pleaded with me to spare no effort to get a visa for him to visit, even if that took a fair amount of money.

I ended the call with tears in my eyes for the brother I missed so, who yearned to visit us with all his heart. Now a thought flashes through my mind—Mr. Yaqoub can surely help Reza. O my friend, my going to you will take me... I stopped myself from saying it, and let myself hope, telling myself, "He'll coddle me if he loves me, even my family's situation will change."

I spent the whole day reading about Mr. Yaqoub via Google—his companies, his memberships on company boards of directors, his holdings in global banks. I examined pictures of him inside and outside of Kuwait.

When I went to the hotel, I felt as if I was embarking on an adventure that was beyond me, a crazy adventure. I thought about going back to the car; I was unsettled and frightened; he had kept after me, asking me to meet him. I imagined that he would attack me the moment he saw me—I was afraid he would grab me and pull me into the bedroom, and what could I do? Would I shout, or push him away and flee? Everything was new to me, and scary, and my mother's face pursued me. But as I sat with him, I discovered that he's courteous, and he did nothing to bother me.

Which of us has become attached to the other? Has he become detached from me while I have not let go of him? What sense does it make for a poor girl to dream of the love of a millionaire? Would I agree to give him the pleasure of love if he asked me to?

I must sleep—it's almost eleven-thirty!

I won't intrude on him; I won't send him another message. Maybe he's completely different from anything I'm thinking—a man of his status, his preoccupations, his position, someone dozens of girls and women would wish for; he won't throw himself at me. But his pursuit has confused me—there must be some purpose behind it. I can't imagine what he wants of me.

I'll prepare myself before I go to work tomorrow, since he's asked to see me.

29

It's been more than two hours that I've been sitting in my office. I can't seem to catch my breath, and my thinking is frozen. All I'm doing is waiting for a call to come.

Uthaiman warned me not to say a thing to Shaikha, but this morning I poured out everything my burning heart held, in her arms. I was lost in my fears, having my breakfast and my coffee, when she came to me. I was surprised that she was awake so early. She said, "Good morning," and I noticed a strange look in her eyes as she sat down opposite me.

"Yaqoub, tell me the truth, what's going on? Why are you running away from me?" I didn't know what to tell her; I was aware of my weakness and my disarray. I felt the need for someone else to bear this killing burden along with me. She said, tiredly, "Don't say 'nothing.' Everything in you says that there is something, something large. Have you married a second wife?"

I sighed, looking at her. I don't know how the words escaped me: "They've kidnapped Ahmad."

I was taken aback by a sudden pallor in her face, while her eyes remained fixed on me, as if she refused to believe what she heard. For a moment I was afraid for her. I got up to bring her a glass of water, and at that moment she burst into tears, weeping as I had never in my life seen her weep. I was afraid that Sahar would hear, so I embraced Shaikha and took her to my room. Her body shook with sobs and somehow my own tears rained down. She noticed and cried out, "Oh my God, you're crying!"

I was shaking and choking on my stifled tears. She stood up and took me in her arms, and I thought to wonder who it was who was comforting the other. I told her what was going on, that Ahmad is being held captive by a terrorist group in Syria or Iraq, that they threatened to kill him, and that I was waiting for their instructions so I could go to them. She assailed me, pleading, "I beg of you, don't go!" She began sobbing again, saying, "I'm begging you! It's enough that I've lost my son. Don't go!"

I told her that I wanted to guarantee his safety and that I wanted to bring him back to Kuwait, since I couldn't bear to see him return to the fighting in Syria. I spoke and she listened through her tears, clinging to her opinion. Then, to my great surprise, she said, "I'm going with you!" I smiled bitterly, but she repeated, "Yes! I'll go with you, come what may!"

"Shaikha, no one is supposed to know about this. I don't know how I'll manage myself, so how could I take you with me?"

I felt that this was the first time we had experienced such closeness and openness. I stood up, ending our conversation, saying, "I have to go to the office." I left the house, fleeing from her and from my own weakness and brokenness before her.

I arrived at the office feeling disgusted with everything, so I sat down facing the sea, adrift amid my fears. I look at my phone every so often, to be sure that the ringer isn't turned off and that the battery is charged.

Why have they been silent since yesterday—have they killed my son? I thought more than once about calling Uthaiman, to ask if anyone had contacted him. But yesterday Uthaiman showed himself a coward when I said, "Come with me." Maybe he's afraid to meet me, for fear I will bring up the subject again. My office phone rings.

"Mr. Yaqoub, Uthaiman would like to see you."

"Have him come in."

"Peace be upon you," Uthaiman said upon entering.

I sensed that he was hiding something. "Have they gotten in touch with you?"

"The brother of the martyr called, warning us not to play with the murderers."

I almost shouted at him, Uthaiman, you're one of them and you're working with them! But instead I said, "What else?"

"He told me they contacted him through the intermediary, and that they will kill Sheikh Ahmad the moment they find that we intend anything underhanded with them." I stared at him, hating his devious way of speaking. "He just now called me, begging me to take extreme care with Sheikh Ahmad's life."

"Didn't he say anything about their share of the ransom?" My angry question shocked him into silence. "Uthaiman, I have the feeling that Ahmad is the victim of a dirty plot, and that more than one party is complicit in it."

He was silent, his face and his eyes tinged with fear, then he answered, "Abu Du'aij, if they call another time, I won't answer them."

I went on staring at him, exhaling my anger. "Do you remember the Egyptian Abdel Shafi, the one you and Ismail defended, and the teacher Omar? I wish I could kill them both! They are the ones who created Abu l-Fath al-Kuwaiti, they are the ones who led my son astray, they are the true killers!"

He rose to his feet, his face flushed, but I motioned to him to stay. “Sit down, I haven’t finished.” An explosive silence hung between us. I felt that he had nothing to tell me, and that I would have to get my son out on my own. I told him, “If Ahmad’s friend or anyone else calls you, have him talk to me.”

30

It's lonely in the hotel suite.

A little while ago I had a call from Shaikha, asking if there was anything new. "Not a thing," I told her. And I warned her sternly. "I don't want any person to know a word of this, not Uthaiman, not Du'aij, not Abrar, not Sahar, not your mother, not any of your sis—"

"I understand. You don't have to give me the list. I won't utter a word." Then she changed the subject, asking me about lunch and when I would be home.

"Don't wait for me. I'll return when I please." I ended the call without waiting for a reply.

It was twelve-thirty when I got to the suite, which seemed plunged in silence. There was no trace of Farnaz's perfume, and I realized that I had neglected her for the last few hours, though I was still pervaded by the sense of having a different kind of connection with her. Without thinking, I sent her a message: "Come over, I'm in the suite." Moments later the reply came: "I'll come by during the break."

I sat alone, anxiety gnawing at my heart. What's happened? Why have they cut off all contact yesterday and today? Has Uthaiman told anyone in Syria about what passed between us? My mouth was dry, so I got up, took the water bottle, and drank a mouthful. Suddenly there was a message on my phone with a link. My shoulder trembled, then my hand holding the phone—had they killed my son? The link took me to a video showing Ahmad, bare as before, tied to a wooden chair, with a large, masked man standing beside him, holding a chain saw. It may have been the same room as before, with its mud walls and dirt floor. Ahmad lifted a face covered with bruises and spoke to the camera in a broken voice: "Baba, please, for God's sake, pay the ransom and don't tell anyone."

I felt my knees buckling, so I threw myself down on the couch. At that moment the phone rang, and the familiar long number appeared on the screen. When I answered, I heard the same awful voice that had spoken to me the last time.

"You've seen your dog of a son, and you've seen how thirsty the saw is for his unclean flesh." He went on, loading his voice with anger. "Within twenty-four hours you'll be in Tehran. We'll give you the details when you arrive."

"Tehran?" I asked in amazement.

"You're not deaf. You heard what I said. If you want your son, come to Tehran. We won't call after this. We expect you in Tehran within twenty-four hours, and beware, beware of deceiving us, or else we'll kill your renegade dog of a son." He was silent for a few seconds, as if checking something, then he said, "When you arrive in Tehran we'll contact you."

The call was cut off abruptly. I felt as if I was stumbling, weak, unable to catch my breath. Once more I threw myself on the couch, trembling all over.

Uthaiman told me that they were in northern Syria or Iraq, and now they wanted me in Tehran! Have I entangled myself in going to their lair? I don't think I can turn back now. They're waiting for me in Tehran—will I be the reason my son is killed? I felt the room spinning around me, and at that moment the door opened and Farnaz came in, closing the door behind her. She stared at me, clearly appalled by my look of defeat and the dazed expression on my face.

"Good afternoon." Fear seeped into her voice. At first I stared at her, then, I don't know how, I stood up and went to her, clasping her to my heart. She stood subdued, my breath brushing her neck. I don't know how long the embrace lasted, but when I came back to myself I found what I had done strange, and I didn't know what to say except "I'm sorry."

"Are you ill?" I lifted my head and looked at her, the girl who had taken my heart, with her sweet gaze, her tender smile, and the small beauty mark on her lip. She tossed down her purse, took off her head covering, picked up the water bottle and poured out a glass for me. "Drink, Mr. Yaqoub."

I took the glass obediently. "If I tell you a secret, can you keep it and not reveal it to anyone?"

Our eyes met. She sat near me and said, "I swear to you that I will not say a single word to anyone."

There was a moment of silence. I looked at her face and her eyes, and saw there something that encouraged me to whisper, as if in fear of someone hearing my words, "This afternoon or this evening I'm going to Tehran."

I saw the look of astonishment in her eyes as the word escaped her: "Tehran?"

I was afraid to tell her the secret of my son, and I don't know... the silence returned.

"Mr. Yaqoub, I swear to God that if you tell me a single word more, I will not reveal it even if they slaughtered me."

I looked again into her eyes. I moved closer to take her head in my hands and kiss her forehead. "I'm going to Tehran because my son has been kidnapped there."

She looked startled. "Your son has been kidnapped?"

Like someone under hypnosis, I told her the story. She was silent, a look of shock on her face. Finally, I said, "I'll have to reserve a ticket immediately to Tehran. If I'm late, they'll kill my son."

"Who will be with you there?" I kept looking at her but said nothing. Then she offered what seemed like a suggestion. "My brother is in Tehran."

I needed a moment to take this in. "Farnaz, this is very dangerous. You did tell me that he's a soldier, but what makes you think he would agree?"

"My brother is on vacation, and he loves Kuwait. I'll ask for his help. I'll beg him to stay with you." A moment of silence passed. "I won't impose any obligation on him. He can excuse himself, or refuse if he likes."

The veil has been lifted, I told myself. This is the end of the thread. My heart became attached to Farnaz to bring me to her brother, and he will take me by the hand to rescue my son.

"Mr. Yaqoub, Reza is a kind man. He won't hesitate to help you."

"Farnaz, please don't involve your brother in something dangerous, something that might harm him and affect his future."

"Have you ever visited Tehran before, or had a project there? Do you know anyone there?"

I shook my head.

"It's not right for you to be on your own!"

"I don't know what's waiting for me there."

"Reza knows every inch of Iran. For more than seven years

he's been transferred from one place to another, from one assignment to another." A silence descended on us that felt transparent. "Please, Mr. Yaqoub, trust me!"

"It's not your affair only. You're speaking for your brother, and he's a soldier."

"I know him. If he realizes that he can't help you, he'll make his excuses."

Silence returned to sit between us. Without another word, she got up and went to her purse—the one I had bought for her. She took out her phone and activated the speaker as she spoke to a young man on the other end. "Hello, Reza."

"Hello, dear Farnaz!"

"Reza, there's a problem. The owner of the company I work for, who is a very kind man, needs help in Tehran. Can you meet him and stay with him?"

"Of course, of course! I'll be at his disposal as long as he's in Tehran."

"Reza, dear, it's a difficult matter and it could be dangerous."

"Is he going to the hospital for treatment?"

"No, no... it's something else."

"Farnaz, you know that I'm on vacation. Let him come, and I promise you that I'll stay with him the whole time, and I'll do what he asks."

I took the phone from Farnaz and spoke to him. "Hello, Reza."

"Hello, sir."

"Please don't take a burden on yourself. It's a difficult matter, and as your sister said, it's dangerous."

He was silent for a moment, and then answered, "Sir, you are from Kuwait, and you're sent to me by my sister. I'll be there for you in whatever you ask."

"I don't want you to say a single word to anyone until we meet."

"Of course, of course."

"You must keep silent, as if you never heard a word. Can you do that?"

"Sir, I'm a military man, and I'll consider your instructions the equivalent of a military order. I won't discuss it or transgress it."

I passed the phone to Farnaz, who spoke to him. "Thank you, dear Reza! I'll call you and give you Mr. Yaqoub's arrival time in Tehran. Once again, please take care of Mr. Yaqoub—don't leave him until he comes back to Kuwait. And there's something else important: I don't want you to tell Mother or Father anything, ever."

"Farnaz, it's done. I'll wait for the man. I'll be there for everything he wants, and I won't say a word to anyone."

"Goodbye, Reza."

As Farnaz closed her phone, I said to myself, it's a matter of following the trail, it's the intuition in my heart.

Silence returned to sit between us again.

31

I've chosen an isolated corner to sit in. The first-class lounge seems quiet.

Yesterday afternoon, I asked Shaikha not to tell Uthaiman about my trip. "If he asks you, say, 'I don't know.'" I hesitated to tell her that I have very real doubts about her brother, that I'm almost certain that he has a connection to the community, and that I plan to call him to account and maybe throw him out of my company when I get back.

I didn't want Marwan to reserve the ticket, as then Ismail and Uthaiman would know about it. I asked Shaikha to reserve it without telling anyone—Kuwait Airways Flight KU515, departing at twelve noon.

This morning, I said goodbye to Shaikha and left the house about eight-thirty. I had two hours before I needed to be at the airport. I drove the car myself, heading for the office; I wanted to give everyone, and first and foremost Uthaiman, the impression that I was in Kuwait. I thought that maybe it would be better to inform him, but something held me back.

Marwan came in with the mail file and put it in front of me. I kept him with me and signed the transactions, then returned the folder to him.

At ten, I left for the airport; I got here an hour and a half before departure.

Yesterday, after I said goodbye to Farnaz and got into my car, I called my friend Daniel, who manages my accounts in a Swiss bank. I told him that I needed to have ten million American dollars at my disposal; I was about to transfer that sum to another party at any moment, as part of a large commercial deal I was entering into. He seemed relaxed as he spoke with me; he asked me when I was coming to Geneva again, then said goodbye. He assured me, "Consider the sum ready for transfer starting now."

This morning, I contacted Farnaz and asked her to have her brother rent a good car and prepare to stay with me for five days. "I want an excellent car, and of course I'll pay for it." I emphasized, "No one must know a thing, neither inside the company nor outside, nor anyone from your family."

She replied that she had not told her brother any more than she had said in front of me. She had told him that I would say more on the way.

I asked Shaikha to buy a new telephone for me, with a new number, and to call me only on that number; I would not answer any other caller. I sent the number to Farnaz, also, saying, "Our calls should be on this number."

The airport café is quiet; I asked the waiter for tea. I haven't had anything since breakfast. I packed a small bag for my trip: underclothes, pajamas, and five thousand dollars for expenses.

Shaikha was hovering over me, tears in her eyes. "Yaqoub, what you're doing is madness, by God!" She was broadcasting her fears. "You're putting yourself in danger by dealing with terrorists!"

I hid my plan to meet Reza from her. "I've bought the ticket and made my arrangements. There's no call to talk about our fears!" She gave in to my wishes, her voice breaking on her appeal. "May our Lord bring you both back safe and sound!"

As I was leaving the company, I had a message from Farnaz on the new number. "Good morning." She wanted to check on me, and repeated that she had told her brother to take good care of me, not to leave me for an instant, and to stay with me the whole time until I came back. She said, "God willing, you will get your wish!"

The waiter placed the tea before me, a small cookie beside it.

I don't know anything about Ahmad's condition. Since the call yesterday, I haven't received any other message from them. The man said, "When you reach the airport in Tehran we'll contact you." Ever since then, I've been wondering how they will know when I've arrived in Tehran.

Farnaz told me that she had sent a picture of me to her brother. When I asked her where she got it, she laughed and replied, "From the albums of Our Lord Google." She told me that she sent a picture of me in a shirt and pants, without any other information.

This trip is unlike any other I've taken in my life. Never once did I think about visiting the Islamic Republic of Iran, although it's no more than two and a half hours from Kuwait. I have the idea that the rulers of Iran have harbored enmity toward the Arabs ever since Khalid ibn al-Walid defeated them and conquered the country in the seventh century, putting an end to the Sasanian Empire, and ever since Saad ibn Abi Waqas completed the conquest at the Battle of Qadisiya. Here my fate is leading me to them at the worst moment of my life.

I don't know what my encounter with Ahmad's kidnappers will be like, or where it will be. I hope they don't harm my son.

Maybe he'll agree to come back to Kuwait with me. Even if he doesn't have a visa, I can contact the Kuwaiti ambassador in Tehran as soon as Ahmad is seated beside me. I won't leave him this time, I'll stay right by his side.

Only now does it occur to me that I did not bargain with them—I didn't say five million, or seven. All I could see before me was Ahmad, bruised and broken, humbly pleading that I pay the ransom. In my heart, he's worth all the money in the world.

O my son, what brought you to where you are? Maybe I should have told Ismail about my trip, but he would certainly take the news to Uthaiman, and I don't want Uthaiman to know a thing. He must have told Ismail about Ahmad being captured, and of course he would tell his group in Syria about my movements. I'll try to concentrate on my negotiations with the captors; I'll tell them, "Deliver him, and you'll get the money!" I'll say I won't transfer the ransom until they give me my son.

Farnaz's brother Reza will meet me and stay with me. I don't know what our meeting will be like, or what he will say when he learns more about the task. I hope he will agree; my situation would be much worse if he refused to accompany me. But he's a military man, and he has every right to keep his job.

From the first moment I saw her I had a premonition, and now it's become clear: she has asked her brother to help me rescue my son. But how will I deal with Farnaz when I get back? How will our relationship continue, and will I still be in love with her?

A hostess from Kuwaiti Airways comes to me. "Sir, are you traveling to Tehran?"

"Yes."

"Please come with me. We have a car waiting to take you to the plane."

"Thank you." I picked up my bag and followed her. I had told Shaikha, "One pair of pants is enough, with a jacket and two shirts." I told the hostess that I would carry my small bag.

"Please go ahead."

I got into the car. Shaikha cried as she said goodbye. "God willing you'll come back with Ahmad!" But Farnaz, in a charged voice, made her wish clear. "I'll come to the suite to meet you and congratulate you on the return of your son." This morning she sent me a picture of Reza with the caption: "My brother Reza, who loves Kuwait."

Here's the plane. As I get out of the car, I'm filled with questions about what's waiting for me in Tehran.

32

They are murderers, and I've blindly, stubbornly insisted on not informing anyone that I'm about to meet them.

I don't remember anything about the two hours of the flight. I was plunged into my thoughts, my anxieties, and my fear of what lay in store, the image of Ahmad always with me. A little while ago the plane landed at the airport in Tehran; everything seemed new to me. At last, here I am in the Islamic Republic of Iran, after decades of hating the thought of it.

I stood before the officer in the airport and handed him my passport. He examined it and asked, "Have you gotten a visa?"

"No."

He began examining me. "You have to get an entry visa."

"I was told I could obtain one at the airport."

He told me to go to another window and handed me my passport, attaching a small paper to it, which he stamped with the word "visa." The second officer asked me about the reason for my visit, and I said "tourism." He took sixty dollars from me, then handed back my passport with the entry stamp.

I looked for the exit sign, feeling a small tremor in my back. I've traveled alone my whole life, but this airport is filled with policemen, and with chadors that cover the heads of the women. I feel as if I'm lost among crowds of people and incomprehensible babble.

When I went out to the parking lot and looked around, I soon saw a young man coming toward me. The picture of Reza appeared in my mind, and he said, "Welcome, Mr. Yaqoub! Thank God for your safe arrival."

He shook my hand warmly. He was in his early thirties, with an open face, an athletic build, and regular features—attractive eyes and eyebrows, and a straight nose over a black mustache. He was wearing a shirt, pants, and a jacket. "Please come with me. The car is ready."

"Is there a café nearby?"

"Yes."

"Let's go there first."

He seemed friendly, speaking with a Kuwaiti accent as he told me, "I was born and raised in Kuwait, and it's my second country."

As we sat down, I was careful to choose an isolated table. He asked for tea, and I said to him, "I must inform you of the task ahead, before we begin." A moment of silence passed, then I said, "You are a security officer, and your work might conflict with accompanying me." His eyes lit up with interest. "My son has been kidnapped here, and I've come to pay the ransom and get him back."

I saw his face change, stunned by surprise. He asked, "Do you know the kidnappers?"

"It's a group from al-Qaeda or Daesh."

"Oh no," he exclaimed, sounding astonished. "Have you informed the Kuwaiti government?"

"No."

"Wouldn't it be right to inform the Kuwaiti ambassador, and the Iranian police?"

"I won't inform any party."

"I'm sorry to say it, but that's very dangerous—both for you and your son."

"They threatened to kill him if I tell anyone. One of them may be observing me now—they know a lot about me."

He was looking at me with amazement tinged with fear when my telephone rang. The familiar voice came to me: "You have entered the Tehran airport. Now you must take a taxi and come immediately to the city of Semnan."

I put the phone on speaker so Reza could listen with me. Since I had not spoken, the voice asked, "Do you hear me? Semnan is two hundred and twenty kilometers from Tehran. You have to take Route 44. Do you hear me?"

"Yes."

"We'll send you the site of a small hotel in Semnan. Spend the night there." Suddenly the call was cut off, and I turned to Reza.

"As I suspected, I'm being watched."

"Uncle." He said that instinctively, so I let him finish. "I don't know what's waiting for you. This is a scary situation, especially because Daesh has ties to al-Qaeda, and they are terrorists who attach no value to any human life."

"You have every right to refuse."

"Excuse me, I'm not refusing to help you. But allow me to be frank: your plan is not a good one. It puts you both in danger."

"You're correct. But I've been in contact with them and we've come to an agreement, and what matters to me is my son's life."

"Mr. Yaqoub, I love Kuwait. My family and I are indebted to it, and you are a Kuwaiti who needs help. I promised my sister and I will keep my promise, and I will be with you until you leave Iran and go back to Kuwait. But I don't support your going alone to negotiate with them." As I was weighing his words, he declared, "Telling the police is the safest way out."

"I'm sorry, but I have placed my trust in God and made my decision. I won't inform any party."

"But your enemies do not know God; they are killers."

"As I said, you have the right to refuse. I have just one request—that you conceal what you've heard from me even from yourself."

He paused, as if contemplating me and weighing how serious I was. "Mr. Yaqoub, I will go with you, even if I still wish that you would change your mind."

"If you come with me and they ask about you at any point, what will you say to them?"

"I'm a taxi driver."

"What about the car?"

"I've rented a private taxi with a license." I watched him, both bold and hesitant. Something in his face reminded me of Farnaz, and something in his tone set my heart at ease. "Mr. Yaqoub," he said, "Iran is a country ruled by secret services of all kinds. The police have many resources of their own that would never even cross your mind, means to pursue kidnappers and reach them. They are more able to deal with the situation and to get your son out, especially if they know that he's a citizen of another country."

"What if the kidnappers kill my son?"

"No one can guarantee what will happen. As I said before, al-Qaeda are killers, and they care nothing for the soul of any man. Excuse me for asking, but what is the ransom they asked you for?" I stared at him, wondering what he might think of me if I told him the sum. He hastened to say, "If you don't want to say, that's your right."

Maybe I should have informed the Kuwaiti Ministry of Foreign Affairs and let them handle the task of bringing back a child of Kuwait. I could have called his excellency the prime minister. Perhaps I've made the wrong decision. Shaikha said, "I've lost my son, and I don't want to lose you!" And Uthaiman rejected the idea that I be the one to negotiate and get Ahmad back.

I feel cold sweat seeping from my body. Reza's voice comes to me. "Forgive me, Mr. Yaqoub, but it's not too late. I can take you right away to the headquarters of the secret services and the police in Tehran, and they can take over the case. You won't lose anything. They will certainly inform the Kuwaiti embassy, and you'll be under their protection."

I am torn, unable to make a decision. They told me again that they would cut my son in pieces with a saw if I told anyone, and now I've told my wife and Farnaz, as well as Reza, who is a police officer. Ahmad had begged me, "Don't tell anyone."

I tell myself that if it's a matter of money, then my son is dearer than all the millions in the world, and if a transcendent force is pushing me to confront my fate, then there's no turning away God's decree. I'm resolved; I've made my decision, and I won't turn back. I asked Reza, "Are you afraid to come with me?"

"No, by God—I'm afraid for you and for your son."

I waited a few seconds, looking at him. Then I said, "As long as you're not afraid, then there's no call for delay."

My telephone signaled a message containing a link, which took me to Google Maps. Reza's voice came to me again. "Uncle, for the last time, I'm cautioning you, I'm advising you. It's your decision and your responsibility. But if you're determined, then drink the tea. Then we'll place our faith in God. The road is long; we might arrive around seven tonight."

Showing him my determination, I stood up and said, "Let's place our faith in God."

33

"Please, sir." Reza took me to a white Toyota and opened the door for me.

I had my phone open to the map that would take us to Semnan, but as we moved off, Reza said, "There's no need for that—I've worked in the city and I know the way. Before we get there we'll use your phone to find the hotel."

How does a person trust another? How does a fond, trusting relationship grow between people? I wondered about this as I stole glances at the young man I did not know, and who did not know me, who was meeting me for the first time in his life and yet complying with my wishes, risking his life and his position in order to help me.

My heart told me the moment I glimpsed Farnaz by the elevator that she was a message and that I should follow the track. Flashes from her eyes attracted me, and now her bother is driving me to my son. Up until now I have not promised him anything, nor did I raise Farnaz's hopes with any promise.

When we got in the car, Reza said, "Uncle, the road takes about three and a half hours. I know a café about halfway there, in an area called Garmsar. We can stop there to have some coffee and rest a bit."

"Fine," I said. I felt as if I was in a dream.

As we drove, I looked at the scenery without any of it staying in my mind. I was forced to come here, and I'm not here for pleasure, for sightseeing, or on vacation. I had the strange feeling that I was far from Kuwait, far from my country, from the people I know, from my relations and my position, far removed from any power or influence. I'm used to traveling on the basis of my importance and my reputation, always finding a welcome and a luxury car waiting. But here I am in a small car driven by a young Iranian who dreams of visiting Kuwait, who could do whatever he likes with me, no questions asked.

What had Farnaz told him? He must know that I'm a millionaire. But what would he do if he knew I had made a date with his sister, taken her to a hotel, hugged her close, and kissed her? I looked at him stealthily, but his silence put me at ease. I'm not good at talking to strangers, and I don't like to be subject to their curiosity and intrusive questions.

"Uncle, I lived in Kuwait longer than I've lived in Iran." I simply looked at him, as if I had nothing to say in reply. Perhaps he understood my anxious feelings of loss and my fear, as he said nothing else.

The road was well paved and the traffic was light after we left the congestion of Tehran. "I came to Iran eight years ago," he said. "And rather than spending two years I served three in the army and a year and a half in the police. Since I'm proficient in Arabic, English, and Farsi, I received advanced training and became an officer."

"Are you happy in your work?"

"God be thanked." His tone suggested dissatisfaction. He fell silent, and I sensed that he was stumbling over something he wanted to say. We were traveling on an asphalt road, carved for the most part between the bare, rocky mountains tinged by colors of yellow and burnt brown.

Our silence continued as we drove on until he let out a complaint. "At work they call me 'the Kuwaiti.' Unfortunately, in Kuwait I'm Iranian, and in my own country I'm accused of being Kuwaiti. And there's a big difference between us in our way of thinking, in dealing with life. Sometimes I find their behavior strange!" He looked at me from the corner of his eye and then went on. "A Persian by his nature is very proud, and fiercely attached to his ethnic origins; in their view, I'm not a pure Persian. So since I graduated, they've kept tossing me from one department to another, from one province to another, from one dangerous job to another. Whenever I told myself that I would settle here, I would be surprised by a transfer to another province. They have promenaded me up one side of the country and down the other, as if they were taking vengeance on me!"

As I listened to him, the picture of Ahmad being tortured pursued me. Just then, the new telephone rang. It was Shaikha.

"Have you arrived safely?"

"I have, God keep you safe."

"Where are you now?"

"I'm on my way to a city named Semnan."

"Is that where you will get Ahmad back?"

"I don't know. I'll call you if anything new happens." I hung up, but she soon called back.

"Why did you hang up? I wasn't finished speaking."

I hesitated to tell her that her voice moved me to tears. Instead, I said, "I don't have any news now. If anything new happens, I'll tell you." Once again, I hung up.

"Uncle, we've come into the city of Garmsar, and we'll soon reach the coffee shop, where we can rest a little."

"Fine." I felt as if I had forgotten my body during the last few days; I was completely exhausted.

We sat in the café for about a quarter of an hour. Everything around me was astonishing: the smell of the place, the voices and accents of the people, their clothes, the looks in their eyes, the tables, the chairs, the tablecloths, the plastic flowers, the television screen . . . I had a cup of coffee, and he took a glass of tea and smoked a cigarette. When I started to pay, I discovered that I did not have any Iranian money. He smiled and said, "You're my guest."

We returned to the car, and as soon as we moved off, he said, "My father tried to get a visa for me to visit, but he couldn't get one."

"God willing, when I get back to Kuwait I'll arrange a visa for you."

"That would be a great favor. I won't forget it." Gratitude was clear in his voice and on his face. "I haven't seen Kuwait since I left it."

It occurred to me to wonder if it made any sense for a young man to risk his life for a visa. Images came to my mind of men, women, and children in traffickers' small boats, drowning as they dreamed of getting to Europe.

Silence settled between us. Uthaiman had told me that Ahmad was in a battle in the area of al-Bukamal, so I told the person who called me that I was prepared to go. I'm from a generation that was raised on the dream of one large Arab homeland, so something inside me still sees any Arab region as part of my country—the people's faces, the tone of their speech, the architecture of their houses, their streets, their trees, their coffee shops, their food, even something in the smell of the air. I never imagined that the kidnappers were in Iran. It would have been easier for me if the site had been in Iraq or Syria, but Iran—nothing links me to it! I never once imagined that I would be forced to come to it, and that my son's rescue would take place in its territory.

I was far away, lost in my thoughts and my fears, with images of Ahmad in my head, when Reza asked, "Uncle, is this your first visit to the Islamic Republic?"

"Yes."

Ever since we first shook hands, he has called me "uncle." Maybe it's a habit he learned in Kuwait, where a younger man will call an older man "uncle." It shows fondness, closeness, and respect, as if the man were his father's brother.

"Iran is beautiful and it has everything, but poverty and want devastate the people."

I recalled that he had lived in Kuwait in a small apartment and was raised by a poor man who drove a one-eight. "Was your life in Kuwait better?"

"Definitely." He answered without hesitation. "Kuwait is a good country."

Sunset began creeping into the car. Ever since I was small I've hated the sunset, when some hidden monster grips my heart. "Uncle, I've come with you as you wished, but I hope you'll allow me a little leeway."

"What do you mean?"

"I know the city of Semnan, and I'm certain that they won't negotiate with you here. It's a congested residential area, with a large contingent of security forces, intelligence units, police, and army. Semnan will be a stopover for us, on our way somewhere else."

"What do you mean?"

"We won't go to the hotel they specified. I know a simple hotel where we can sleep without anyone asking for your identification. It will be enough for me to show them mine."

"What about Ahmad? I'm afraid they'll hurt him."

"Mr. Yaqoub, they are much more dependent on you now than you are on them. They are your prisoners now. Believe me, they won't kill your son now, because the ransom is many times more important to them than killing him."

Darkness had taken us unawares, filling the car. Reza's words only increased my uncertainty. It was the first time I had felt so weak, as if I were a small child. I wished I could cry.

"Uncle, please trust me." I looked at him; he was the only one offering to help me now. "They want you to stay in Semnan, and we will stay there. If they know you did not stay in that hotel, that means the hotel is under their control and in contact with them, and we should not be an easy prey."

I said nothing, telling myself, Yaqoub, you are a small boat, a piece of wood tossed by the waves. You made a mistake in your decision, and your stubbornness has plunged you into something you don't know. Neither your money nor your influence means a thing now!

"We're reaching the outskirts of the city of Semnan. What do you want me to do?"

My voice came out weakly. "Do as you think best."

"We'll go to the police."

"No, no, no. We'll go the hotel you spoke of."

34

When we arrived in Semnan yesterday evening, he took me to a small hotel. He stopped the car and said, “Wait for me a few minutes. Of course you can get out of the car.”

He was clearly leading me now; I had given myself over to him with no objection. I told myself that I had never been as weak and broken as I am now, and could only wonder what tomorrow would bring. Once again, I was beset with the fear that I had made a tragic mistake.

The private telephone rang, showing the number of al-Khayyam, and I rushed to answer it. “Farnaz,” I said. “I’m with Reza, I’ll talk to you later.” I hung up as Reza was coming toward me.

“I’ve reserved two connected rooms, and now I know a restaurant that serves good Iranian food.”

His words reminded me that I was hungry and that I had not had a meal since I woke up. “I am hungry. But first let’s go someplace where I can get some Iranian money.”

He hesitated for a moment and then said, “There’s no need for that. You are my guest, and I’m happy to be with you.” I smiled, and he added, “I’m returning some of Kuwait’s kindness to me.”

“Thank you very much. And let’s go to the currency exchange.”

The exchange was near the restaurant, where I ate ravenously from hunger and fatigue.

I slept dead to the world that night. At five in the morning I received a message, which took me to a video. It showed Ahmad being thrown on the ground of the earthen room, his hands tied behind his back and his feet bound. Bruises and wounds covered every part of his body, and a huge man was kicking him. A strange tremor passed through my body. There was a bitter taste in my mouth, and the smell of blood rose to my nostrils.

I felt the silence surrounding my room. Reza took two adjoining rooms, separated by a door. When we went up to the second floor, he asked me to choose which room I wanted; I told him it didn't matter.

As we were getting out of the car, it seemed that he was trying to hide something from me. I took care not to learn what he carried, but he surprised me by putting his hand into his breast pocket and pulling out a handgun. "This is my revolver—I brought it with me as a precaution."

I called him when the message came to me, and before he arrived, a second message came: "You did not sleep in the hotel we specified yesterday. You will regret any dirty tricks you try to play on us. We will meet you in Mashhad at two-thirty this afternoon."

I showed Reza the two messages, and he said, "Mashhad is about seven hundred kilometers away." He scratched his head and added, "We will have to leave immediately to be there in time. It's a long road, and it could take eight hours."

As we left the hotel, he said, "We'll eat on the road."

He was waiting for my response, so I said, "I'm not thinking about eating."

He settled our account at the hotel, and we got back into the car. I was still like someone hypnotized, seeing everything around me as if through the glass of the present moment. I told him that they knew I had not slept in the hotel they specified, and he answered that they might own the hotel, or at the least it might belong to someone collaborating with them. Semnan seemed full of traffic as it met the morning. For a moment I missed waking to the calm and luxury of my room, my house, and my garden.

"I don't think they will negotiate with you in Mashhad."

Reza's voice called me back, and I responded, "They said they would."

"Mashhad is a very busy city. It's the second-largest city in the Islamic Republic and the tomb of Imam Ali ibn Musa al-Rida is there. It's also in the grip of the intelligence services, and I think it's very unlikely that they will be there."

I looked at him, as if he were showing me the plan for my day. "What do you think?"

"When we arrive in Mashhad, our real journey will begin. Maybe they'll take us to an area called Birjand. I think so, but I'm not sure."

"Birjand?" Something about the sound of the word captured my attention.

"It's a city south of Mashhad, in the southern part of Khorasan. It's considered a frontier area with Afghanistan."

My heart began to beat fast. I asked him, fearfully, "Are they going to pull us into Afghanistan?"

"No, we'll stay in Iran. But the frontier area is dangerous and full of al-Qaeda and their helpers."

My heart beat even faster. As if he understood what I was

feeling, he said, "Uncle, I worked in the area of Birjand for nearly a year, and I know it like the back of my hand. But I still think that contacting the police would be safer for you and for your son." He said what he had to say, then drove on in silence.

O Ahmad, why are you doing this to me? The question came to me, and with it the image of Ahmad being thrown face down on the earthen floor. Have you tortured anyone Ahmad? Are you tasting what you've done to others? Were you harsh with innocent people, as al-Qaeda is with you now? Why have they held you? Is it because you are the group commander? Or because you are Abu l-Fath al-Kuwaiti? Or do they know how rich I am?

"We'll arrive soon in a city called Shahrud. We'll stop to have breakfast, but we won't delay. Tea and maybe a sandwich and then we'll be on our way."

"As you like."

My God, I've become obedient! Farnaz gave me to her brother, and he's leading me as one would a child. I've become weaker and weaker, just when I was at the height of my powers! What is it that breaks a man's spirit and brings him to a state of helplessness he could never have imagined?

"Excuse me, what kind of sandwich would you like?"

"Coffee is most important."

"We'll have coffee and take a cup of tea with us for the road, then we'll have lunch in Sabzevar later on."

"I'm not thinking about eating."

He went into the restaurant while I stayed in the car. He came back carrying coffee, tea, and sandwiches, then quickly sat behind the wheel and started off. He was saying, "It's a long way, and we mustn't be late."

I thought about his determination and kept to my silence. How would I repay this young man for all the help he was giving me? I would not promise that I would get him a visa, so as not to impose a burden of gratitude on him.

"Reza, I'm grateful to you for all you're doing for my sake."

"Pardon me, but I've had a question ever since yesterday."

"What is it?"

"I have a friend in Mashhad who is an intelligence officer, and who lived for some years in Kuwait. Would you allow me to speak to him, and would you allow him to come with us?"

"No." I answered immediately, and then added, "I agreed for you to be with me because you are Farnaz's brother, and because I trust you."

There was a moment of silence as the car devoured the space separating us from our destination. I reached for the water bottle I had brought from the hotel; my mouth was dry.

"As you like, sir. It's just a thought."

I asked him to slow down, then said firmly, "Please stop for a moment."

He slowed to a stop, then I asked him to turn off the motor. I looked at him; something in his face and the look in his eyes reminded me of Farnaz. I told him, "Reza, you are not obligated to come with me. You can set me down here and I'll figure out how to manage myself."

He just looked at me. When I said nothing more, he restarted the motor. Before he set off, he turned to me and said, "I made a promise to my sister and to you that I would not leave you until you return to Kuwait. May God keep us both."

35

There is no god but thou: glory to thee: I was indeed wrong!

O God, you are the mighty, the avenger, O God, hasten my deliverance! My God, help me to bear the torture of the tyrants, for the sake of the majesty of your will, in obedience to you, to draw near to your noble face, O God! O my God, honor me with martyrdom, O God!

Ever since I arrived here, there has been nothing but interrogation and torture. Martyrdom would be a mercy for me, the longed-for meeting with the beloved, the chosen, together with his pure companions, and a paradise as broad as the earth and the heavens.

For days I was blindfolded, bound hand and foot, and crammed into the trunk of a car, as it passed through potholed streets, turning off only to resume the journey, not stopping except at night. Then I was permitted to relieve myself in some waste land, and they gave me some bread and water. After a long journey I guessed we were traveling in Iraqi territory, since that's Daesh country. I was thoroughly shaken when I learned that they told my father to go to Tehran!

During the first days of their interrogation, they kept me from sleeping; whenever my strength gave out and my eyes closed, they came to torture me and poured a bucket of cold water over me. I fainted more than once. They asked me about the leaders' meeting places, citing names I knew and others I did not. They dwelled on arms depots and our relations with the American army.

They tortured me until I wished for martyrdom, asking me about the sources of the group's financing. Sometimes I was silent and other times I dodged the questions. They gave me beatings beyond what I could bear. I often thought that my spirit was leaving my body, and I pronounced the profession of faith.

"O God, I have wronged myself greatly. No one forgives sins but you, extend your forgiveness to me and have mercy on me, you are indeed the all-forgiving, the merciful!"

I was surprised when they asked me for my father's telephone number, since I have not carried a phone for over two years, and I don't remember it. I told them I did not know it. More than once I felt my spirit nearly return to its creator under their torture, as I swore, "By God Almighty and Most High, I have not memorized his number! You can get it from Ibrahim." But their answer stunned me and brought me to tears. "He got his reward, he croaked." I didn't know whether to believe it, but I wept for my brother Ibrahim, the martyr, and prayed to God that he was among the companions of the Prophet (God bless him and give him peace), and would be resurrected with the martyrs, the pious, and the righteous.

They handed me over to a huge brute, who beat me and kicked me in every part of my body, shouting "Speak!" But I didn't know what I should say. They took my torture to extremes, imagining that my father was the one who transferred money to us. I didn't want to reveal the role of my uncle to them, so after I nearly died I told them, "Call Abu Bilal, he'll get my father's number."

In the last few months it has occurred to me that there's no solution for our conflict with Daesh, either now or in the foreseeable future. We hope they will turn to God in repentance and come to their senses, but if that does not happen, then the only solution is fighting. Every time, I tell myself again that it's clear that they won't repent or come to their senses.

My God, I'm still thinking about how I was captured and fell into their hands. There's no escape from God's will! I remember that my brother Ibrahim was behind me, and that God (all praise and glory to him) had supported us so we achieved the goal of the operation, blowing up their headquarters and killing those enemies of God and of religion. Then they began firing on us, bullets were raining down from different directions. I knew my back was protected, and I heard Ibrahim's voice crying *Allahu akbar*, and that's the last thing I remember from the battle.

I hear the door opening. O God, O my savior! "You're going to perish at our hands, you enemy of God!"

Two men came toward me, each one holding a stun baton. I know this damnable weapon.

One of them comes to me and hits me with it. Ah! Ah! I feel my limbs flying in pieces in the air, then falling to the ground. Once again there's pressure on my body, then the fragments fly… Ah! O God! I testify that there is no god but God!

"You will tell the damned usurer, your father, to come. You will only tell him to come, any other word from you will condemn you and him. Got it?"

"Ah! Ah!"

"Do you understand what you have to say?"

"Ah! Ah! I'll say it! Father, come, please come!"

Every part of my body is trembling. I can't draw breath, I can't open my eyes, as if the tears and blood...I can hardly see anything. I don't know what they'll do with the video of me. Maybe they'll lure my father to pay blood money. I hope he doesn't come—I'm afraid he'll be killed.

My God, "Do not entrust me to myself even for the blink of an eye." My God, you are my glory, grant me martyrdom.

I remember when I drilled for nearly a month to blow up a truck in the unbelievers' camp. I memorized the way there, and a little before zero hour they stopped me and gave the operation to one of my brother jihadis, and in it he attained the face of God, may he be praised and glorified, and was martyred. Three months later I was assigned an explosion near some barracks; the explosives were placed around my waist and loaded onto the truck. I bade farewell to my wife, rejoicing in my heart over how close I was to leaving this corruptible world for the everlasting hereafter, to meeting the beloved Muhammad and his noble companions in paradise. A few hours only separated me from attaining martyrdom and meeting the beloved there. But once again instructions came at the very last minute; the operation was stopped and then given to a brother who was my partner, but who carried it out alone, by the will of God. That was just before I was named as the commanding emir. Ibrahim, may God grant him mercy, said to me, "Maybe they were testing your steadiness," adding, "It's not right to sacrifice a brave leader and someone who funds the community!"

I hear their voices. My body is still shaking. I may have peed on myself; I feel liquid below me.

I don't know where I am. My God, I have none but you, lord of heaven and earth. O my God, grant me relief! O thou who created all by a word. O God!

I don't know how my father ever agreed to risk his life. They should have contacted the group and made a deal with them. I wish my father would pull back; I don't want him mixed up with them. God forgive him, he's the one who drove me away! Taking usury, oppressing me, battling unjustly with Shaikh Abdel Shafi and insulting him.... *Our Lord! Make us not a test and trial for the Unbelievers, but forgive us, our Lord! for Thou art the Exalted in Might, the Wise.*

O my Lord! bestow wisdom on me, and join me with the righteous; grant me honorable mention on the tongue of truth among the latest (generations); and place me among the inheritors of the Garden of Delight. Forgive my father, for that he is among those astray; and let me not be in disgrace on the Day when (men) will be raised up. My father was unjust. For a long time my uncle talked to me about his usurious, immoral contracts, his tyranny and arrogance in dealing with everyone around him. He fell short in upholding God's law in his household, among my mother and my sisters, and when I could not bring him back to the highroad of righteousness, I hated him and fled his house, praying to God to guide him. I resolved to flee, to preach the true religion of God, hoping to become a martyr, to meet the beloved, to enter everlasting paradise, to find the beautiful houris.

The hardest trial for a man is to be tried by the people of his house. Perhaps God, may he be praised and glorified, has brought my father here to atone for his sins. *O our Lord! cover us with Thy Forgiveness—me, my parents, and all Believers, on the Day that the Reckoning will be established!*

I can barely breathe, as if one of my ribs has been broken.

Ah! They threw me on the ground and left. I don't know how long my torture, my captivity will go on. We have captives from them, I remember that, maybe seven of them. My jihadi brothers must surely have gotten in touch with them, but I don't know what's going on between them and the jihadis.

Ah! O God, O Lord, honor me with martyrdom! O God, I confide myself to you. I had wanted to die on the field of battle.

I feel cold. I'm lying on a dirt floor, in all my filth.

Here comes that big brute again. *And We have put a bar in front of them and a bar behind them, and further, We have covered them up; so that they cannot see.* There is no god but you, all praise to you. I have been among the unjust. O God, receive me well. O God, I have greatly wronged myself, no one forgives sins but you, give me your forgiveness and have mercy on me, you are the forgiving and the merciful!

Ah! His kick to my side has nearly killed me! I'm suffocating, I can't draw breath.

Ah! O God, O God, help me, O God! I attest that there is no god but God, and I attest that Muhammad is God's prophet. . . . Ah!

36

"We've entered Mashhad."

Just as Reza informed me of this, a message came: "We repeat: beware of any treachery!" Seconds later another message arrived, with a link that took me to a video showing Ahmad cowering on the dirt floor in a corner of the room while two masked men beat him with stun batons. One of them hoisted him and tossed him a distance of two meters, and he fell trembling to the ground. "Father," he moaned. "Come. Come, in the name of God!" I felt my mouth go dry and my chest breaking in a flood of tears.

"What just came?" I handed the phone to Reza.

He slowed the car to a stop. "Uncle Yaqoub," he said, "it's war between you and them, and they are killers." I gazed at him, and he gave me a small bottle of water. "Here," he said. "Drink this." I took a long drink. "It's now two-thirty, and it will take us less than twenty minutes to get to the center of town. I expect you'll get new instructions from them." I nodded, unable to answer him. "We'll get into town and have our lunch and wait for their instructions."

As the car moved off again, I thought of my conversation with Farnaz the night before. She had called when I was asleep, saying she wanted to check on me. I don't remember what I said to her. Some fate placed her in my path; if it had not, how would I have managed without her brother?

He drove the car with confidence and calm. Unbidden, the question came to mind—had I wronged Ahmad and put both of us in danger when I agreed to this expedition without informing Kuwait's Department of Foreign Affairs or the Kuwaiti embassy in Tehran? The phone rang, and my heart skipped a beat. "Hello!" I shouted, expecting a call from the kidnappers.

Shaikha's voice came to me, with all her fear. "What's happening? How are you, Yaqoub?" I wished she could be here with me so I could hug her. "Yaqoub, why are you silent?"

"It's nothing. We're on the road to Mashhad."

"Who's with you?"

"A young man who has lived his whole life in Kuwait. He's been helping me since I got to the airport."

"Thank God. That's reassuring. Will he stay with you the whole time?"

"He's determined not to leave me until I'm at the airport on my way back to Kuwait."

"God keep you both! Please give him my thanks and gratitude."

"I will."

She asked anxiously, "Are you going to pick up Ahmad in Mashhad?"

"I don't know, I'm waiting for new instructions."

Her voice changed. "Uthaiman asked about you, and I told him you're at the beach house."

"Good, good. I'll give you any news as soon as I have it." I hung up, for fear that my husky voice would break and give away my fear.

"Uncle, what would you like to eat?"

"Anything. Nothing."

"Excuse me, but you must eat. Perhaps you don't like Iranian food?"

"Anything at all, Reza."

We had just begun eating when the call came. A hoarse voice I could barely hear said, "You are in Mashhad, and your accused dog is in his filthy pit. Take a taxi and come immediately to Birjand. That's where we will give you the renegade enemy of God."

I felt the food stick in my throat. I was about to speak when another call came. "Father, please, for God's sake, come to Birjand right away."

"Of course, of course, I'm on my way." The call was cut off, and I stared into nothing.

I gave the information to Reza and he looked upset. As we were wiping the food off our hands, he said, "It's a long way, about five hundred kilometers. We'll arrive tonight at nine or nine-thirty."

"I can help. I can take a turn driving."

He called the waiter and asked him to wrap up the food, then he got up. "I'll go to the bathroom, then we'll take off."

We left the restaurant, him carrying a large cup of coffee. He smiled and said, "The traveler's friend." As we got into the car he said, "It's true that Birjand is an Iranian area, but al-Qaeda has a very active presence there."

I said nothing. The car devoured the road. Reza was silent, sipping his coffee from time to time.

It occurred to me that I don't know a thing about what I'm involved in—I don't know the road, I don't speak Farsi, and I've never dealt with terrorists before. My heart beat fast as I thought of what was happening to my son.

I didn't deserve all this pain, Son. May God not forgive those who stuffed your head full of destruction, violence, and killing, and took you to the field of battle! I pictured Ahmad in my mind, surrounded by his group, dressed like them, a frown on his face, carrying a machine gun.

I noticed the unpleasant sunset, and asked Reza, "Wouldn't you like to rest?" He answered, as if just becoming aware of his surroundings, "Yes, yes. The town of Torbet e-Heydariyeh is ahead of us. We should come across a coffee shop where we can sit for a while."

I don't know how much ground we had covered or how long we had traveled, but I was aware of Reza slowing the car to a stop so I could get out. I left the car with my head spinning from fatigue. A strange odor pervaded the area.

He came back with a bottle of juice and brought out an apple from a paper bag, offering it to me. I took it without comment while he had another.

Darkness descended heavy and gray on the road. Reza told me, "At our next stop, in the town of Gonabad, we'll have dinner."

At some point I dozed off—maybe it was half an hour later. I apologized to him, but he said, "It's good that you had a little rest." I noticed that he was slowing down, and I asked him where we were.

"We're in the area of Gonabad. This restaurant might be okay."

When I got out of the car, I noticed the darkness. I disliked the smell of the restaurant and how crowded and noisy it was. I chose a small, distant table next to a wall. I looked up and noticed a wall clock and realized that it was nine-thirty.

I've lived my whole life obsessed with time—how did I come to lose track of it? Everything in the restaurant was strange and repellant; I hardly recognized myself. I was sitting in a roadside restaurant, plunged in poverty and loud with the incomprehensible gibberish of Persian. Afghan dress dominated, and that there wasn't a single woman in the place. Reza came over with a tray of food, saying, "I hope you'll like this."

I smiled and thanked him. It occurred to me to wonder how I would ever repay him fittingly, and his sister, too. I suddenly felt hungry and began eating with an appetite sharpened by the misery I was going through, dipping my bread eagerly in the lentil soup.

I was in the bathroom when the message came: "We'll wait for you in the town of Zabol. We'll give you your filth of a son after we receive the money."

I went back to Reza and gave him the phone. He had barely finished reading the message when another one came, so he gave the phone back to me. "Before the dawn prayer you'll get your son. We're waiting for you—take the taxi and come to Zabol immediately."

"We won't go now," Reza said firmly. "I was sure they would suggest doing this at night. Zabol is an area bordering Afghanistan, and by night it's controlled by gangs belonging to al-Qaeda."

I felt that I was helpless to manage my own affairs, and that I had made a major mistake when I had stubbornly insisted on coming alone.

"Mr. Yaqoub, we can't even trust some of the police here because they collaborate with al-Qaeda." He said that to alert me to the extent of my involvement and my position of weakness.

"What do you suggest?"

"We'll spend the night in the car, and at first light we'll head toward Zabol."

I was a lost child. Reza was taking me by the hand and leading me where he wanted. If it weren't for Farnaz and him, I would have perished.

"What do you think?" he asked, as my mind wandered.

I was sorry for him. "Reza, you've done nothing wrong. There's no reason for you to be involved with me."

A reproving smile flickered on his face. "Mr. Yaqoub, we're beyond that now. You and I are in the same boat."

It pained me that I was compromising the future of a young man who had no relationship to my son. He scrolled through his phone, then informed me, "Zabol is about three hundred and sixty kilometers from here; it will take us four or five hours to get there. If we leave at five a.m., we might get there by ten."

"We'll spend the night here?"

The question hung in the air until he answered, in a tone I did not understand, "I don't think we can find a hotel, and if we did find one it might not be safe." I was used to being the one making plans for myself and others. "We can't risk anyone recognizing you. This area is mined, and everyone is a spy for al-Qaeda. Forgive me if we spend the night in the car."

We went back to the car. There was nothing but complete darkness around us. Reza calmly started the motor, and the odor of blood came to me sharply.

37

"I'm sorry, Yaqoub!" I said to myself.

I never for a moment imagined that I would spend a whole night stretched out on the rear seat of a car. In the darkness, Reza drove to what looked like a garden beside the road, and we spent the night parked under an ancient tree.

The only distraction was the birds, which attacked us with their chirping before dawn, as if they were reminding us of what was waiting for us.

"Good morning," called Reza. I don't know when he fell asleep or when he woke up, but there were blue circles under his eyes. "We'll stop at any café or shop we come across on the road, to get tea or coffee, and then we'll go on to Zabol." He said this crisply, in a tone that went straight to my heart and frightened me. I told myself that Reza was aware of the approaching danger and was acting as an officer.

I noticed two messages on my phone: "You're late, you coward! Come on the road from Jadeh Zahdan to Nehbandan." My heart missed a beat as I read the second message: "We're waiting for you with your accursed son. Your deadline is the *adhan* for the noon prayer. We'll slaughter him as soon as the call sounds."

I showed Reza the messages and begged him to hurry.

He set off, driving in silence, looking upset and tired. I felt my mind betray me; I had no power to think about anything. I had my coffee while he drank a large cup of tea and smoked a cigarette.

I looked again at the two messages, and said to him, "The last message said to come on the Jadeh Zahdan-Nehbandan road."

"That's the one we're on," he said.

I was at a loss to interpret the look on his face. Was he angry with me, or angry with himself for going along with me? Had he spoken to his sister and now blamed her for entangling me with him? It seemed to me that it was best not to discuss anything with him, that it was better to leave him to his own thoughts.

"Uncle, how will you pay the ransom to them?"

"I don't know." I realized that they had not sent me any account number or information about the payment method. "They told me that I'll transfer the sum to their account."

I looked at the dashboard clock; it was eight-thirty. "Could we stop for another coffee?"

"This is a poor area. If we come across a restaurant or a shop, we'll pull over."

It was clear that the geography of the region had changed; the road had become a single lane, where two cars could pass only with difficulty. Barren land surrounded us on either side. Suddenly the odor of blood came over me.

Reza had begun to slow down, then he stopped in front of a small shop. He got out hurriedly, without speaking, and came back with two cans of Coca-Cola. "I didn't find any tea or coffee."

"You're spending your money on me." The phrase escaped me, in my embarrassment.

"Don't say that."

A new message came through. "This is the link for the meeting place. We're waiting for you. When the call to the noon prayer sounds, we will slaughter your cursed son and toss out his stinking corpse."

My heart beat fast; I had no words. I heard Reza asking, "Another message?"

"Yes." I handed him the phone, but he asked me to read it. "The road here isn't safe."

I read him the text. "Open the link and we'll go to them," he responded. "We won't begin the transfer operation until we see your son. Write to them, 'I want to see my son.'"

I did as he asked, and the reply came quickly: "You'll see him at the transfer point."

I read that to him, and he asked me to write back, "I must see him standing on his feet, then I'll transfer the money to you." I typed out his words, sent the message, and waited for their reply, or for any clarification from Reza. My heart was beating very fast.

I stared at him as he concentrated on the road, cautiously following the map in the link. His face wore a grimace, while the rancid odor of blood took my breath away.

We had begun to enter into back streets. "All these areas belong to them. They use them to grow narcotics."

"We have to be sure that Ahmad is with them, and that they have not hurt him."

"That's why I said to show him to us standing."

We drove onto a dirt road, and I received a message from them: "What color is the taxi you've come in?"

"They are asking for the color of the car."

"We've almost reached the place. Give them the description of the car," Reza replied.

"It's a white Toyota." I sent the message and saw that we were now on a dirt road with a pitted surface. It was surrounded on both sides by tall trees with trunks like ship masts and dense foliage that hid whatever was behind them. There were no other cars or any movement except for ours.

"We've arrived," Reza said, stopping the car under the shade of some trees. He turned off the motor and lowered the car windows.

The scent of Farnaz came to me strongly, but Reza soon raised the windows back up and checked to see that the doors were locked. He then reached for his revolver and placed it under his thigh.

My mouth was dry, with a bitter taste in it. The phone rang.

"Are you the stopped car?"

"Yes." I placed the phone on speaker.

"We're coming. Your accursed son is with us."

My heart palpitated. I was about to turn around, but Reza signaled to me to stay where I was.

I felt as if the place, the car, the trees, the birds, the movement of the air, the scent of Farnaz, the sky, our very breath—all was suspended in an explosive moment of silence.

What would their car look like? My heart was racing. Would I see Ahmad?

I heard Reza's voice: "I think they're coming."

A small, dirty red car drove past us. I thought I saw Ahmad in the rear. The car stopped about two hundred meters away and a call came: "We're here in the car with your accursed son. Transfer the money to this account and we'll set him free."

I immediately received a message with an account number.

I closed the phone, not knowing what to do. Reza said, "Before making the transfer, ask them for your son to walk out and stand in the middle between us."

My phone rang and a voice said roughly, "Have the taxi driver get out and move away from the car."

I hung up and looked at Reza. He said quickly, "Let your son come out and stand between us, let him remain standing while they receive the ransom and move away, then we'll take him. Do not get out of the car yourself, ever, no matter what happens." He said this forcefully, his eyes seeming to occupy his whole face. "Let your son walk out on his own strength, transfer the sum, and do not budge from where you are."

He took his revolver, opened the door, and calmly crossed to the other side of the street, where he chose a rock and sat down on it.

An unwelcome tremor seized me, and the phone rang. "If the call to prayer sounds, we will cut your son's throat."

"Let my son come out so I see him standing before the transfer."

The call was cut off. I sat in the car, my heart beating fast. A heavy silence stifled the whole place—there was nothing but my breath, the scent of Farnaz, the sweat of my body, my fear waiting for the sound of the call to prayer.... They will kill my son. I wished the *adhan* would be late.

I can't call them. Reza is hunched on the rock, looking toward their car.

The door of their little car opened slowly, and one of them got out, his face masked. He was dragging Ahmad behind him. Ahmad was wearing Afghan pants and a white undershirt spotted with blood. The phone rang. "Your son is before you as you asked.

We will tie his hands and feet. You have five minutes to transfer the money."

I stared for a moment at Ahmad, who was standing with his head hanging down. With trembling fingers I wrote a message to my friend Daniel, the bank director, asking him to transfer ten million dollars to the account number, which I copied. The message flew off. My phone rang. "We won't wait long. If the call to prayer sounds, we won't miss the obligation of the noon prayer."

They will kill my son to the sound of the *adhan*.

Everything was stifled in silence: the car, the road, the trees, Reza, the scent. Again the phone rang. "Have you transferred the sum?"

"Yes, I've transferred it to your account."

The call was cut off. I sat with my rapid heartbeat, my breathing, my sweat. The silence shrouded the trees, the potholes in the road, the air, the scent, my son with his head hanging down, and Reza where he sat. The phone rang again, and I heard Daniel wishing me a good morning.

I tried to remain calm, though my voice was cold as I answered.

He said, "I have received an order to transfer ten million dollars."

"Yes, it's for the contract I told you about."

He was silent for a few second, then asked me, "Is everything okay?"

"Yes. Please just transfer the sum."

Once again silence. Then he said, "Okay, fine."

I hung up and once again I sat gripping my phone, my heart pounding, my hands trembling, my breathing ragged, and my eyes fixed on my son, in the midst of silence, mummified trees, still air, the scent of Farnaz, the pitted road, and my fear of the sound of the *adhan*. Reza had told me not to move, not to get out of the car.

I received the notice from the bank: "The transfer has gone through." I sat for a moment, then I opened the car door to get out and go to Ahmad. I hear Reza shouting, "No, no, no!"

The small car moved off rapidly as I ran to Ahmad, Reza shouting behind me, "No, Uncle, no . . . !"

There was a distant echo of the muezzin's voice: "*Allahu akbar, Allahu akbar.*"

Suddenly a shot rang out from the trees behind Ahmad, shattering the silence. There was blood in my nose. My son fell.

Kuwait, July 17, 2021

Translator's acknowledgments

My heartfelt thanks go to all who have given me their unstinting help with this project: Taleb Alrefai, Wendy Munyon, members of the Third Coast Translators Collective, and members of the Northwest Literary Translators. As always, the work is dedicated to the memory of Farouk Abdel Wahab Mustafa.